"It's tremendous. With echoes of Charles De Lint's *Someplace to be Flying*, it's fresh, fast-paced and wholly immersive. Love it!" **Joanne Harris, author of *The Gospel of Loki*, *Chocolat* and many more**

"Astonishing, riveting. Powerful mythic fiction that makes you remember why you read this stuff in the first place." **Ellen Kushner, author of *Swordspoint* and many more**

"*Birds of Paradise* sits in a place between Plato and John Wick, a place which frankly I didn't know existed. And it is profoundly human too: whoever has ever known loss will resonate with it." **Francesco Dimitri, author of *The Book of Hidden Things***

"A beautifully written novel by one of the UKs most exciting new voices." **R. J. Barker, author of *Age of Assassins* and *The Bone Ships***

"A meaningful tale told with style, subtlety, and a deep understanding of the world and all its ways, *Birds of Paradise* joins the past to the present, the oldest stories to the new, without putting a foot wrong. It's a beautiful, thoughtful read." **Aliya Whiteley, author of *The Beauty* and *The Loosening Skin***

"This is a profoundly felt and richly imagined novel; a fragment of myth from an older time which, as you turn it around in your mind, you know instinctively must be true. A beautifully executed and original work of art." **Una McCormack, *New York Times* bestselling author of *Star Trek: Picard – The Last, Best Hope*, *The Undefeated* and many more**

BIRDS
OF
PARADISE

BIRDS
OF
PARADISE

OLIVER K. LANGMEAD

TITAN BOOKS

Birds of Paradise
Print edition ISBN: 9781789094817
E-book edition ISBN: 9781789094824

Published by Titan Books
A division of Titan Publishing Group Ltd
144 Southwark Street, London SE1 0UP
www.titanbooks.com

First edition: March 2021
10 9 8 7 6 5 4 3 2 1

A CIP catalogue record for this title is available from the British Library.

Printed and bound in the United States.

The king! With beak and talons
The king! In the form of man
Nothing escapes those eyes
He sees everything

Cult of Luna – 'Ghost Trail'

PROLOGUE

Adam tends to the garden. He works among the flowers where the bees dance. Around his ankles, and up his legs, and across his shoulders coils the snake, its tongue flickering in his ear. Beyond the grove a hill rises high and the twin trees stand at its apex, knowledge and life overlooking all, with their roots buried deep in Eden's rich earth. The birds overhead are of every colour and they fly high above the trees and call out to one another, and beneath them in the river and the lake swim and play the shining fishes, and among the trees wander the beasts and fowl that walk the earth, and all and everything belongs to Adam; the earth and the plants and the trees, all made for him, so that he might love and care for them; his paradise.

The low-hanging branches of the trees at the edge of the grove shift and Eve appears, her hair so long and dark, her eyes bright. As she approaches she digs her fingers into the skin beneath her breasts, beneath her ribs, until she pierces her flesh and she can grip hold of her ribs. Her ribs she pulls upwards, outwards, until they jut from her in glistening red and white nubs, and her skin tears away, revealing her lungs inflating and deflating, and her beating heart, thudding its own rhythm besides. From her open chest she tears her heart, pulling the arteries from it, dripping blood with every pulse of it, holding it out to him.

Uncoiling the snake, Adam lets it drop and takes hold of his own chest, digging his fingers into his flesh just as she did. He has one rib less and has to worm his fingers around to find purchase, but he manages to get a good grip and rips himself open. For Eve, he tears his ribs aside and reveals his own lungs and heart, so that they are both exposed to each other, breathing and beating in rhythm together. By touch he finds his heart and pulls it from himself, twisting each artery until it breaks and the pulsing organ is free. It is a heavy heart, bigger than Eve's by far, but he offers it to her just as she offers hers to him, and in that way they make their exchange, their blood pouring into Eden's soil and feeding the twin trees.

Eve's heart is so small. Its beat is the fluttering of the wings of a butterfly. He presses it into his open chest tenderly, pulling his arteries and knotting them around the heart until it stays in place. Then, one rib at a time, he pushes his chest closed, and smooths his ragged broken skin over the hole. Eve is struggling to fit his heart into her chest, so he helps her, pushing and pressing until the heavy trembling organ remains in place, knotted beneath a net of veins, and then, together, they close the opening and seal his heart inside.

When they are both shut, her heart in him, his heart in her, they embrace, she so small, so delicate in his broad arms. There is no weakness to him; her heart has made him stronger, for all its tender fluttering. Eve, too, grips tighter than he has ever known her to, as if she might sink into his skin and become him, return from whence she came. Eden's bright sun sinks, and Eden's silver moon rises, and as dusk becomes night becomes dawn becomes day, the snake coils around them both, tighter and tighter, like rope, until they are bound so closely together that Adam no longer knows where he ends and she begins.

I

Cinema still seems strange to Adam. He's always been a great admirer of literature, but he still struggles to get his head around moving pictures. The problem, he thinks, is that he's too used to the ambiguity of naked words – the way that he's allowed to be the director of the story when he's reading it. Watching a film is like watching someone else's idea of how a story should look, and he prefers the pictures he makes in his mind.

The film he's watching is about a group of plane crash survivors, marooned on an island. The characters are covered in layers of artfully arranged filth, and when they grimace their teeth are pearly white. They deliver lengthy monologues, and die handsome deaths, and Adam becomes preoccupied with the scars across the backs of his hands, shining in the light cast by the projector.

White rivers through dark skin.

Eventually, a scene draws his attention. One of the survivors has whittled a spear out of a stick, and is standing waist deep in a river. The survivor lashes out with his crude harpoon, and raises his catch triumphantly. The camera zooms in on the fish, speared and still flailing, its shining scales refracting the sky into all kinds of colours. The camera pauses on the fish as it suffocates, and Adam realises that he feels as if the spear through the fish is jutting through his chest as well. The scene changes, but the sensation of being skewered does not fade.

Today, Adam is working security. He has been charged with escorting a young actress by the name of Cassandra Coleman, whose real name is Sally Ainsley, to and from the film's premiere. From here, he is able to see her, sitting between a grizzled-looking veteran actor and the film's writer, whose name is Damon Darcy. Cassandra is doing a stellar job of ignoring the way Darcy keeps brushing his leg up against her own; the black trouser of his impeccably fitted suit against the silvery scales of her dress. Whenever she has a scene, Adam watches the way she mouths along with her lines, eyes glassy.

"Adam," she says, when the curtains have closed. "I want to go home."

But of course, they can't go home. There's still the after-party. So, Adam becomes her shadow and guides her there. Cameras flash and microphones are thrust into her face, and she bears it bravely, all the way to the limousine.

"What did you think?" she asks. "Was I good?" She's looking out of the window of the limousine. Adam thinks that she was the best bit of the film, but he stays quiet because she isn't expecting an answer. The night lights of Los Angeles streak across her face in red and green and blue, and she pulls her white fur collar up around her shoulders, and she looks so delicate that she might shatter.

The party is too bright and Adam feels exposed beneath the

hot lights strung from the roof of the marquee. Champagne is flowing freely from bottles to glasses to throats, and everyone seems like exaggerated versions of themselves. The more Cassandra drinks, the smaller she becomes. Darcy's hands rush eagerly across her shoulders and down her spine, making the scales of her dress shimmer, and she does her best to laugh at his jokes. "You and me, baby," he's saying. "You and me. I'll write you in."

She makes to turn away, but he grabs her wrist. Adam's hand is upon his shoulder in an instant. "Hey, man," says Darcy, trying to grin at him. "Hey now."

Darcy squirms uneasily beneath Adam's grip as he's led through the marquee. His red face is reddening further. "Hey, shit. Look, man." He struggles, jabs an elbow out and nudges a waiter, who spills a tray of champagne. Through an open archway decorated with fairy lights, they emerge into the smoking section, where Adam releases him.

"Shit." Darcy wipes the champagne from his suit. "Look what you did! Don't you fucking know who I am?" He digs into his satchel and hefts out an ornament. It looks like a miniature replica of a typewriter, cast in gold. He waves it triumphantly at Adam, eyes bloodshot, nostrils flared. "Do I look like just anyone to you? Anyone you can just push around? Look at you. What have you ever done? This is a fucking Golden Typewriter." Of course, Damon Darcy takes his screenwriting award with him to parties. "Who the fuck do you think you are?" he demands, trembling.

Adam takes the trophy from him. He can still feel the spear

grating against his ribs. He can still see the writer's hand, lustily caressing the scales of Cassandra's dress.

"Hey! What the fuck? What the fuck are you doing?"

When Adam kills Damon Darcy, he feels divorced from the action, as if he is simply watching another scene from the movie. There is the motion of Adam's arm, and the glint of gold as the typewriter flashes through the air, and the crunching of the writer's bones. There is no passion in the murder – it simply feels like the way the script plays out. A repeat of something he has done before.

When the deed is done, chaos reigns around him.

Adam stands, drops the trophy, and returns inside. Everyone is running away from him. For a brief moment he glimpses Cassandra – the glittering of her silver dress, and the flash of terror in her wide eyes – and there he finds relief; he no longer feels as if he is flailing on the end of a spear. His relief is brief – no more than the slightest ripple through the placidity of his apathy – and when it leaves, he takes a seat at the heart of the abandoned marquee. He looks at his hands and the blood turning his bright scars red, and wonders why all of this feels so familiar.

The authorities arrive. They tear down the tent with their cars and their boots, and they surround him. Dozens of rifles are pointed at his scarred skull. Adam kneels, and presents his wrists, but they don't have any handcuffs big enough, so they use zip-ties.

They haul him into a van, close the doors, and leave him in darkness.

* * *

"Hey, pal. You paying attention?"

Over the past two days, Adam has seen a lot of different faces. Some are kind, but most are furious. He lets the interrogations roll over him – lets their words go unheard. He finds a hidden place inside himself and goes there. Even when they try fists, their blows go unfelt. It's been a long time since Adam last saw his own blood, and their knuckles don't draw it.

"Listen. You're fucked. You know that and I know that."

This man has a drooping moustache, hiding his red face. Behind him, another man, clean shaven, is leaning against the wall. Both have their sleeves rolled up. The moustached man has laid out photocopies of documents on the interview table. They spark recognition, and for the first time Adam begins to pay attention.

"We need your help with something else. What can you tell us about these?"

Some of the documents look ancient. Crumbling at the edges. Their presence means that the LAPD have searched Adam's apartment – turned it upside down, probably.

"My garden," he says.

The detectives exchange a glance. "What about your garden, pal?"

Adam realises his mistake immediately. If they haven't dug it up yet, they definitely will now. He leans back and thinks about his cherry tree. He remembers it as a sapling, no more than a twig. Leaves, so small. He remembers the seasons as they passed over it – remembers the way he would fall asleep against it as it grew tall. He remembers the taste of its cherries.

"Look," says the man with the moustache. "These certificates don't make sense. You don't make sense. You've gotta help us out here."

Reaching for the closest couple of photocopies, Adam reads them. The first says that Adam's name is Adam Reynolds, and that he was born in Massachusetts a few decades ago. The next one says that Adam's name is Adam Thompson, and that he was born in Kenya almost a century ago. He remembers both of those lives as if he had read about them once in a book – as if they were other people that occupied his head for a while.

"What do these mean, pal?"

They are keepsakes. That's all. Mementos nobody was ever meant to find.

Embedded into the wall is a mirror. In it, Adam looks like the shadow of a giant. "I'll tell you if you give me a book to read," he says, because he knows he can tell them anything. They won't believe the truth.

"Sure." The man with the moustache leans back, opens his arms, inviting Adam to speak.

"I got made before death."

The rest of the interview goes on as before. Their questions bounce off his skull. Before long, he is led back to his cell by an armed quartet of officers. The cell is far too small, but it has a window that lights up in the evening, and Adam is surprised to find that today somebody has left a book for him to read. He makes a note in his head to try and remember the officer with the moustache. Then, he sits on his bunk and begins to read.

The book is nothing good – a well-thumbed pulp noir – but

Adam lets himself become immersed in the words. He watches the book's city rise in his imagination; builds the streets, fills them with people and rain. The book's protagonist sails out to the middle of a lake, and there, with a hook, fishes out a sunken corpse, and for a brief moment Adam feels the curve of the hook viscerally, through his chest. The feeling fades as he continues, as the book's characters come to life for him. He reads, and he reads, until the room grows bright.

The sun is setting.

When Adam looks up, there is the silhouette of a bird across the floor, made enormous by the sun. But before he can turn and see it, it flaps its wings and takes flight.

* * *

Recently, Adam's been thinking about Eden a lot. The problem he's been having is that he's not sure which bits of his memories are real. He distinctly remembers waking up early one day and walking through the field of long grasses; the way the grasses cut little red lines across his palms, and the way the waters of the lake at the base of the hill sparkled as if all of Eden's stars had been poured into it. But when he remembers that morning, it feels as if he's wearing shoes. It's not a case of being unable to recall the feel of the grasses beneath his feet, which he knows he should remember; more that there is something faulty with his memory.

The problem, he thinks, is the tangle of thorns growing in his head. He can feel them scratching at his skull, and all the thick, twisted coils of them are making it difficult for him to remember things properly. He's not sure what the tangle of thorns is – but he does know that it hurts to remember certain things. In fact, the deeper into the thorns he tries to remember, the sharper they get. There is something terrible at the heart of the tangle, he thinks – the root cause of all the dreadful needling growth – and he's not sure he wants to find out what it is.

* * *

Adam is put into a cold white room with a single table, a single chair, and four lawyers.

Three of the four lawyers are speaking to him simultaneously, and Adam only has the vaguest idea of what they are saying. They have interchangeable faces, as if they have been cast from the same mould, and he is only able to tell them apart by the colour of their ties. The lawyer with the yellow tie is telling him that he should plead guilty; the lawyer with the blue tie is telling him that he should try for a plea bargain; and the lawyer with the red tie is telling him to plead insanity. Adam sits in his chair, idly runs his fingers across the metal surface of the table, and repeatedly glances at the quiet fourth lawyer, feeling like a man who can see an oasis in a desert, but mistrusting what his eyes are telling him.

The fourth lawyer leans against the far wall, and is absorbed in the screen of his phone. He is wearing a suit that looks as if it cost more than the suits of all three of the other lawyers combined. It is a black suit, with a black shirt and a black tie, and his hair is black and tastefully tousled, and the rims of his rounded designer spectacles are black as well. He is pale, and small, but his shadow is cast long before him.

All at once, he lowers his phone and raises a hand towards the door. "Out," he says. Then, "Bring me a chair."

The three other lawyers are immediately silenced. They leave with their heads bowed. Only the lawyer with the blue tie briefly returns, to deposit a chair opposite Adam. The lawyer in black unfastens his jacket and sits, and the temperature in the room seems to drop. There is a long silence as he observes Adam, punctuated by the sound of his fingers drumming rhythmically on the metal table.

"Rook, I'm not—"

"Shut up," says Rook.

Silence reigns anew. Eventually, Rook removes his spectacles, and places them on the table between them. "Fake," he says. "They create a narrative for me. They tell my clients that I have spent a great deal of time reading and straining my eyes in order to learn the many nuances of law. They give me an air of superiority and, because of that, I remain unquestioned. Just one of the many significant little details I have laboured at in order to create the perfect disguise."

He leans forward. "Do you know how much effort it takes me to have all the certificates and passports made? This government has a lot of new systems in place – all manner of gates through which a man must pass to prove that he is, indeed, the person that he claims to be. Every year, my role in our grand masquerade grows more complex and, as such, more precarious. Every year, we take one step closer to discovery and extinction. Tell me, Adam. What drove you to murder a celebrity?"

"I don't—"

"Shut up. It was a rhetorical question." Rook leans back, returns to drumming his fingers. "I'm sure you're well aware of the ire I harbour at being dragged down here to fix this. I have a life, Adam, which I am quite proud of. I have a life which you have threatened by your actions. Yes, I know that the police have found a whole selection of your old certificates, and yes, I am angry that you've failed to follow my very clear instructions on how to dispose of them. Fire, Adam. The great cleanser. As simple as striking a match and setting them alight. Poetic, even: that, much like the phoenix, you should be reborn into a new life as the old one smoulders. Their discovery threatens my life, and the lives of all those whom I protect. Do you understand the damage which you might have caused, had I not been so swift in rushing down here?"

"They're not—"

"Shut up." Cleaning his spectacles, Rook perches them back upon his face. "The question remains: what should I do with you? The obvious answer is that I should leave you in prison for at least a couple of decades, that you might learn some kind of lesson from the mess you've created. Indeed, I have an ongoing arrangement with Barracuda which should keep him behind bars for at least thirty years yet. Perhaps it would be best if you joined him, and were given time to reflect. That being said…"

Adam considers the idea of a lifetime spent behind bars. It would be quiet, he thinks; an opportunity to do a lot of reading.

And maybe, given time and patience, he could find the cracks in the walls of his confinement and grow things there, like lichen, or moss, or tiny mushrooms. It would be a long, patient, soothing time, free of the pressure of having to remember things.

"Perhaps," says Rook, weighing the word. "Perhaps it would be better were you to be free, and abroad, away from prying eyes. Out of my hair, as it were. I do have a matter that requires the attention of someone other than myself, and you may very well be able to help with it." Rook makes a pyramid of his hands. "It would be a simple enough operation. An escalation of your crimes to the federal level, which would necessitate moving you to a far more secure location, remote from Los Angeles. And in the act of moving you, an opportunity would come to free you. You would be a fugitive, of course, but I imagine that you might lose the authorities with the appropriate assistance." Pausing for a moment to think over his plan, Rook smiles to himself. "Yes. Very good. I think it the best option. You are clearly not in your right mind, but I still believe there's enough of the man you once were in you to be useful. Let's try giving you an errand." He stands, fastening his jacket closed.

Adam finds that he is disappointed by Rook's decree; he had rather liked the idea of staying in prison for a while. "What's the job?"

"Oh." Rook focuses on Adam again. "I need someone to find my brother. His spending habits have become peculiar as of late, and I have been unable to contact him. Indeed, my only means of tracking him is by following his withdrawals, which have been growing steadily more substantial. It's... unlike Magpie to spend my money. I've never known him to not have his own. And while I am well aware of my brother's eccentricities, this is unusual, even for him. I'd like someone to track him down, and either have him contact me, or questioned; I'd like to find out where my money is going." Rook knocks on the door, waiting to be released. "Last I knew, he was in Scotland."

"Okay," says Adam.

Rook peers at Adam across the top of his spectacles, looking as if he's been struck by a thought. "When was the last time you spoke to Eve, Adam?"

Her name is like a spark in Adam's brain. A point of light, reignited.

"I don't know," he says, truthfully.

"Mmm," says Rook, briefly studying Adam's face, searching for something there.

The door opens, but before he can leave, Adam asks, "Did she name you? Or did I?"

"She did," says Rook, and then he is gone.

* * *

Adam is denied bail and transferred to a holding facility pending trial. They don't have an orange jumpsuit big enough for him, so he's made to wear one two sizes too small. The other prisoners watch him pass in silence – step back from the bars of their cells.

He's given his own cell. It has a low barred window, through which Adam can see a single leafless tree, standing darkly against the scrubby ground at the centre of the facility. Once a day, he is brought out to the yard to stretch his legs, but he spends most of that time beside the chain-link fence, peering beyond the enmeshed links and trying to get a better look at the tree. It needs some care, he thinks. It's not getting enough water, and the sun is blocked off from it eight hours a day.

The only time of day he is allowed around the other prisoners is at lunch. The sudden sensory rush after being in his cell is always overwhelming: the rattling and clattering, the conversation and movement; all the stink of a hundred bodies devouring cheap slop in various dull arrangements. When he lines up with his tray, he is given space to move. The prisoners here don't meet his eye, but the servers are generous with their portions.

Usually, Adam finishes his tray, but on the third day the kitchen serves fishcakes and he loses his appetite. A recent riot means that cutlery is forfeit for the foreseeable future, so that the prisoners must eat with their hands, and Adam becomes preoccupied with the slivers of fish clinging to the fingers and lips of everyone around him. He feels as if he is on the verge of remembering something – the reason why killing the writer felt so familiar. Lunch ends, and the sensation fades.

After the fourth day, two prisoners come and sit with him. The first is muscular, with so many crudely drawn black tattoos that he is running out of untouched skin; the second is slight and downcast, looking as if he has lived through a lifetime of sorrows. "Hey, man," says the tattooed prisoner. "You the guy that killed that writer. I know you. Seen you all over the news."

The sullen prisoner swirls his porridge around in its bowl with his finger. "I'm Earl. This is Throat."

"Yeah, and you Sullivan. Adam Sullivan. Pleased to meet you, man." When Throat grins, he flashes a complete set of golden teeth. "Fuck that writer, man. Way I see it, you did the world a favour. He's been puttin' out shit for years. Wish you'd done it three films ago." He laughs. "You all right, man. You all right. Way I see it, guys like us, we gotta stick together."

Adam peels his orange. "Guys like us?"

"Yeah, man." Throat gestures broadly around the room.

No matter where Adam goes, he's always singled out for the colour of his skin. He places his half-peeled orange down for a moment and turns his wrists over, studying his scars. "You were all once me," he mutters, but the words aren't really meant for Throat and Earl. They're just a reflection of a thought he's had for a long time.

"Listen, man," says Earl, after sucking the porridge from his finger. "Some guys have been saying your lawyers are Corvid & Corvid. That shit is expensive. More important, they don't even got a phone number."

"My man's got connects." Throat slaps Adam on the shoulder. "Ain't that right?"

Adam returns to his orange, pulling it apart and digging around in the segments, tugging the seeds free. He lines the seeds up on his tray as he eats, and then gathers them up, sifts through them on his palm like a fortune teller interpreting bones. The orange is old – barely edible – but some of the seeds might still grow, under the right conditions.

"You got a number I could call?" asks Earl, but Adam doesn't answer. Two of the seeds seem viable. Adam places them carefully into a pocket.

Adam returns to his cell, lays back on his bunk, holds each of his two seeds up to the light and thinks about orange trees. He remembers that he had an orchard in northern California a whole lifetime ago, and he grew a lot of orange trees. He remembers walking among them; treading between bright shafts of light and hearing the hum of bees; plucking a ripe specimen and tasting the fruit; the sharp citrus tang, and the juices rolling down his chin. He clenches his fist and feels the two seeds buried between the folds of his palm, as if they have been planted there and might grow.

*　*　*

Two days later, Adam is moved.

Men in dark suits and dark sunglasses put him into the back of a black armoured van, and he is chained down opposite an armed guard. The guard's name is Tom, and he's talkative. So, as the van rattles away through LA, and the palm trees they pass make the white sky strobe through the small slotted windows at the top of the van, Adam listens to Tom's story.

For a while, Adam forgets that he is Adam, and becomes convinced that he's Tom. He marries Tom's wife, and the wedding is bright and beautiful in his mind. He has his first child, and then loses her at the age of three during the hurricane that ravaged the East Coast back then. But he and his wife remain together, and battle on through their grief, and move to the West Coast to start anew. They have a second child, and he's fifteen now, and while they do struggle – working for the FBI doesn't pay as well as it used to – they are happy, happier than they've ever been. Tom is happy, and Adam is happy, and he doesn't want the story to end.

Yet Adam's absorption is interrupted by a distant noise, which Tom doesn't seem to notice.

The slotted windows are bright across Adam's face as he returns to reality, and he stares through them, trying to see what it is that has broken his concentration. It was a sound so familiar. There is nothing but the white sky, at first. But there – something dashes across, too quick to see. It might have been a bird. An enormous, monstrous bird.

There is a scream cut short from ahead, barely audible over the engines of the van's escorts. Tom is at once alarmed, gripping his shotgun tight. "What's going on?"

Suddenly, his radio blares into life – confused voices yelling over each other – and from outside the van, cackling gunfire is audible. Tom stands shakily and swings his shotgun around, trying to see through the slots. "What's happening?" he shouts into his radio. "Tell me what's going on!"

There's an inhuman shriek, and claws the size of pickaxes come through the roof of the van. Tom is thrown to the floor. Blinding daylight flashes through the slashes raked through the steel, and the van shudders, tottering on two wheels before slamming back down to four.

Adam breaks free of his chains. Tom, panicked, aims his gun, but Adam grabs it by the barrel and red lines are slashed across his face as the blast skims him.

There's another animal shriek, and claws strike the side of the van. This time, it teeters and then tumbles – hits the side of the bridge and falls from the edge.

Grabbing Tom, Adam cradles him like a father with a son. Sunlight whirls around them as the van spins, plummeting. Tom is screaming, and struggling, but Adam holds tight. They hit the water, and it's sudden and cold, filling the van and filling Adam's lungs as the impact pushes his breath from him. They sink, in a rush of torn metal and froth.

The gaps in the roof aren't big enough for Adam to escape through, so he breaks the lock on the back door, struggling against the icy water making his fingers clumsy. Grabbing hold of Tom, he swims; powerful strokes, free of the van. He can see motorbikes and cars hitting the river around them; ragged bodies tugged away by the strong current, red rushing from them and mingling with the debris of the motorcade.

There are fish in the water. Silvery fish, that dart to avoid the falling wreckage.

Suddenly, Adam remembers.

There was a valley. A mountain valley, in a country a long way away from here, back when it wasn't even really a country – just the edge of a continent – where he and Eve lived, and made their own little paradise. There was a waterfall that beat his shoulders when he bathed beneath it, and there were so many birds in the trees that there was never a moment of silence, and there were the soft songs that Eve sang when she floated in the lake, gently rippling the waters with her fingers. Crane lived with them there, and she would often be seen circling the big blue sky, or stalking the edges of the lake; and so too did Pike, the lake his kingdom, his brilliant silver scales each a tiny mirror reflecting lost Eden.

They raised children there, he and Eve. Adam would teach them how to survive: taking them foraging in the forest, and showing them all the different kinds of berries and fruits and vegetables, and the marks that all the creatures left. And Eve would teach them how to love: showing them how to delight in Crane's graceful, slender movements, and telling them how to be gentle and patient with Pike, so they could feel him glide around their legs, tickling them with the swish of his silky tail.

A stranger came to the valley, Adam remembers. A coarse man, wearing furs around his waist, and carrying a heavy pack filled with salted meats and dried teas. Adam bade caution, but Eve welcomed the stranger with all the kindness she knew how to give. They shared tea down by the lake, and ate of some of the salted meats, and the stranger told them about the world beyond the valley, which was full of marvels that Adam mistrusted and Eve delighted in. Eve slept well, but Adam stayed awake, troubled by the weapon the stranger had brought with him: a long spear with a tip made of polished metal, which gleamed deadly in the firelight.

As the days progressed, and the stranger took advantage of Eve's kindness, eating readily of their stores of food, Adam began to notice that Pike was absent. This was unusual; the great fish was often to be seen agleam in the lake at the heart of their valley. Adam went down to the waters, and there he waded, and swam, and searched the underside of every pebble for Pike, but he was nowhere to be seen. It was true that the river at the edge of the lake eventually made its way to the sea, and that in all likelihood Pike had simply gone swimming, but it was unlike the kindly fish to leave without bidding anyone farewell. Emerging from the lake, a heaviness set upon Adam the likes of which he had not felt since Eden. He went to go find the stranger.

The stranger had set up camp on the far side of the lake, near the waterfall, and there he was now, surrounded by bones and the ashes of burnt-out fires, working at something with a length of twine. There were flecks of cooked fish-flesh still clinging to his equipment, and there, smeared across his spear, the webbed fibres of a silvery fin. For the longest time Adam simply stood, observing the stranger, consumed by an emotion he did not recognise. The stranger said things to him that he did not hear, and then, so full of pride, showed Adam the results of his labours. It was to be a gift, the stranger said – a wonderful gift to reward Adam and Eve's hospitality – as he raised the necklace he had been lacing, composed of Pike's brilliant scales.

Adam had taken the scale necklace from the stranger. Then, with it bunched in his fist, he had murdered the man with it.

The movement of his arm. The crunch of the stranger's bones.

The recollection is sharp, and painful: a single thorn belonging to the tangle in Adam's skull.

Adam gasps for breath as he breaks the surface of the river.

There's the bank, nearby. He swims across and hauls himself free of the river, collapsing to his knees upon the pebbles, coughing up water and feeling his lungs burn. Tom, the FBI man, might be alive, might be dead. He wipes the river from his eyes and looks around.

The broken bridge. The dead everywhere, torn to ribbons. The bright white sky. The quiet scrublands. They must be miles away from LA.

Nearby, a naked, powerfully built man is watching the river wash the blood from his bare feet. His hair is long, wild and unkempt about him, and there is something regal about the way he holds himself – as if he is superior to everything he beholds with his wide wild eyes. His feet are marred with gore, and ribbons of flesh wriggle in the shallows, caught between his toes.

"Owl." Adam's throat is raw, so he tries again. "Owl."

The ragged man's head snaps around, unblinking eyes fixed on the sound.

Adam stands cautiously, keeping his movements slow, and Owl's eyes follow him, every twitch. "Where's Rook?" None are living around them. It looks as if Adam is the only survivor of the attack, apart from Tom, who stirs still – somewhere between life and death.

"Yonder," replies Owl, gutturally. Walking unsteadily across the pebbles, he makes his way over to Tom, and then places one of his bloody feet upon the dying man's neck. There is a crunch as he pushes down. Beyond, the blue lights of the armoured van still flash beneath the waves, distant glimmering sparks of blue; but everyone is dead.

Owl makes his way towards the scrubby brush at the edge of the embankment, trailing blood across the earth. He walks as if he is unused to using his legs. There, he raises an arm prophetically, as if answers await Adam beyond the ridge.

Adam leaves the river, but at Tom's corpse, he pauses.

"Sorry," he says, and he's surprised to find that he means it.

II

Leaning against a bright white muscle car is a girl in a summer dress who only has one leg, and even though she is wearing a pair of huge sunglasses the same black as her long hair, she shades her eyes against the sky. Behind her, the Pacific sparkles, and before her, the California road is empty and being swept by a veil of desert dust. Adam twists the silver bracelets around his wrists until they break, and drops them as he approaches – leaning over to do the same with those around his ankles.

"Orange doesn't suit you," says the girl, when he's close enough.

Adam shrugs. "They only had orange." He looks left, and then right – no cars on the road. They are alone.

"I got you some clothes. Extra-extra-extra-*extra* large. The guy in the shop gave me a funny look." There is indeed a duffel bag at her feet. Adam takes it and pulls out a white T-shirt, a pair of black sweatpants and some running shoes. He pauses with them, glancing at the girl, but she laughs. "You don't need to be coy, Adam. I've seen it all before."

The clothes fit, miraculously. He wanders across to the river nearby and throws his jumpsuit in, before returning to the car.

The girl is inside and waiting for him, and when he slips into the passenger side, she starts the engine. "Rook wasn't kidding," she says. "You look different."

"What about Owl?"

Back near the edge of the river, a monstrous silhouette is moving. Owl has changed – is now something between man and bird. He spreads his wings and they glint in colours of bronze and gold, and then he moves out of sight suddenly – a ferocious strike at something. "He'll catch up," she says. "He's got some cleaning up to do. And besides, I don't think he likes being in the car. He was irritated all the way down." She inclines her head at the back seat, and Adam turns to see the torn white leather there.

Pulling out onto the highway, she drives them away.

"There's a new set of papers in the glovebox for you."

As promised, Adam finds an envelope. He opens it and draws out a new driving licence, birth certificate and passport, as well as a credit card and some cash. "Simon Davies," he says. "Rook hasn't called me Adam."

"I think you pissed him off."

"Mmm." Adam folds the documents away and studies the girl. It's difficult to see her features behind her enormous sunglasses, but she has a way of looking as fragile as porcelain, yet holding herself as if she's forged out of steel. Her prosthetic leg starts just below the knee, and it's made of a clear material, which makes it look as if it's both there and not there at the same time. "I like your leg, Crow," he tells her.

"Me too." She smiles.

They drive in silence for a while, with the Pacific to their right, until Crow steers them up a ramp and onto a highway, joining a stream of other cars. A set of police cruisers hurtle past, sirens blaring, but the muscle car's windows are tinted and none of them slow. Shortly after, a helicopter also sweeps by. Then there is the open road, and Crow lowers her window – dark hair curling and uncurling in the wind.

Adam begins to relax. "What now?" he asks.

"Rook didn't tell you? You're going to help me find Magpie."

"I figured I'd be doing it by myself."

"It's my job," says Crow. "You're just the muscle. The brawn. I've been doing the PI work for Corvid & Corvid for a long time now, and I think I'm pretty good at it. So you just sit back and try to not think too hard." She turns towards him and lowers her sunglasses, peering over them and pinning him in place. "Don't kill anybody unless I tell you to, okay?"

"Got it."

"Good." She turns back to the road.

The sun is behind them now, and setting. Soon it will be night. "Where are we going? Rook mentioned Scotland."

"We'll end up there eventually. But I want to stop off in Louisiana first. Corvid & Corvid have been looking after Owl's assets since he's been on sabbatical, and I was going through the papers and noticed that somebody's been paying to keep the power on in his old Louisiana property. Traced it back to Magpie. They're big bills, too. He's been using a lot of electricity. So, Owl and me want to go see what he's been doing. It's going to take us a day or two to get over there, though, so you might want to get comfortable. It's going to be a long drive."

Shifting in his seat, Adam leans back and yawns. Truth be told, the car is comfortable. "When was the last time I saw you?" he asks.

"French Riviera, I think. You read about it in a book and wanted to go on holiday there, so I came along. Do you remember?"

"Yes," Adam lies. When he thinks about the Riviera, he thinks about the hot sun, and the mild chattering of the brightly dressed holidaymakers, and the slow boats made wavering by the heat rising from the water. But he's not sure which bits of his memory belong to the trip, and which belong to the book. He doesn't remember Crow at all.

"You fell asleep on the beach, and nobody could wake you up or move you, so we just left you there. I came back in the morning and the water was up to your chest, and you were half buried in the sand, but you were still sound asleep. There were crabs crawling over you, and fish in the pools made by your hands. I wish I'd taken a picture. You sleep like the dead, Adam."

"Guess I've got a lot of death to catch up on." It's meant to be a joke, but it comes out morbid, as if there's a truth to it.

With the oncoming dark, Crow removes her sunglasses.

As the last remnants of the day ebb away in red and yellow, Adam closes his eyes. Already, his brief time in jail is beginning to feel like a dream – as if it happened to someone he read about in a book once.

* * *

When Adam wakes, the car is dark and he's alone.

He steps out into an empty parking lot. There are no lamps – only the blue and pink neon sign revolving nearby, illuminating the trees and the car-less highway. Adam finds a place to sit on the kerb beneath the trees, and listens to the wind as it rustles the loose autumn leaves.

Soon, Crow returns. She hands him a greasy paper bag, and a large cardboard cup, and sits down next to him, removing morsels from her own bag and biting hungrily into them.

They devour their meals in silence.

When they're done, they stay sitting for a while, and Adam sips at his coffee. Crow is staring up at the sky, looking preoccupied, with the neon sign playing across her features.

"Doesn't it bother you?" she asks, eventually.

"Doesn't what bother me?"

"Being stuck to the ground."

He feels it starting in his stomach – an unfamiliar sensation that grows upwards from there, to his chest and then his throat and his face, bearing fruit as it tumbles from his mouth. When it stops, Adam tries to remember the last time he laughed, but finds that he is unable.

"How are you, Adam?" Crow is studying him, her smile fading.

"I'm fine," he says.

"Really?"

Adam finishes his coffee, and considers the question. "Honestly? I feel like I'm missing a limb. But every time I count them, they're all there."

Crow arches a brow.

"Sorry," he says, realising his mistake. "I didn't mean…" The problem is that he doesn't consider Crow's leg to be missing, as such. The fact that she only has one leg is as much a part of her as the colour of her eyes, or the way she smiles.

"It's okay, Adam. I know what you mean." Crow touches his shoulder. "When was the last time you visited Eve?"

Her name, again – like a candle lit. "A long time," he says, because he honestly can't remember the last time he saw her. Lifetimes ago. Too long ago.

"Well, we are going to be in Scotland. So why don't we go together, after the job's done? I imagine Magpie would want to see her, as well."

"That sounds good," says Adam, but he finds that he is hesitant – afraid that he might disappoint her, somehow. These days, he feels as if he has more in common with his shadow than the man he used to be. Still – he has to admit that it would be good to see Eve again. "Thanks, Crow."

"Your turn to drive," she says, handing him the keys.

*　*　*

Hours and days pass behind the rumble of the muscle car's engine.

Eventually, Crow turns into a long driveway, through rows of bent-backed trees and overgrown shrubbery. The muscle car rumbles down the rough track, and ploughs a route through the long grasses hiding the way.

All at once, the house is revealed.

It looks wrong. The ivy-wreathed pillars supporting the balcony look as if they are of different lengths, and each heavily cracked window seems unevenly spaced, and the very foundations appear off balance, as if the house has subsided slightly.

"Ugly place," says Adam. Black birds take flight from the balcony all in a rush as he and Crow step out. Together, they take a moment to breathe in the humid swampy air, and listen to the eerie tomb-like silence engulfing the remote house. There are big planks of wood barring the enormous front doors shut. "Doesn't look like anybody's been here in a while."

"Magpie won't have used the front door." Lightly, Crow pulls at a plank, and part of it comes free – a sodden, rotten pulp. She drops it and rubs at her palms. "Open this up for me."

It takes little effort to clear the doors of the remaining planks. That done, Adam finds the doors locked, so he wrenches at a handle until something snaps, forcing them open. A waft of stinking, moist air assails them as the doors grate along the cracked stone floor, as if Adam has peeled back the skin of a fruit to find it rotten inside. The interior is wretched; though once grand, most of it looks as if it long ago ripened in the humid Louisiana air – the wallpaper is peeling, the bannisters are warped, and the carpets are brown instead of red.

A pair of fierce eyes peer at them from an enormous ruined portrait. "Owl," says Adam, and he stops before it, trying to decipher the scene. There are all manner of folk around him, some wearing the clothes of servants, others wearing the clothes of the wealthy, and everyone is smiling before a colourful backdrop of drooping bright trees. Only Owl is sincere – he's tall, and broad at the centre of the painting, wearing a brocade coat that already seems out of date.

There's something familiar about the style of the painting: the once-vivid colours, and the way that each subject is so vibrant, as if the portrait is a doctored photograph with the saturation turned up not on the colours, but on the people. At the corner of the painting is a faded signature, which Adam peers at, deciphering the flourishes and curls into a name that might be 'Butterfly'.

"How long has Owl been on sabbatical?" Adam asks.

"Oh, uh…" Crow considers the question. "When was the Boer War?"

"Not sure."

"Since then, anyway. A while now. I'm surprised he still remembers language, honestly." She peers up at the painting, with a frown. "I need a bath," says Crow. "And so do you. You still stink of the river."

"Reckon the plumbing still works?"

"I'll go stoke the boiler, you go run the taps, and we can find out."

Adam tests each step as he lumbers upstairs, but the wood doesn't give. Whatever damage there is to the house, it seems only skin deep – the foundations are holding. Opening doors at random, he eventually comes to a long bathroom; white tiles stained by years of neglect. The bath is enormous, and has clawed feet. Turning the taps, he waits for the water to run clear, and then plugs the bath.

Wiping at the mirror with a ruined rag of a towel, Adam sees an unfamiliar face staring back at him. It is, of course, his own face, but there's something wrong with the eyes. There's a deep weariness in them. Searching through a cupboard, he locates a pair of rusty tweezers and uses them to pull at the pieces of shrapnel embedded in his forehead. Blood drips from the open wounds, and he wonders if the long lines scratched into him from the shotgun blast will leave scars.

The pipes groan, and steam rises from the bath; the plumbing is working, after all.

Crow arrives and throws the windows open, so that all the noise of the forest encroaching on the house drifts inside: birds, and insects, and the distant sound of traffic. Then, removing her clothes and her prosthetic leg, she sinks into the bath with a sigh. "Let me know if you find any soap."

Adam opens a few more cupboards, finds a crusty amber lump and hands it across. Then, peeling off his own sweaty layers, he lowers himself into the tub opposite Crow. The water level rises and splashes over the edge, and Crow uses his knees to prop her legs up, so that she can scrub at them each in turn.

"Surprised the plumbing still works," says Adam.

"We tried to maintain the place for a long time after Owl left, just in case he ever felt like coming back. Thus, the electrics. We gave up a couple of decades ago, though. Owl seems happy the way he is. Or maybe 'happy' isn't the right word. Content."

"Do you know what made him give this place up?"

Crow passes the soap across the back of her neck. "I'm not sure it was any one thing," she says. "I visited him three times while he was here. The first was when he'd just arrived, off the boats and looking for a place to settle. He only spoke

French back then, and he seemed excited, about America, about exploring, about building his own place, somewhere among the trees here. I think he fell in love with this bit of land as soon as he set eyes on it. I stuck around while he built the house, and he was up every morning at the crack of dawn, doing twice as much as the rest of the labourers: importing the strongest, finest trees, and embedding them in the strongest, finest chunks of stone, and hammering tiles into the roof all through the day, lord of his land.

"The second time I visited, he was speaking English. Heavily accented, mind you, and he still insisted on wearing his old brocade coats, like he was determined to remain as French as possible. He had a lot of servants, all of whom were beloved to him, and he had friends all over the country, always visiting and marvelling at his wonderful house, and his wonderful forest, and his wonderful hospitality. I stayed for a few months, and he lavished me with expensive gifts imported from Europe, and took me all around town in his ridiculous coach, introducing me to all the shopkeepers and judges and mayors, and they all had nothing but good things to say about him.

"Then, the third time I visited, he was alone at the house. Barely speaking any more. The roof tiles were falling off, and nobody was coming to visit him, and he was spending his nights out among the trees of the forest, flying around and hunting. I don't know what happened, but I do know that it was long enough between visits that everybody he introduced me to the last time would have passed on. He was still kind to me, though, even up to the point where he stopped pretending to be a person any more."

"Just Owl, again," says Adam.

"Just Owl." Crow smiles.

When Adam feels somewhat cleaner, he heaves himself free of the bath, towels himself down with a stiff piece of coarse cloth, runs his clothes under a cold tap, and shrugs them back on, enjoying the way they steam against his skin.

"You should take a look around," says Crow, still soaking. "I'll join you soon."

Doing as he's told, Adam goes to explore, finding a few bedrooms with rotting sheets and open windows. Birds have made their nests on the dressers and among the silverware, and the Louisiana climate is present throughout; there is little divide between outside and inside. Eventually, he opens a door into a library, but his excitement is short-lived. Every single book is no more than a useless, ruined pulp. Adam mourns the loss of all those words – all those worlds, ruined by neglect.

The truth is, he can imagine Owl alone here, slowly growing weary of his books, of his grief. It would be nice, Adam thinks, to fly out into the forest, into the sky, and leave all that weight behind.

While making his way back to the staircase, Adam notices a pair of eyes watching him from behind a semi-closed door. Pushing it open, he enters an enormous chamber filled from ceiling to floor with shelves upon shelves of taxidermised animals. They are hideous, he thinks – twisted parodies of the creatures they once were – birds and beasts of all kinds fixed into unnatural poses, dead eyes glaring open forever. But they are eerily untouched by the rot inflicting the rest of the house. They seem like a recent addition.

"Adam!" Crow, calling him.

She is waiting in the main hall. "I found some animals," he tells her, as he makes his way down. "Taxidermy. They look new."

She laughs. "Magpie's definitely been here, then. But I found something else."

Through a dripping, drooping kitchen, Crow leads Adam to a metal door, half hidden between piles of rusted tin cans. The door is untouched, and looks strong, and beyond it there is a stone staircase illuminated by clean bulbs, leading below. There is a touch-pad beside the door, flashing green, and Adam frowns. "Was there a code?"

"No code. It was open."

Down the steps, the air is dry and crisp. The whirring of machines filtering out the Louisiana humidity becomes more apparent as Adam descends, until he emerges into an enormous rectangular chamber, perhaps the length of the entire house. The walls are made of cold stone, and so is the floor, and the low ceiling is lined with rows upon rows of bar lamps, currently dark. Otherwise, the chamber is completely empty.

"Watch this," says Crow, and she flicks a switch. The bar lights all flicker on, and they are bright and blue.

Adam crouches, running a hand along the empty stone floor. "Ultraviolet."

"What do you think?"

"Drugs."

"That's what I thought, but it doesn't add up. If it was drugs, then Magpie would be making money, not spending it. Whatever he was growing here, I don't think it was drugs."

"What, then?"

She shrugs. "You're the gardener."

Pacing the long chamber, Adam searches the ground and the walls for any clue, but they're naked – maybe even scrubbed clean. He pauses at the centre, and turns on the spot, but he can find no reasonable explanation for the hidden greenhouse.

There is a muffled thump from upstairs, and a loud cry, echoing down the stairwell.

"Owl's here," says Crow. "Time we got going."

"Where next?"

She flicks the UV lights off, and the chamber is darkened once again. "Scotland," she says, as she climbs the stairs.

Back in the main hall, Owl is waiting. He is perched on the bannister at the top of the stairs in his native shape – all bird – beneath an open crack in the roof, through which sunlight pours. The feathers of pigeons drift around him, and he flicks his golden wings, and for a moment, just for a moment, he is the lord of his house again.

*　*　*

The closer she drives to the coast, the smaller Crow seems.

She's foregone her summer dress and put on some shapeless practical clothes, and she hides behind her sunglasses. Passing cars reflect across the black lenses, and she is silent, even as Owl makes soft noises and tears up the back seats with his claws.

In his native shape, Owl is still regal. He paces from claw to claw restlessly, and his head revolves, peering with enormous yellow eyes at the trees and the overcast sky. Adam finds it difficult to resolve the bird with the man or the monster. They seem like discrete things – like individual elements of a trinity with nothing but a name to join them.

Eventually, the Gulf of Mexico comes into view.

Adam has always preferred the West Coast to the South Coast. Here, there are no impressive cliffs or beaches. The land simply seems to come to a gentle end. Crow shivers in her seat at the sight, driving with her hands gripping the wheel too tight, and directing it down a disused slip road into an abandoned fishing town. They pass ancient, crumbling brick buildings being reclaimed by the sea. The skeletons of fishing boats lay out like beached whales. "It's funny," says Crow, quietly. "How quickly things fall apart."

Parking up beside a broken pier, they exit the car. Adam opens the back door and Owl flutters out, coming to rest on his shoulder. The feathers of his wings are soft across Adam's skull, but his claws are sharp and dig into Adam's skin. Together, they make their way to the edge of the pier and admire the cold, grey Gulf.

Crow folds her arms and tries to hide in her hoodie.

"You okay?"

"Yeah," she says. "I just… I really don't like flying. I mean, I don't like planes. They put me on edge. I don't get how you do it. I don't get how you can just sit there cramped up in a big tin can, all strapped up in neat little rows, blind to the sky, flying too fast. I keep thinking: it's going to fall; it's too heavy; I'm trapped and when it goes down we're all going to sink into the sea and I'm going to drown because I can't get free."

"You'll be fine. Nothing's going to happen."

"You've got to make sure I don't do anything stupid on the plane, okay?"

"Sure. But what about me? I'm still a fugitive."

"Oh," she says, smiling bitterly. "Don't worry. They're usually too busy bullying brown people to look for anybody who's actually dangerous these days."

With a soft thump, Owl lands at the edge of the pier. His feathered head turns to and fro as if he might take in the whole sea. Then, with one great heave of his brilliant shimmering wings, he takes flight. Adam watches him until he becomes a copper glinting, and then no more than a black dot, soaring away over the Gulf in the direction of the Atlantic.

"He's going to meet us in Edinburgh," Crow says.

"Why don't you fly with him?"

"Well. I've done it a couple of times, but I'm not really built for that kind of flight. I get too exhausted, and then I'm useless for weeks afterwards. Besides, someone's gotta look after you." She removes her sunglasses, and the face behind them is timid, as if she left her confidence behind at Owl's house. "You're not yourself, Adam."

Crow places a hand on Adam's arm, and the touch seems tender, meaningful in a way that feels strange. Adam remembers a time when it was his job to watch over the animals of Eden. It was his honour. But here, in this strange, cold, bitter world, everything is backwards.

* * *

The departures lounge at New Orleans International is bustling.

Adam is fond of airports. Over the last few years, he's spent a lot of time ferrying celebrities to and from LAX, and waiting in various terminals for them to arrive. Today, he sits at the heart of the departures lounge, among the rows of benches, and listens to everyone speaking, letting their voices flow into him unfiltered. Adam likes all the languages he hears mingled together at airports, some of which he understands, but most of which he does not. If languages were a tree, he thinks, then small fruits would be rolling from their mouths, and the roots of the language tree would be the language he spoke in Eden. Adam doesn't remember any of the words he spoke in Eden. He's not even sure his name was Adam, back then. He does remember how easy it was to speak, though, as if every word came not from his head, but from some other organ deep inside him, as essential as his liver or lungs. And when he named something, which was his great honour, the name gave that thing more meaning than a simple utterance: it gave that thing an identity. He supposes that Edenic might not much resemble any of the languages he can hear here at all; that the languages being spoken all around him are likely to be as far removed from the first language as their speakers are from their distant progenitor.

Crow is somewhere else in the airport, awaiting the boarding announcement. They are to be aboard the same plane, but they've had their tickets booked separately, to smooth Adam's escape. Soon their plane will be called, and Adam knows he will have to face security. So far, however, he has attracted no attention at all.

At last, the announcement comes.

There is a queue for security, and Adam is made to remove his shoes as he passes through. Of course, he sets off the metal detector, but that's no surprise. A man waves a hand-held detector over him and it beeps at every bullet and broken blade and piece of shrapnel still embedded beneath his scars, and when they pat him down he tells them that he's a veteran and has had several of his bones replaced with metal parts. They accept his explanation with no further questions, and suddenly Adam is queueing to board instead, and lacing his shoes back on. He tries to spot Crow in the queue, and notices her near the front, so hunched up in her hoodie that she seems smaller than she is in his memory.

On the plane, they manage to find seats together, despite having been booked separately.

They are in standard class, and everyone seems a little too close together. Adam's knees are crushed against the seat in front of him, and to his left Crow is clutching his arm with both of hers, and there is an elderly Scottish lady leaning in to his right, who is insisting on making conversation.

"Do I know you?" she asks again, peering at him through thick glasses.

"No, ma'am."

"I'm sure I do."

"We've never met."

The lady stares for a few moments longer, and then smiles. "You have a nice face."

Adam turns back to Crow. "Maybe you should try and sleep."

"I can't sleep. If I sleep, I'll die, and I'll wake up dead."

The plane begins moving, and every small jostle makes Crow clutch at Adam's hand tighter. She is clearly terrified, and he's not sure what to do about it. He considers trying to say something comforting, but he's never been very good at words.

The plane takes off, and a child a few seats up starts shrieking. "I'm sorry," says Crow. "I hate this. I hate being trapped. I promised myself I'd never let it happen again."

"Again?"

Crow's voice is very soft. "He was the son of a Gupta; handsome, charming and intelligent. He was interested in architecture and astrology, and he'd take me to see temples and palaces during the day, and name all the constellations at night. He loved treasures, and he treated me as if I were a finer treasure than any of his jewels or spices. I fell in love with him, and he confessed that he felt the same way, so I showed him my feathers, and he professed his wonder, and adoration, and lavished me with praise in every way he knew how, and had a room made for me, in his palace, where I could roost undisturbed, and fly from the window at all hours. In time, he told me that I should keep wearing my feathers always, because he loved them so much, and some nights, he began closing the window to my room, and locking the door, because his enemies were close, and he was afraid they might try and hurt me. Then he started locking me in every night, for my safety. Eventually, he only unlocked the door to let me out while in his company, because he so feared for my life, and he would watch me as I flew laps around his lavish courtyard. Then, at last, he had a chain made for me from the finest silver, and looped it around my claw, so I would be tethered to him whenever he let me out. He said that it was a symbol of our undying love for each other."

"What did you do?"

Crow absently touches her prosthetic. "I escaped."

"I'm sorry."

"What for?"

"If I'd have known…"

"But you didn't. Nobody did. I let it happen. That's the problem. I let it happen."

Adam places his hand on top of hers. "I'm sorry."

"I know," she says, so quietly it's almost a whisper.

Soon, she is asleep; exhausted, perhaps, by the retelling of her story. And lulled by her breathing, Adam, too, drifts away.

The first time he wakes, it is night, and most of the passengers around him are tucked up under tiny blue blankets. The elderly lady is leaning against him and snoring, but Crow is wide awake again, and glaring out of a window as if she might smash the glass with the intensity of her gaze. Her grip on his arm has strengthened, and every time there's the slightest tremble of turbulence she twitches, as if ready to leap from her seat.

Sleep takes Adam again.

The next time he's awoken, it's by noise. There is the overwhelming rushing of air, and books, and crisp packets, and plastic cups whirl everywhere around him. Adam's seat is shaking horribly, and bright daylight gushes in through the windows. Oxygen masks dangle, swinging and bouncing with each jarring jolt of the plane, and Adam can see everyone around him pulling them to their faces. Feeling light-headed, Adam grabs at his own oxygen mask and straps it on, trying to take stock of what's happening. There are people in the aisle clinging on to the seats to remain steady, and there are even more people at the front of the cabin, trying desperately to close the door. Beyond that gaping portal is the open sky, blue and white in rushing abundance.

With a Herculean communal heave, the door slams shut.

The shuddering of the plane continues, and the screaming of the passengers suddenly becomes audible. Everyone is panicking and trying to breathe. There are marks on his hand where Crow gripped him tight, but her seat is empty. He tries to stand, still feeling dizzy from the sudden loss of cabin pressure, but only succeeds at bouncing his skull from the low ceiling. So, instead, he turns to the elderly Scottish lady, who is breathing heavily, her face pale. "Have you seen the girl who was sitting next to me?"

"It was her," she says, breathlessly. "She opened the door."

"Where is she?"

"She jumped," says the lady, her eyes wide. "She jumped out of the plane."

III

It used to be that any journey of profound distance could be measured in lives lost.

Sickness, weakness, starvation and accident were chief among the causes of death. To be elderly and embark on a long voyage or pilgrimage was to flip a coin, and to begin a journey while weary or starving or inflicted with illness was to invite death. The wind could fail, or your engine might, or even your feet. The weather might dry you or drown you or freeze you. Your food and water, if not properly kept or foraged, might poison you. Over the next horizon might be new diseases, waiting to strike you down. Your horse might break a leg or throw a shoe, or, without enough care, you might overwork your animal and have it just plain give up on you. One slippery section of deck and you might tumble overboard. One drunken argument with one of your fellow travellers, one border guard in a bad mood, one gang of robbers or locals or colonists and your journey might end short of its destination.

Sitting in the busy arrivals lounge, Adam tries to get his head around the fact that he is suddenly in Edinburgh. It doesn't feel like he's earned his passage here. He still feels like he's in America. California, even.

Up on the big screen, Cassandra Coleman weeps dramatically into a handkerchief. She's being interviewed about her time with Adam. The questions keep coming up in the subtitles: did she suspect that Adam was a killer? How well did she know Damon Darcy? What was it like being so close to both victim and murderer? Cassandra does her very best to seem both strong and upset simultaneously, and the effect is compelling. Even now, Adam appreciates her acting. She will go far, he thinks.

"Excuse me." It's the elderly lady he sat next to on the plane.

"Hello again," says Adam.

"Would you help me with my luggage? My grandson's waiting outside, but I'm struggling a little, and you seem like a big strong man." She smiles.

"Sure thing, ma'am." Adam takes her suitcase and hauls it along easily, following in her wake.

"That girl," she says, "on the plane. Did you know her?"

"Not really. I only met her when I sat down."

"Why do you think she jumped?"

Airport security, and then the police, have already spent a couple of hours asking him the same question. Adam gives her the same answer he gave them. "She seemed scared."

"Selfish, though, don't you think? Her family must be so upset. Now they'll have to organise her funeral, and spend the rest of their lives wondering what they could have done. She shouldn't have done it. Do you know what I do when I get sad?" She grips his arm and leads him past crowds of people. "I go for a nice wee walk. Cheers me right up. Or maybe I'll go see a movie, or go have a natter with a friend! You don't see me throwing myself out of a plane when I get sad. Such a waste of life. Oh look, there's Bobbie! Hello there, Bobbie!" Adam places the case down beside Bobbie, who frowns suspiciously up at him. Then he and his grandmother go on their way, out into the cold Scottish day.

For a moment, Adam stands at the threshold, before the automatic doors that will lead him out of the airport. The first time he arrived in Scotland, it wasn't called Scotland. In fact, it wasn't even called Caledonia. When he and Eve first set foot in this country, all that time ago, it didn't have a name to any but its few inhabitants.

Adam and Eve had been living in Rome for a few lifetimes, and they had grown weary of the place, of the very idea of civilisation. Together, they had watched emperor after emperor ruling over a slowly growing empire, shaping it with their successive whims. So, she and Adam began to talk to the traders, to find the limits of the empire, and some forgotten corner of the world where they might start anew. There was word of an island far to the north, called Albion, and though the south of it was known to be occupied, there was little news of the northern reaches. Tales reached Adam of wild lands, almost untouched by human hands.

It took them the better part of a year to travel through the empire, and across to Albion. They hitched rides with trading caravans, and rode horses, and sometimes simply walked, until at last they came to the fringes of the mainland and could see, across the sea, the suggestion of their island destination. Adam spent a season making a boat worthy of crossing, built out of the sturdiest trees he could find. He traded for good sailcloth, and tapped trees for sap to seal it, and Eve wound endless cord for him, to help rig his sail. Then, on the darkest night of the year, they waited for dawn, and when it came, they set sail across that cold and forbidding sea.

Strange, to set foot on a new shore; to feel the sand beneath your feet.

They spent a while together simply exploring the south of Albion. There were pale peoples here, who had begun trading with the land across the sea, and were aware of the advancing empire. They didn't seem to care much for it. There were more tales of the north, of wild, unfriendly people who did not often trade, and hard lands, rich with forests so huge that they touched shore to shore; and mountains and shale and endless rain, assailing visitors until they left. Eventually, Adam and Eve set sail again, following the coast north and further north still, day by day, moon by moon, until winter began to give way to the first signs of spring, and at last they arrived in the north.

Adam sailed up a broad river-mouth, paddling with oars carved from the branches of an oak. The air was calm that day, he remembers; the river was still, and Eve trailed her fingers in the water, among the curious silver fish that followed the boat. There was none of the forbidding atmosphere that Adam had expected. The forests were indeed thick, and the mountains he could see in the distance were indeed rocky, and every now and then he was assailed by a light drizzling rain, but there were finches and starlings singing in the trees, and bluebells and snowdrops clinging to the shores, and every now and then the sun would break through the clouds and warm his weary arms.

They landed in a knell, and there stepped out into the land that would one day be called Scotland. Eve was tired from the journey, and spent the first few days there wandering not very far; simply recovering. To help cheer her, Adam made her a crown. He went among the frosty bluebells and snowdrops, which were wilting with the end of winter, and picked a great many, and carefully wound them into a rich blue and white and green crown, and shyly presented it to her. She kissed him, he remembers, and wore her crown of flowers until it disintegrated, coming apart while she bathed in a stream.

Adam blinks, emerging from the memory. Before him are the automatic doors. He thinks he will make Eve a new crown of flowers, when he sees her next.

At last, he steps out into Scotland.

* * *

It's a grey day in Edinburgh. From Waverley Bridge, where Adam's bus stops, there's a nice view of Edinburgh Castle. Adam pauses there a while and remembers the configuration of the rocks around its base as it was – the way the moss clung to them, long ago. Running his thumb across the tips of his fingers, he recalls the sensation of gripping hold of that moss, made slippery by the morning mist. Adam used to live in this city, he knows; whole lifetimes ago.

He's not sure where to start looking for Magpie, so he lets his feet take him through streets simultaneously familiar and unfamiliar. The curve of the pathways and the feel of the cobbles that line them is the same, and sometimes he stops and presses his hands against patches of brickwork. There is memory in the stones of the city. The rest is strange to him, though; the shops, and the people, and the vehicles now rumbling up the hills. There were horses, the last time he was here. He remembers their breathing and soft noises, and the movements of their muscles and tails. Driven onwards by his recollections, he heads south through the city.

When he reaches the veterinary school, it is much the same as it was. It rises before him, a towering design at the head of the autumnal Meadows, and the stone steps leading up to the entrance are worn but at familiar heights. For a little while, Adam sits on those steps. He used to work here; one of the few men in the city capable of hauling an entire horse through the long halls. Most of those horses were dead, he remembers; specimens for students to dismantle, but there were a fair share of live horses, along with cattle and the occasional dog. He worked here so that they would all have an ally close at hand. Someone to offer comfort to the sick, and someone to offer respect to the dead. Those were good years, he thinks – kind years, recovering from the bloodshed of a war he barely remembers fighting in.

The veterinary school is no longer a veterinary school, however. When he heads inside, he finds its halls filled with art instead of medicine. The place is now called Summerhall, and where students once learned the art of healing there is now dancing, and painting, and small libraries. At the back of the place, the stables are now microbreweries, lined with massive vats. Adam goes to the central courtyard, which is now a pub, and sits at one of the benches, watching the patch of grey sky above and trying to find something in it to help him anchor his memories.

Time passes, in contemplation.

"Adam."

The voice startles him from his thoughts. The source is a woman he does not recognise, newly arrived to the courtyard. She is wearing a revealing white dress, and she seems to fall out of it at odd angles, shifting within it as if she is uncomfortable wearing any clothes at all. Upon her head is a thick crown of flowers, and draped loosely over her shoulders is a fur shawl that draws Adam's eyes irresistibly across it. As she comes closer, Adam notices that she is wearing heavy amounts of make-up, and has dyed her hair a rich spun gold. There is a look in her eyes that might be hunger.

"Adam," she says again, with a smile that cracks her powder.

"Do I know you?"

She sits down opposite him on the bench, spilling from her dress. "Not yet. But I hope we'll be friends. Maybe more." She licks her lips. "We have a mutual acquaintance. If my information is correct, then you've been sent by Corvid & Corvid to find one of its errant partners. Magnus Corvid."

It takes Adam a few moments to realise that she's talking about Magpie. Magnus Corvid must be his current alias. "That's right," he says.

The woman leans forward, offering her hand, and she smells

like an entire orchard. "Ada Sinclair. It is *such* a pleasure to meet you."

Adam doesn't take the hand, but this does nothing to deter her. She leans back, eyes travelling over every scar of him. "My husband and I also have a vested interest in locating Magnus, which is why I'm here. We would be interested in offering what little information we have on his current whereabouts, along with a proposal. I suppose that we're offering a kind of partnership, if you like. Would you be interested in coming to meet my husband? I have a car waiting out front, and the trip isn't too far. I promise that it will be worth your while."

This close, Adam can see the crow's feet marking the edges of her eyes. This woman has gone to great lengths to try and appear much younger than she is, he thinks. He studies her for a few moments longer, trying to make up his mind about whether to go with her. He doesn't like the way she beholds him, as if he is a piece of ripe fruit that she might devour. But then he finds himself examining her shawl again. It's draped loosely across her skinny shoulders, and shifts with the light; sometimes a burnt ochre, sometimes a deep wine red, and sometimes a fiery orange, as if all the colours of sunset are present in the rich layers of fur.

"Your flowers," he says, eventually.

This seems to take the woman by surprise. She touches her crown. "Lovely, aren't they? My husband and I dabble in botany."

"They're all out of season."

Ada Sinclair's smile broadens, as if Adam has confirmed something to her. "Yes," she says. "Yes they are. Come with me and I'll show you why."

* * *

The back of Ada Sinclair's car is spacious, but she chooses to sit beside Adam with one of her legs pressed against his. The out-of-season crown of flowers rests on the seat opposite, a symbol for something that Adam doesn't yet understand. Ada keeps one hand on his wrist, and whispers sweet words to him, and her breath smells of fruit and faint rot. The only thing keeping Adam where he is is the feel of her fur shawl as it brushes against his neck – the luxurious softness of it is soothing, somehow. The car's driver is a hunched and elderly black man in an ill-fitting suit, who keeps glancing at Adam in the rear-view mirror with an expression he is unable to read. Adam ignores the driver, and ignores Ada, and ignores the crown. He stares out of the car window at the grey sky as it clears, revealing patches of blue and a silver crescent moon. He is uncomfortable seeing the moon during the day; it looks wrong, he thinks. He catches himself reflexively raising his hand to the window, as if he might push that moon back below the horizon where it belongs.

Adam loses track of the car's route, but it eventually rumbles down a long road between high hills and into a deep basin. A broad and mighty river must have formed this valley, Adam thinks, but there's no sign of it now. Instead, the basin is agleam with greenhouses. There are so many of them reflecting the shifting sky that they are difficult to look at. The greenhouses hum with artificial light, and sump pools glisten oily between them, and beyond the panes are endless neat rows of green shrubs with gemstone-like fruits gleaming from their branches.

"Wonderful, isn't it?" breathes Ada Sinclair, and her eyes are like those fruits: glassy gems. "The market is ripe for this kind of agriculture. People want local produce, but they also want apples in the dead of winter, and blackberries in spring. Something we're happy to provide, at a premium." She runs her fingers up his arm.

The car passes among the endless greenhouses, and as they flash past Adam finds himself wishing for the return of the river that carved this valley. It would be better that all of this were washed away, he thinks. Yet, eventually, there is a break in the greenhouses, where there is a wilting meadow and a set of stables. A pair of horses watch the car pass, munching at hay. "One of my husband's hobbies," whispers Ada into Adam's ear. "We keep stables, and kennels as well. Perhaps you might like to join him on a ride sometime? He would be pleased to have you, I'm sure."

There are larger greenhouses along the track, containing entire orchards which glisten with moisture and heat, wavering beneath the lamps that sustain them. Adam tries to focus on the moon again, but as he attempts to locate it in the sky he notices a new building at the edge of his vision. It looks like another greenhouse, but grown out of all proportion, large enough to contain an entire forest; it bristles with spires, and its panes are uneven shatter-shards, and its jagged tiers scrape at the grey sky.

"What *is* that?"

"Our little pet project." Ada Sinclair licks her lips. As the car passes the orchards and mounts the rise that leads up the house, the spined greenhouse comes fully into view. It has been built at the rear of a grand mansion, but utterly dwarfs it – it could be a collection of glass knives, Adam thinks, aimed at the sky. "My husband will be inside," she says. "It is my absolute pleasure to be able to take you on a tour." There is a flash of yellow, and Adam notices that the enormous shatter-pane greenhouse is still being worked on. There are men in high-visibility jackets operating machines with tracks to the rear of it, manoeuvring more uneven shards of glass into place.

The car's elderly driver pulls up at the mansion's entrance, and opens the rear doors for them. Adam steps out into the shadow of a yacht, resting shining and white on a trailer. Horses, and hounds, and yachts, and endless greenhouses, he thinks, watching as the driver helps Ada Sinclair to her feet. He's not sure what any of this has to do with Magpie yet, but there is a lot of money here. The mansion looks as if it's the oldest building in the valley, and Adam is willing to bet that the Sinclairs have been here for a while. A few generations, maybe.

"Come, Adam." Ada ushers him out of the yacht's shadow and into the house.

The mansion might as well just be a reliquary, Adam thinks. There are statues, and paintings, and artefacts in cases everywhere. As Ada meanders from treasure to treasure, he finds himself distracted by an especially enormous portrait, encompassing almost the entire wall of a drawing room. The portrait depicts a silver tree with golden leaves and ruby fruits, and around its trunk winds an enormous green snake. Among the tree's coiled roots stand a pale man and a pale woman, genitals obscured by artfully placed fig leaves, and the two of them sup greedily on the tree's fruits. The sky beyond the tree is pinpricked with dazzling stars and angelic figures, accusatory fingers aimed at the pair eating from the tree. Adam spends a while absorbed in the painting. It's not that the painter got him so wrong, he thinks. He's more uncomfortable with how little the representation of Eve resembles her. There is nothing of her grace, her intelligence, her loveliness in the painting.

When Adam emerges from his thoughts, Ada Sinclair has changed. She is now wearing a robe so thin that it reveals the few angles of her he had yet to see. Without her fur shawl, Ada seems diminished – less trustworthy than Adam had initially thought. He finds himself suddenly wary of her. "Marvellous, isn't it?" she smiles, lips glistening. "The original, no less. But let me show you something even more marvellous." Taking Adam by the hand, she pulls him gently through tall corridors.

At the very rear of the mansion is a great glass airlock. Visible through its thick panes is the interior of the overgrown greenhouse, which is bursting with greenery. A meadow rolls away from the airlock and up to a low rise, where thriving trees bloom green as if it is still summer inside. Tiny flowers emerge from the meadow, and artfully arranged bushes and copses enrich every angle of the artificial hills that roll away to every side. Adam approaches the glass, feeling something shift inside him at the sight of that magnificent garden. Yet, when he presses his hand against the nearest pane, it feels strange beneath his fingers.

"This isn't glass," he says.

"My husband's recipe," says Ada, as she keys numbers

into a pad and cycles the airlock. "We had it patented a few years ago. It's very, very strong. We have government agencies coming in every now and then to ask after it. They think we're building a bunker."

"Are you?"

"No. This is a vault."

The glass airlock whirs, and then they are inside. The interior of the greenhouse is rich with scents, the air thick with pollen and insects and warmth. Adam spends a while simply breathing it all in. Above, the knife-like tiers of the greenhouse capture and refract the sky, arranged to maximise the little light coursing from the distant autumn sun. Ada shuffles out of her sandals. "You can remove your shoes," she says, sweetly. "You can remove as much as you'd like, here."

Adam glances at his shoes: plastic white crushing the long grasses.

"I'm fine," he says.

There's so much to take in. As Adam follows Ada further into the greenhouse, he finds himself trying to absorb as much of the place as possible. There are groves and orchards and trees of all kinds; artificial hills and small, glittering rivers; common flowers, and rare flowers; humble, tiny leaves, and enormous, fan-like leaves casting shade, all artfully arranged so that nothing quarrels with anything else for light. Temperatures subtly shift as they move from hill to valley, and so does the light. Adam catches sight of delicate mirrors clicking into place in order to cast better sunlight on certain sections. They must be automated, he thinks. In fact, the whole place seems especially designed to provide the optimum conditions for every living thing planted within it. It's been painstakingly designed.

Eventually, Ada leads Adam to a gentle grassy slope above a silvery river. This meadow is dotted with daisies, and sitting among them is a small man wearing a white dressing gown. The man rises, and each part of him is fleshy and wrinkled and round. What little white hair he has left is a white halo around his pockmarked scalp. He seems bewildered when he catches sight of Adam approaching, small mouth twitching beneath his white moustache, and he looks to his wife for confirmation. Ada nods, and with that he advances, raising his hand. "You must be Adam," he says, tiny eyes agleam. "My apologies. You look different to how I imagined. I'm Frank Sinclair."

Adam's hand engulfs Frank's.

"You'll have to forgive the robes. Usually my wife and I like to explore the greenhouse as God intended, as it were, but we thought we'd spare you the sight." He winks. "And you'll have to forgive the drilling, as well. Still a couple more sections to be built, and they're hard at work on it nearby. Too many apologies, I think. Come – if you're thirsty, you can drink from the stream. It's perfectly safe. We have machines that purify it."

"I like your greenhouse," says Adam.

"Yes," says Frank Sinclair.

"He's here about Magnus," says Ada.

"Of course. Of course." Something of Frank's smile fades. "What a devil old Magnus is. Impossible to get hold of. I'm told that you're here searching for him. You'll be glad to know that, so far as our sources are concerned, he is still in the country. In fact, my wife and I are very much interested in getting in touch with him ourselves. Which is why we thought we'd reach out to you." He clears his throat. "We'd like you to extend an offer to him on our behalf, when you find him. But tell me: do you know what it is that Magnus has been trying to buy from me?"

Adam shrugs. "No."

"Ah, then you're in the dark. Let me illuminate you." Standing, Frank brushes the grass from his dressing gown. "This way," he says, and he steps with bare feet across another hill, with Adam and Ada in his wake. "When next you see him, please let him know that I'm finally ready to hear his offer. I know I've snubbed him in the past, but all of this costs money, and with the greenhouse so close to completion I think it's time I raised a bit more. Of course, for passing along the message and acting as our agent in this matter, I think we can make an arrangement to suit you. How does five per cent of the final deal sound? I imagine it'll be in the millions."

"Millions?"

"Yes." Frank smiles again, the tips of his lips becoming visible at the edges of his bristling moustache. "Five per cent, then?"

"Sure."

Over the hill is an octagon of wooden decking overlooking a shallow lake, with carven pillars at each point, and at its centre rests a tall table with a bell jar upon it. It is to the bell jar that Frank goes, his feet leaving moist footprints across the pale wood. "Here," he says, and he runs his hands lightly across the glass.

Inside the bell jar is a crisp white flower, speckled with dew. Its leaves are a vibrant green and unblemished, its thick stem is punctuated by wickedly sharp thorns, and its petals are each a perfect paleness. As Adam beholds it, he notices that the rest of the greenhouse seems to fade away. Worse than that, the trees and grasses and river all suddenly seem fake, as if nothing except the rose is real. "It's a rose," says Adam, and his words feel inadequate.

"Not just any rose," replies Frank, reverently. "It doesn't age, and it doesn't die. My grandfather found it in the middle of the Saharan Desert, half hidden beneath the sand. Even there, in that barren place, it grew. Without the right conditions it wilts a little, and you can see the marks the desert left on it if you peer closely, but… give it the right light, and the right water, and enough earth, and it blooms forever. A moment in time, caught." There is a twinkle in Frank's eyes.

Adam frowns.

"When you find Magnus," says Frank, "Tell him that I'm willing to sell. We can arrange a meeting, and you're welcome to come along, if you like."

"Sure," says Adam, unable to take his eyes from the rose.

"Good." Frank releases a long breath. "Very good. We'll have our driver take you where you need to go. Any destination in mind?"

"Back to Edinburgh."

"All right. Best of luck to you, Adam. I hope that you manage to find Magnus, and that we'll meet again soon." Frank takes Adam's hand and shakes it energetically. "It's been a real pleasure to meet you. No, an honour. It's been an honour." He smiles, creasing his ruddy face. "Oh! But before you go. There was one last thing I wanted to tell you. Only a small thing. I just wanted to remind you of one of my favourite passages of the Bible. Genesis one: twenty-eight. Do you know it?"

"Yes," says Adam, but he's unable to recall the passage. He's never been too fond of the Bible. It doesn't do Eden nearly enough justice.

"Wonderful," says Frank Sinclair, and this time, when he smiles, he shows a row of tiny teeth, like a small dog. "Then we understand one another. I'm so glad to have met you, Adam."

When Ada Sinclair takes Adam by the arm, and gently leads him away, back towards the airlock and the house, he can still see the rose in his vision, as if it's been scarred there. The greenhouse seems dull now, its every arrangement so artificial and poised. He thinks that he would like to go back and sit with the rose for a while longer, and admire the curve of its petals. And as the car pulls away from the house, the rose remains lodged in his thoughts – a phantom flower blooming through his brain, thorns prickling down his throat as he swallows.

* * *

The Sinclairs' driver stops for fuel on the way back to Edinburgh.

It's cramped in the car, so Adam stretches his legs by wandering through the service station. It's a place between places, and it shows in the vacant eyes of the drivers, and the staff stuck behind their desks; nobody looks as if they are actually here. The station is bizarrely labyrinthine and features more empty shopfronts than occupied ones, so that in places sounds echo. There is a set of garish slot machines, where a single wiry lady sits, slotting coins and pulling a lever. From time to time a little bell rings and the machine vomits a stream of silver coins at her. Without pause, she feeds them back into the machine.

Feeling hungry, he orders a burger and chips. The car's driver places an order as well, and they sit with their little plastic trays together.

"What did you get?"

"Burger and chips. You?"

"Same."

The burger is tiny. Adam lifts the soggy bun to reveal some sad, limp lettuce and a single joyless, juiceless wheel of tomato, beneath which sits a round grey slab of anonymous meat, half hidden by a perfect square of counterfeit cheese. The chips are hollow. Thoughtfully, he munches at them, thinking about how eating meat used to mean something.

The life you would have to take.

There was a respect, there. A respect built from years of care: of watching the cattle and seeing them grow fat and healthy, the decision to slaughter a weighty one. Or the respect earned of the hunt: the chase, the blood, the fall. And by your own hands, you would have to dismantle the body. Cutting, and tearing, and plucking, and dissecting, so that you knew your food intimately.

Through the window, Adam can see a flock of black birds pecking at piles of rubbish. They flap among skittering crisp packets, and their feathers are ruffled by the passing of trucks.

He tries to count their legs, but all of them have two. Somebody throws a plastic bag filled with cardboard coffee cups onto the pile of rubbish, and they take off all at once, flapping into the grey sky.

IV

When Adam is back in Edinburgh, he goes to a park and sits on a bench beside the rail-tracks to watch the magpies at play. They balance on branches, fanning their long tails, and they flap across the grasses, flicking the white tips of their wings, and sometimes, if Adam sits still enough, one will perch on the back of the bench beside him, bobbing up and down.

When a train rushes past, they all fly away.

He twirls a fallen feather between his fingers, studying it like a detective might: opalescent blue infused into black. There is only one way he can think of trying to find Magpie, but he will have to wait until after dark. So, Adam sits on his bench until he gets too cold, and then goes in search of a coat.

Everywhere he tries, the coats are made for smaller people. At last, he comes to a crowded vintage shop, and at the very back finds an ancient military overcoat which fits well enough across his shoulders. At a mirror, he stops. There are dark patches across the breast where medals must have once hung.

Further along the road, there's an old second-hand bookshop, and he picks up a book at random. It's a collection of memoirs written by a nineteenth-century entrepreneur, heavily embellished, but still charming in its way. He reads until the light starts to fail, and then continues reading until the shop's owner tells him that the place is about to close. He pays, and goes out into the dark city, the book in his pocket.

At a crumbling graveyard beside an abandoned church, he breaks the lock on the gate and makes his way among the tombstones. Well beyond the street lamps, he comes to a vine-encrusted slab, which he clears with his hands. The moon isn't casting enough light on it, so he traces the letters with his fingers. *Here lies Captain Adam Carris*, it reads, and the dates beneath it have been worn away by time. Hauling the lid back, he searches the empty interior by touch, fingers feeling the earth and the worms curling. But there is something in there, after all. A small metal box.

Pushing the gravestone slab back into place, he sits beneath a gnarled old oak and pries the box open, holding the contents up to the half-moon. The silhouette of a rusted, skeletal key is there between his fingers. He places the key into a pocket, and begins to relax.

The moon is snuffed out by clouds, and it begins to rain. Beneath the graveyard oak, Adam falls asleep.

* * *

Awoken by dry leaves falling on his face, Adam opens his eyes to behold the cold sun. His extremities are numb, and there's a thick layer of frost covering him. He flexes his fist and shards of ice fall from his fingers. More leaves tumble across his shoulders, and he looks up to see the source of all the rustling. An enormous pair of yellow eyes glare down.

Stretching to break through the frost, Adam stands. He stamps his feet until his toes start tingling. "Have you seen Crow?" he asks.

Owl makes a soft noise and shudders in the cold, splaying his feathers. With a thump, he hops across to a lower branch, so that they are level.

"I'm gonna try and find Magpie," Adam tells him.

He leaves the graveyard by himself, feeling Owl's gaze follow.

Soon, the life returns to Adam's limbs. He feels as if he's been asleep for centuries. The remnants of his dream start to come back to him – he remembers the smell of gunpowder, and the screaming of gulls, and the booming of cannons. There was a pain in his neck, too. He rubs at the place, and feels a long scar there.

At a DIY centre, he tests a few different sledgehammers until he finds one that feels good. With the sledgehammer wrapped up in several plastic bags, he returns to central Edinburgh and the old tall houses there, stacked up against each other. He has a bit of trouble finding the right house, but eventually manages to make his way there by trusting his feet. In the front garden there's a dead apple tree.

The windows are all different, and so is the door, but the stonework is familiar. Adam rings the doorbell and nobody answers. This street is empty of cars; everyone is at work. Gripping the handle, he leans against the door and quietly breaks the lock. Wood splinters and he steps inside.

The walls seem thicker. He runs a hand down the striped wallpaper and feels the tiny bubbles, the multiple layers behind it. Further in and there's a family portrait: three happy children, a slender, thin-lipped woman, and a rotund, moustached man. In the living room, the fireplace is metal instead of stone, and Adam realises too late that he's leaving enormous muddy footprints across the fluffy white carpet. He flicks toys aside with his sledgehammer to make space.

Tapping the pristine back wall with his knuckles, he finds the right place. Then, hefting the sledgehammer, he gets to work.

It doesn't take long to smash through. Dust rises, and broken brickwork is scattered everywhere, revealing a hollow compartment beneath the ruination. Below the rows of ragged clothes hidden in the wall, there is a reinforced wooden chest.

Dragging the chest out and wiping the dust from the lid, Adam is surprised at how well preserved it is. Engraved above the lock is the legend *Property of Captain Adam Carris*, and he idly traces the letters with the tips of his fingers, as if they are scars etched into his skin. Then he takes the ancient key from his pocket and unlocks the chest.

Inside, there are rows of ornate powder pistols. Eight of them are arranged along belts, each intricately and uniquely decorated. But it isn't the pistols that interest him. Rummaging around among the bags of coins and papers and ledgers at the base of the chest, he finally locates what he came here for: a thick, leather-bound book.

Sitting back on one of the room's stained white sofas, he flicks through.

Pages upon pages of names and addresses are written down in his old, clumsy handwriting. Adam runs his finger down the rows and knows that every single name he touches belongs to someone dead. Dead, dead, dead – the word repeats itself in his mind like a mantra, and as he reads on, through further endless addresses, he feels as if he's slipping deeper and deeper into a dark hole. Dead, dead, dead. Everyone in the book is dead.

There is a tapping at the window, and Adam blinks, disturbed from his thoughts. Owl is perched outside, glaring at him.

Adam hefts open the window and Owl hops through, spreading his wings for balance. Copper and brass feathers flutter everywhere, and papers scatter. Dust whirls around. Owl lands on the metal mantelpiece, and his head swivels to and fro, taking in the wreckage of the room.

"We can go soon," Adam tells him.

Dead, dead, dead. As he skims through names, it feels as if spectral hands have emerged from the pages and are choking him – the ghosts of everyone he knew back then, back when he was a captain and earned a great many of his scars. Adam tries not to think about ghosts, because the thought of them usually overwhelms him, but the book forces it upon him. Dead, dead, dead.

But there, a name.

He pauses, his finger poised beneath the address. Not dead. He taps it to make sure that it's real, but the name and address remain solid. Of course, it's been decades – more than a century, even – but it might be possible. He reads it aloud for Owl, but mostly for himself, to confirm its reality. Then he closes the book and places it back into the chest.

Glancing around at the dusty room, and the hole in the wall, he wonders what he should do about the house. Of course, the owners should be able to sell his old pistols for a lot of money – they were antiques when he hid them, and he supposes they must be very valuable – but he would still like to do something for the people here.

He remembers the dead apple tree outside. At the base of the chest, among the papers, he locates a small wooden box and sifts carefully through all the seeds contained inside. Doing so eases his mind – brings him back from the terrible place the book of dead names sent him. There are maybe two or three seeds that might still harbour life, he thinks. He looks at them, so small, in the palm of his hand. As he leaves, he places them carefully into the bowl beside the door, artfully arranged in order of potential, and outside in the front garden he pays his respects to the old, dead apple tree, running his hand down the bark.

"Come on, then," he says, and Owl emerges from the house, flapping mightily into the sky. "Time to visit an old friend."

* * *

Adam takes a train out to Arbroath, and a bus from there.

Where the road becomes a track, he walks instead. The forest is a striking gold colour – the trees are dripping a wealth of leaves – but he doesn't like it very much. Adam's never been fond of autumn because it heralds winter, and he always finds himself worrying that winter will never end. So, instead of admiring the forest, he thinks about spring – about the white and blue buds that will emerge among the roots of these shedding trees once winter has passed.

As he walks, he considers the first time he met his contact in Scotland – the owner of the name printed in his book of dead names. He and Eve had settled in a low valley far to the north, which was sheltered from the northern winds. Rocky mountains rose around them, and the river at the heart of the valley wound a complex route around the pine-gripped low hills. The best bit about the valley, Adam remembers, was the way odd little growths sprouted here and there – ash and alder and even a single apple tree, hidden in a mossy knell. Wolves serenaded them at night, their distant calls echoing from the mountainsides, and sometimes Adam would wake and see the silhouette of a stag high on a rise. A large family of beavers moved in upstream, and Eve would watch them for hours, while whittling branches of her own with a stone knife.

One night, Eve woke Adam. The stars were bright overhead, and so were her eyes, agleam in the last embers of firelight. "Listen," she said, and Adam did, to the far-off rumbling of thunder, to the gentle rustling of the pines, to Eve's breathing, her chest pressed close to his. But at the very edge of hearing there was another noise: a muffled thumping and grumbling from further along the valley. It continued for a while longer and then stopped. "I've been hearing it every night since the new moon," Eve told him.

In the morning, Adam went to investigate.

There were tracks rutted in the undergrowth, and branches snapped from trees, and the apex of the disturbance was around the lone apple tree, small and twisted and sour and desperately clinging on to life in its knell. It seemed, to Adam, as if there were considerably fewer apples than his last visit. So, that night, he waited in the dark beside the tree until the mysterious apple-eater arrived, and there, grumbling through the undergrowth, tusks pale in the moonlight, emerged an enormous, bristling beast.

It was Pig. Eden's own Pig.

Pig hefted his considerable bulk up to the apple tree, and there heaved his flank against the trunk, thumping at it until apples began to fall. Then he quickly snuffled them up, his stomach making satisfied gurgling noises with every swallowed morsel.

As quietly as he was able, Adam approached the tree, and took an apple from a branch. Then, crouching, he extended the fruit as an offering. "Pig," he said, and the name felt as good as a fresh, sweet apple in his mouth.

Pig grunted in warning, and then grunted in curiosity, and then, finally, grunted in recognition, and carefully, so carefully, took the apple from Adam's hand and munched at it, grumbling in gratitude.

Always, after that night, Adam would return and pick apples for Pig, and then they would sit beneath the apple tree, and watch the changing weather together.

The hills of this valley are high on every side, and at their uppermost they are powdered white. Soon, Adam is in the shadow of the hills, and he knows that he's descending into the valley, towards his destination. Where there's a break in the trees, he stops and considers the view of it.

At the centre of the valley is a second sky. The golden

forest continues for miles ahead, clinging hold of steep slopes interspersed with stretches of evergreens and rocky outcroppings, and the loch it surrounds is a mirror. In those still waters are clouds, and small patches of blue, and a second set of slopes and trees, as if there is another valley beneath the valley. A flock of birds wheel overhead, and they too are doubled in the loch.

But Adam isn't here for the loch. There is another place in this valley, nestled not far ahead – a place built by people. He's here for the monastery: the holy gatehouse to the valley. Moving on from the view, he rejoins the track and follows it around. The loch used to belong to the church, he remembers. The last time he was here, there was the pealing of bells.

Yet the monastery has changed almost beyond recognition. The treeline is much closer than it once was, and some trees are embracing the old walls. There wasn't a tower before, and now there is – weathered stone pointing at the white sun – and there are even more crumbling extensions, including a stained and cracked conservatory with broad leaves breaking out of its panes. All is overgrown, and Adam steps across tufts of yellowing grass where it sticks out from between cracks in the concrete.

Somebody has painted two enormous canary-yellow lines across the outer wall of the old chapel, as if to say *No Parking*. There's the sound of flapping wings as Owl comes to a landing on its weathervane, which creaks and turns slightly. From there, he beholds the ruins and all that lies beyond them – a proud sentinel.

One of the doors to the entrance hall is ajar, and Adam raps his knuckles on it as he steps inside. The sound echoes through the place, and he might have imagined it empty were it not for the art supplies heaped up everywhere. The hall is filled with cans of paint, and brushes, and rollers, and canvasses, and easels, and enormous white sheets protecting statues.

There is more peculiar painting across the walls in here, too. The huge figure of an elderly man on a bench feeding pigeons covers one entire section, and the artistry is exquisite. Adam admires it for a moment – it might have been a photograph, vividly filtered, had it not been painted across old stone.

Further in, where there is a broad stone staircase leading up, there are canvasses covered in similar pieces. Here, a crowd of commuters waiting at a set of traffic lights in the rain; and there, a jogger splashing through puddles. Always, the paintings are picked out brilliantly, in bright colours which defy the ordinariness of the scenes, and the skill with which they have been depicted is dazzling. Adam turns on the spot, lost in their moments.

"What the hell? Adam?" There's a girl on the stairs, dressed in paint-splattered overalls. Her hair is pinned back with pencils, and beneath her broad-rimmed glasses is an expression of astonishment. She rushes down the last few steps and flings herself at Adam, laughing as she embraces him. "Why didn't you call ahead? If I'd have known you were coming, I would've tidied up a bit."

"Hey, Butterfly," says Adam, and her name feels nice to say.

"It's been so long. Way too long." She releases him and steps back. "How are you?"

"I'm okay." He looks around at the paintings, at her. "I was expecting someone else."

She grins. "When were you last here?"

"There were monks."

"Wow." Butterfly raises her eyebrows. "Come on. I'll make us some coffee. Are you alone?"

"Owl's outside."

She glances at the door. "He still…?"

Adam nods.

"Fair enough. This way." Down a long corridor, they pass more canvasses in better stages of completion, hung up at intervals. "This place has been a lot of things since you were last here," Butterfly says. "Pig turned it into a hotel after the monks left. Then, when he got fed up of that, he converted it into a boarding school. Both were pretty popular, from what I hear. There's still a set of swings outside. They were pretty rusted up, but I managed to get them working again." They turn into a broad kitchen which looks as if it was once meant to serve an entire garrison. Butterfly only seems to be using one corner of it. "After that, I think he just let the place rest for a good long while. Didn't know what to do with it. He's been letting me use it as studio space, and it's been great, honestly. There's no phone signal down here, so I'm cut off. A bit of peace and quiet."

"It's good to see you," says Adam, sipping at his coffee once it's been made.

"You too." She smiles at him. "Want to see my new project?"

"Absolutely."

Down another corridor, they come to what must have once been the main hall. It's filled at every angle with unframed paintings – on easels, and hung on the walls – and all of them are brilliant. "I call it 'Forgotten Moments'," says Butterfly. "It's a project I've been working on for ages now. Meant to immortalise those bits of people's lives they won't remember." She narrows her eyes thoughtfully. "It has its problems. As soon as you paint a forgotten bit of someone's life, then it isn't forgotten any more. It's a funny sort of paradox. Plus, this isn't real immortality. The paint will fade, and the canvasses will stain. No matter how hard you try, they won't survive – not really. But I'm still happy with how it's going."

There are forgotten moments everywhere. A boy sifting through change in a butcher's shop, a man reading a newspaper through the window of a train, a woman sipping at a hot drink in a café. Each picked out in Butterfly's dazzling bright style. "They're brilliant," says Adam.

"Thanks."

One of the paintings makes him stop. Upon it there is a wild figure – tousled black hair, and well-cut clothes – bent over and tying his shoelace. There is an extraordinary tension about him, as if at any moment he might leap from the canvas.

"Magpie."

"Yeah," says Butterfly, tilting her head. "It's a problem piece. Doesn't really match the rest. There's something about him that makes him difficult to capture. It's like trying to paint a storm – no matter how hard you try, you can't pin down the true kinetic intensity of it."

"Was he here?"

"Yeah. He came by a couple of weeks ago. Stopped for lunch."

"I need to speak to him. Do you know where he is?"

"Uhm." Butterfly bites her lip, thoughtfully. "I don't, I'm afraid. He didn't say. But you could always ask Pig. I'm sure he'll have more of an idea than I do. He's been living in Glasgow, but he'll be here in the morning. He always comes over for Sunday lunch." Peering at Adam, she pulls a pen from her pocket and doodles a curl down her forearm in ink. It looks like one of his scars, he thinks. "You and Owl are welcome to stay the night. In fact, I insist. I think I'd like to paint you, and for that I need you to have a forgotten moment."

Adam smiles. The expression feels strange across his face, as if he's pulled on a piece of clothing that doesn't belong to him. "Okay," he says. He has plenty of forgotten moments for her to choose from, he thinks.

* * *

Adam is woken by errant leaves of paper blustering across him. They drift silently across the chapel, tumbled by some stray gust, and the sliver of dawn light leaking in through the gap in the roof makes them glow yellow. Perched upon the chapel's ruined font is Owl, looking like some mighty figure of mythology. He's crouched upon his haunches, naked and human and muscular, half wreathed in shadow, and his wide yellow eyes are fixed on the far corner.

"What is it?" Adam asks.

"Listen."

Silence returns. Except, as Adam turns his head, he hears something in the distance. An engine, approaching down the track. He stands, stretching and shivering the papers from his shoulders and lap; they are pages dislodged from a ruined Bible, he notices. At the entrance to the chapel, he pauses and turns to see Owl flap up through the gap in the roof, golden light across his bronze feathers, back in his native shape.

A beaten looking minivan rumbles up the track, crushing leaves beneath its wheels. It comes to a halt in the monastery's cracked car park, engine hissing and ticking as it cools. Hefting himself out from the driver's side door is an enormously overweight man looking deeply uncomfortable in a Hawaiian shirt – tugging at the collar of it. When he rolls the van's rear door back, a stack of notebooks spills out and he curses, gathering it all up in his huge arms before chucking it back in.

"Hi, Pig."

Pig turns, small eyes seeking. "Adam? What are you doing here?" He clenches his fists, his whole body tensing. "Saw you on the news. What you did."

There is power in those arms, Adam thinks.

"Pig!" Butterfly hops down the monastery steps two at a time. With her bright tie-dye T-shirt and rushing rainbow hair, she is all the colours of summer.

Pig's expression softens at the sight of her, and when she throws her arms around his neck and kisses him on his stubbly cheek, the tension ebbs from him. "'Ello," he says.

"I love your shirt."

Pig's cheeks turn pink. "Thought you might."

"Did you bring lunch?"

"Of course. Of course." Pushing stacks of paper aside, Pig

reveals a picnic basket with a polka-dot blanket draped over it. "Didn't reckon we'd be having company, though."

"It's fine. I'm not that hungry anyway."

"Well, then." Pig clears his throat, eyes passing from Adam to the chapel's weathervane, where Owl perches. "Shall we wander down? Looks like it might be a warm one."

Pig leads the way through the forest, with the picnic basket on one arm and Butterfly clutching hold of the other. Beneath the trees she chatters to him – small nothings that make him smile. Adam follows at a polite distance, feeling as if he is intruding.

The forest breaks at the edge of the loch, where there is a shallow cove. A pair of weather-beaten deckchairs are set out among the pebbles and Pig settles into one, warped wood creaking beneath his weight. Butterfly wanders over to the lapping waters and removes her sandals, rolling up her jeans and paddling in the shallows.

Adam takes the other deckchair.

The loch is so still that Butterfly is mirrored in it. Both of her sift through the waters for coloured stones, raising each to the light and considering the way it plays across them.

Pig watches her in silence for a while. Then, turning to Adam, he says, "You're not here to cause trouble, are you?"

"No. Not at all."

"Good," says Pig. "See that you don't."

Butterfly finds a shining silver stone and pockets it.

"Hungry?" asks Pig. Sifting around in the picnic basket, he produces a couple of thick-cut sandwiches wrapped in cling film.

"Thanks." When Adam bites into his sandwich, he is surprised by the filling. "BLT?"

Pig chuckles. "Vegetarian bacon," he says. "Think they make it out of mushrooms or something. You can get sausages and pork chops and all sorts these days, all made out of plants. Don't know how they do it, but I'm not complaining."

"Tastes like the real thing."

"Good to know." Pig munches away. "Seriously, though. Why are you here, Adam?"

"I'm looking for Magpie."

"Magpie?" Pig's prodigious brow folds. "What do you want with him?"

"Rook sent me."

"Rook. Ah." Pig brushes crumbs from his chest. "Well, now. That's different. I owe Rook. We all do. Funny the power a few bits of paper can have, ain't it? The right bits of paper can mean all the difference between a good life and a bad life." Pig rubs at his stubbled chins. "I last saw Magpie a couple of weeks ago. I'm doing a bit of teaching in Glasgow, these days. Nothing fancy, just getting kids through their sums, a bit of algebra. It pays the bills – enough to maintain this old place, at least. Magpie, though. He showed up out of the blue at my school, holding this big old roll of papers under his arm. Told me he was working on a project and wanted my opinion on it."

"What were the papers?"

"Not a clue. Looked a bit like the blueprints of a greenhouse. Weird looking greenhouse, though. He was asking me all kinds of questions about the structure and materials and weaknesses, but I don't think I was much help. It's been a while since I did any architecture."

"What then?"

"Not much else to tell, I'm afraid. I invited him to Sunday lunch out here; figured Butterfly would like to see him. He came along, but he seemed pretty distracted."

"Do you know where he might be now?"

"Well." Pig squints at the sky. "I picked him up and dropped him off at a hotel in the West End. Could be he's still there. Can give you the address, if you like."

"Thanks. That'd be great."

The sun slowly rises overhead, warming the cove, and Butterfly soon returns from the loch bearing a wealth of coloured pebbles. She sits cross-legged on the polka-dot blanket and shows Pig and Adam her collection. Then, when she is done, she and Pig go to the edge of the loch and throw her pebbles back into it one by one.

Adam takes his leave while they're distracted. He pauses at the treeline, considering whether or not to say goodbye, but when he turns back to see Butterfly and Pig, wading and skimming stones together, he decides against it. He thinks he would prefer to try and fix this moment in his fractured memory: the sound of their laughter, and their shimmering reflections rippling in the great mirrored loch.

A moment of true happiness.

V

Queen Street railway station is mostly composed of scaffolding, and the rest of Glasgow is much the same. Adam wanders through crowded streets where the buskers are so close together that their voices compete. He knows that he must reach the West End of Glasgow, but his feet don't seem to know these streets very well and he finds himself repeatedly getting lost, veering down alleyways where the wrecks of burned buildings squat beneath flapping expanses of blue tarpaulin. Eventually he decides to follow the sun, peering up through the grey smog and grey sky to find it glowing white there. Glasgow makes Adam feel clumsy; he keeps accidentally colliding with people in the street, no matter how carefully he navigates the crowds.

The last time he was here, the sky bristled with chimney stacks, he remembers.

No matter where he walks, the path crunches beneath his feet, either with dead leaves or crisp packets or bits of broken glass. Homeless people call out to him from every corner and shopfront, asking for change, and charity workers dance across the paving, trying to get him to stop, to listen, to donate.

Adam raises his collar and practises unseeing the city, passing through an enormous park with a murky fountain. At a bridge he pauses, observing the frothing brown flow, interspersed with the occasional white flash where discarded wet-wipes tumble between the ducks.

At last, he comes to the West End. Everything here is slightly cleaner, the faces he passes are slightly younger, and the buskers are positioned slightly further apart. The homeless are more demanding: they raise their hands and curse Adam when he offers them nothing. There is laughter here, and music drifting from open windows, and the trees cast their leaves thick across the streets as if they might bury the city.

He's not quite sure where to go, so he asks a young guy with a clipboard offering free eye tests for directions, and is told the hotel he's looking for is based on the other side of the Botanic Gardens.

As Adam passes through the black gates of the Botanics, a silhouette descends from the grey sky, and Owl perches among the tall trees, amber eyes sweeping over the yellowing grounds.

Deeper inside the gardens, white bunting is strung up across the bushes, and people dance to music. It's a wedding, Adam thinks. He catches the briefest glimpse of the bride as she is swept across the lawn, spinning with the music, and tries to remember if he ever married Eve. The idea of promising to love her forever seems superfluous, somehow.

There is a marquee set up on the central lawn. Tipsy men and women in their wedding best laugh and flirt between the flower beds, twitching to the live band performing on a stage nearby. Staff meander through the throng with trays of bubbling champagne while screaming children run around their feet, and somehow nothing is spilled. The white table covers, and white flowers, and white teeth of the bride and groom all remain white. There is only one smile that catches Adam's attention: the metallic grin of the man sat at the bar, turning a fluted glass between his fingers.

This man is wearing a sharp suit that somehow complements every angle of his especially angular body, and there is a golden pince-nez perched across his nose. His tousled black hair wavers in the breeze, and even though he is sitting perfectly still, he seems in motion, somehow. Half of his smile is white, and the other half is silver.

"What happened to your teeth?" Adam asks.

"A boy with a rock," says Magpie. "I was tired after a long flight and decided to roost in an old oak at the back of a long garden, imagining I was safe there. I was wrong." Throwing his head back, he drains his glass. "I must say," he says. "I knew that someone would show up eventually, but I didn't expect it to be you. How are you, Adam?"

"I've been better. Whose wedding is this?"

"No idea. But I do like a good wedding. A pleasant way to pass the time."

Adam examines Magpie's expression, but there's no trace of irony in it. "Rook wants to know what you're spending his money on."

Magpie's smile flashes. "I expect he does."

"Ran into your friends, too. The Sinclairs."

This seems to take Magpie by surprise. His smile fades. "You did?"

"They took me on a tour of their greenhouse."

"You must be kidding. They actually let you inside?"

"Showed me a rose. Told me they wanted to sell it to you."

Magpie laughs hard enough that his pince-nez tumbles from his nose.

"Is it real?"

"Is what real?"

"The rose."

"Yes," says Magpie, carefully. "It's real. As real as you and me." Magpie leans down and snatches his pince-nez from the ground, brushing the grass from it as he regains his composure. "Tell you what," he says. "You help me break into the Sinclairs' greenhouse and recover the rose, and I'll do better than telling you what I've been spending all my brother's money on. I'll show it to you. How does that sound?"

"Are you serious?"

Magpie's semi-silver grin somehow makes him look as if he is holding a dagger. "Perfectly."

Adam observes the wedding: the dancers as they move among the dry leaves gently tumbling from the trees, trampling the green lawn with their heels. Then he studies his hands and the scars that run across them, white on black. If the rose is real, he thinks he would like to see it again, more than anything.

A part of Eden he never expected to survive.

"Sure…" he says, at last.

"Wonderful." Magpie throws Adam a set of rusted car keys.

"I'm parked beside my hotel, just a little further along. I'll finish up here and meet you there in, say, half an hour. My car is the green one."

Wandering towards the far entrance to the Botanics, Adam pauses beneath a yellowing grove of trees where the noise of the wedding party is muffled. He turns on the spot until he locates Owl, those intense eyes following Adam's every movement. "You should go find Crow," Adam tells him. "Let her know we've got Magpie. I'll keep an eye on him."

There is the softest hoot of what might be acknowledgement.

As Adam exits the Botanics, he hears the beating of wings behind him.

It takes him longer than he thought it would to locate Magpie's car. The problem is that none of the vehicles parked outside the hotel are green. There are plenty of silver cars, and black cars, and blue cars, and even one abandoned hulk covered in a layer of moss, but nothing painted green. Adam turns the keys over in his hands, searching for the button to unlock the car's door and make its lights flash, but the keys are so old that they lack electronic components.

When he tries the keys on the door of the overgrown wreck, they work.

Moss covers the chassis in enormous patches, and a few errant roots dangle through the cracked sunroof. Adam circles the car, and is surprised to find that it still has one remaining hubcap, held in place by a single bolt.

Magpie arrives looking ruffled, cheeks ruddy.

"Think you need a new car," says Adam.

"Nonsense," says Magpie, brandishing the bridal bouquet. "It still works fine."

As Magpie slips in behind the wheel of the car, he hands the bouquet to Adam. The tightly arranged set of flowers are already crisping slightly at the edges, and as Adam turns it over in his hands, searching the petals for their colours, he considers the rose – the memories that might still cling on to it like errant particles of Eden's soil. When he's recovered the rose, he'll take to it to Eve, he thinks; he'll present her with it again, the same way he did all that time ago in the garden, so proud to have found something so gorgeous to show her.

* * *

At the outskirts of Glasgow, Magpie pulls in to an enormous but mostly empty car park. A concrete complex stands ahead, gleaming glass reflecting the grey sky. As Adam crunches across discarded receipts and flyers towards it, he realises that he is surrounded on all sides by highways. The highways curve like waves, and the cars upon them seem to rise and fall like ships, making this place an island.

Adam remembers the white harbour of Kos.

The ships arrived from mainland Greece and far beyond, white sails flying against the shining white sea. The sands were white, and so were the stones of the harbour, and Adam worked as a labourer, hauling cargo to and from ships and helping to make repairs. Sometimes, when the harbour was quiet, he would wade into the sea just to feel the weeds writhe around his legs and crustaceans scuttle across his feet. Eve worked further inland, at a new school devoted to the study of health. Ever since they left the garden, she had been troubled by the idea of death, and here, on this island, were people claiming that diseases and illnesses might not be divine judgement at all, and that there may even be rational ways of curing them – of prolonging life. Of course, Eve, as a woman, was not allowed to join in the debates, but she found work as a servant and sat in on the conversations when she could. The debates, she told Adam, were mostly philosophical in nature, and while physical specimens were not closely examined, the school at Kos still gave her so much joy. It was progress, she told him, towards discovering the true nature of illness. Adam knew that she secretly hoped to one day find out that death was no more than a disease that could be cured. Meanwhile, he was happy because she was happy, and content to spend his days idling among the ships.

The automatic doors at the entrance to the complex grind open, and beyond them is a cavernous shopping centre. Tinny music drones from frayed speakers, and light is cast unevenly across the tiles from the yellowed windows above. Most of the shopfronts are vacant and mirror-black, but somebody has taken the time to arrange flowers in front of them. As Adam passes by, he notices that the flowers, though bright, all have plastic petals and wire veins. There's even a layer of dust across them. "Behold a mausoleum," says Magpie, and Adam thinks he's right. This place is a mausoleum: a mausoleum for a century that he barely remembers.

Those few shops that are still open cast warm glows, promising sales and discounts and relief from the tomb-like halls. Downcast mothers wheeling prams and shoppers clutching bags move furtively through the enormous empty space, their footsteps echoing. Where there's a fenced-off play area, three children huddle in a corner. Their play-set casts long shadows, and the colours of the plastic castle have faded into sickly greens and yellows.

Stepping over the fence, Magpie sits on a plastic log in a pillar of sunlight. From somewhere inside his sharp coat, he retrieves two small marionettes. The first is a proud knight, with shining silver armour that flashes the same way that Magpie's crowns do, and the second is a fair maiden with a white dress and a length of braided yellow hair. In the cavernous hall, the marionettes are aglow. Fascinated, Adam watches as Magpie's clever fingers operate them, bringing them to life. Slowly, the children break free of their huddle and emerge into the light, to sit and watch and even laugh.

The knight is foolish and clumsy, swinging his sword at shadows and banishing them only by accident. The maiden dances, whirling and wheeling through the gloom and sending shadows scattering in fright. The marionettes turn and leap and collide, and Magpie smiles all the while, black eyes glinting. Eventually, the children begin their own games. They become clumsy knights and graceful maidens themselves, and by their joy the tomb-like shopping centre is brightened.

"I like your marionettes," says Adam. "Did you make them?"

"Antiques," says Magpie. "I started collecting objects of

mummery a while ago. Masks and bells and puppets." Pocketing the marionettes, he continues through the shopping centre. "They do come in useful, every once in a while."

Through a set of double doors is an octagonal food hall, where the light of the sky reaches every corner. The flowers here are real, and there are even a few aquariums embedded in the walls where exotic fish flit. The food stands here are shut down; the garish signs belonging to each franchise no longer glow. Yet at the rear of the hall is a single long countertop, upon which gleam fresh fruits embedded in sticky pastries, among overstuffed baguettes and piles of oranges ready to be squeezed into glasses. If the shopping centre is an island at the centre of a sea of traffic, then this is the verdant grove at its heart, Adam thinks.

"How did you find this place?"

Magpie orders fruit juice, and pancakes, and pastries. "I've had a lot of time to kill recently," he says, "so I've taken to tasting every corner of this little country." They take seat at one of the wooden benches overlooking the sea of traffic. Cars roll up and down the highways silently beyond the panes, and Magpie follows them with his eyes as he munches at a tart.

"Why are we here?" asks Adam.

"Lunch," says Magpie. "We can't go breaking into the Sinclairs' vault on an empty stomach. And it would probably be prudent to put together a plan, as well."

Adam tries one of his pancakes. It tastes great, he thinks.

"Perhaps," says Magpie, "you should draw a map of the place."

"Got a pen?"

Magpie considers the question carefully, as if there's real weight to it. "No."

"Then I can't draw you a map."

"Describe the layout to me, at least."

The pancakes really are very good. The cream is freshly whipped, as well. As Adam considers the layout of the Sinclairs' greenhouse, he finds himself beginning to arrange napkins, and when he has run out of napkins he uses the salt and pepper shakers, and the ketchup bottle, and the wooden box they came in, and the menus, and even their plates. Soon, he is so absorbed in creating his map that he forgets to finish his food. The corner of a pancake becomes a lawn, and a trickle of syrup becomes a river, and his knife and fork become walls.

"There," he says, when he's done.

Magpie wipes cream away from the corner of his mouth, hardly able to contain his smile. "Where's the rose?" he asks.

"Here." Adam points at a small blob of cream.

"Hmm." Swirling his fruit juice around in its glass, Magpie observes the map thoughtfully. "What…" He leans forward, tilting his cup at a torn-up pile of napkins. "…is that?"

"Construction site. They're still building it."

"Ah." Magpie's grin broadens. "There it is. That's how we'll get in." Draining his cup, he withdraws a huge wad of cash from his coat. Loosening the elastic band around it, he selects two large notes and leaves them on the table. "Lunch is on my brother," he says, with a chuckle. "Come on, then. By the time we get there, it should be dark."

"You want to go there right now?"

"No time like the present!"

Adam studies his crude map a little longer. "It's not much of a plan."

"Trust me," says Magpie, his expression sobering. "It will work."

Lingering a few moments more, Adam sifts through his pockets until he finds a few errant notes. They are mostly dollars, but he leaves them anyway – an apology for the mess he has made.

On his way back to the car, Magpie stops beside a fountain. The fountain itself is still, but there's a body of water beneath it, made shimmering by the silver and copper coins heaped at the base. A lot of people made wishes here, once, Adam thinks. Removing his coat and shoes, Magpie steps over the rim and wades through the water. Then, rolling up the sleeves of his shirt, he fishes out handfuls of coins and heaps them on the fountain's rim. When he deems there are enough, he emerges, and dries himself off using the edge of his coat.

"For the parking meter," he explains, with a wink.

* * *

It is a warm night. One of the last warm nights of autumn, Adam thinks.

Magpie has parked up at an abandoned petrol station, and has balanced the rusted nozzle of a derelict pump in the fuel tank of his mossy car, his delight at the act echoing from the empty hills. Now, he is busy changing, pulling on a black turtleneck and black overcoat, with the headlights of the car gleaming in his silver crowns. Adam wanders through the petrol station to pass the time, enjoying the way that grasses and even a few small trees have sprouted up from the cracks in the concrete. The sky is cloudless overhead, but while the moon is a soft pale blur, there are barely any stars visible. Adam stands in the ruins of the car wash and wonders at the glow on the near horizon; it looks as if a bright city lies just over the hills.

"Take this," says Magpie, handing over a wrecking bar.

Adam considers the twisted piece of metal. It seems small in his hand.

They set off, wading across the dry grasses gripping the hills. The trees they pass beneath cast long shadows that deepen the closer they draw to that glowing horizon, and what few stars there were above are gradually snuffed. When at last they mount the final hill, the intensity of light from the view beyond provokes an artificial twilight; the moon has become a yellow sun, and the sky is a bruised purple and blue. A kingdom of glowing glass lays before them, hundreds of greenhouses bright against the night. And up on the rise stands the greenhouse vault, spired and palatial and almost too dazzling to look at.

Without pause, Magpie descends the rocky slope and becomes a silhouette between the greenhouses. Adam follows, feeling uneasy. There should have been a fence, or a wall, or some kind of perimeter, he thinks, but he has yet to see any security at all. There is nobody visible patrolling the estate or the greenhouses. When he reaches the valley floor, he hunches down, trying to make himself smaller. The greenhouses give him so many faint shadows that they shift and multiply beneath him, and the heat emanating from the glass is so intense that he finds himself unfastening his coat against it. Magpie splashes through an oily sump pool, and Adam tenses, waiting for the noise to alert someone to their presence.

There is no response.

Parked outside the mansion are a handful of sleek, expensive-looking cars, gathered in the shadow of the yacht. The home's stately windows are aglow, and shadows shift beyond them. "Looks like they're having a party," says Magpie, as he crunches across gravel. He leaves deep footprints in the flower beds as he tramples across the garden and around the edge of the vault. Ahead, the bulky yellow shapes of construction vehicles sit idle in the greenhouse's glare, light reflecting from stacks of reinforced panes yet to be installed.

The construction site is still. Materials lie around on pallets, trenches yawn, and the great yellow trucks and diggers cast complex shadows across the torn ground. Yet there's something about it all that increases Adam's uneasiness. It feels like he's back in Hollywood, watching a scene being filmed. The site feels like a film set – as if somebody has posed everything to make it seem like it really is a construction site, and not a collection of props.

Magpie doesn't seem to notice. He continues without pause.

"There." At the edge of the greenhouse, there is a long shard of glass that looks as if it might be loosened with enough pressure. Magpie flicks it with a finger and it rings like a wine glass being struck. "See if you can get that open."

Kneeling down, Adam applies the wrecking bar. The glass slides aside.

"This is too easy," he says.

"Do you think you can get through that gap?"

Adam turns, lowers the wrecking bar. "This is a trap."

"Of course it is. I'm not stupid, Adam."

"Then why are we here?"

Magpie's smile fades. "They're going to underestimate you," he says, and the light of the greenhouse glints in his dark eyes. "They don't know you like I know you."

"You have a plan, then?"

"I have you."

Adam weighs the wrecking bar again. It seems so small. But then he thinks about the rose again: waiting, just inside. Crawling through the gap, he enters the greenhouse. The heat hits him so abruptly that he takes a few moments to breathe, wiping away the sudden sweat on his brow and getting his bearings. He has emerged into a tangle of trees with tremendous palm leaves that drip moisture across him – this must be a tropical wing of the greenhouse.

Standing up beside him, Magpie takes a deep breath and grins his dangerous grin. "Exactly how I pictured it," he says. "Come on, then. Take me to the rose."

Pushing aside fan-like leaves, they emerge into a humid clearing, humming with insects. There are no paths, so Adam navigates from grove to grove, getting his bearings by following the shatter-shard greenhouse roof until the sight of it starts to seem familiar. Still, nobody stops them. Even as Adam crushes young plants beneath his shoes, there are no guards, and no guests, and no Sinclairs.

Through a long glass corridor gusting air, they emerge onto the bright lawn with the octagonal section of decking, aglow even in the depths of night. And there upon it sits the rose in its bell jar, every bit as crisp and pure and perfect as before. As they approach, Adam realises that the rose is positioned at an angle by which they might be ambushed from three different sides. It's been cleverly placed, he thinks.

From somewhere inside his dark coat, Magpie reveals a loupe. Wrinkling his nose, he places it against his eye like a monocle and leans over, posed as if he's a jeweller inspecting a particularly intricate piece of jewellery. Adam admires the rose, and now that he's here, seeing it for the second time, he knows he was right to come. He can feel it evoking old memories in him already.

"The genuine article," mumbles Magpie. "I can't believe they were foolish enough to—"

"Hello again, Adam."

The voice comes from the top of the grassy rise, but the first person Adam notices is the Sinclairs' elderly driver as he advances from between some trees nearby. The driver is barefoot and pads silently across the lawn; he aims a hunting rifle at Magpie's head. There is something in his poise that tells Adam he has training with firearms. The driver comes to a halt at the foot of the octagonal veranda, eye across the iron sights of his gun.

At the top of the hill is Ada Sinclair, at the fore of a crowd of elderly men and women. All of them are completely naked, except for Ada, who is wearing a single article: her wondrous fur shawl, draped across her shoulders. The party's eyes flick from Adam, to Magpie, and back to Adam.

"Which one is it?" A greying man with a protruding belly asks.

"Step forward, Adam," says Ada.

Glancing at Magpie, Adam notices that he's removed his loupe. He is observing the crowd of naked people with an expression that Adam does not recognise. It might be contempt. Unsure how to proceed, Adam takes a step forward, as commanded.

"Bloody hell, that's the first man?"

There's muttering among the crowd.

One of them says, "Looks more like a fucking gorilla."

Laughter ripples out.

"We weren't expecting you quite so early," says Ada. "Frank was hoping to be here when you arrived. He'll be joining us shortly." Despite her nakedness, she still wears powder and concealer and mascara. In fact, most of them are made up – desperately trying to appear younger than they are. "It's good of you to join us, Adam. We've been waiting for you. You don't need to feel ashamed here. You can remove your clothes if you like. Enjoy the warmth of the greenhouse, like the rest of us. Don't pay any attention to Thompson's comments." She smiles, cracking the powder around her lips. "He's an old rogue, and he'll learn to love you just like I do. I hope you'll forgive the gun, as well. While I can vouch for you, I can't vouch for the creature you've brought with you. Now – if you'd be so kind…" Ada slowly makes her way down the hill, at the head of her procession. She halts a few paces away from the decking, and deposits the object she was carrying with her on the ground before it. It's a gilded cage. An intricate piece of work.

"Tell your fowl to get in the cage," she says.

Adam feels his brows curl into a tight frown.

"Dominion, Adam. Genesis one: twenty-eight. God told you to 'have dominion over the fish of the sea, and over the fowl of the air, and over every living thing that moveth upon the earth'. Exercise your dominion. Tell your bird to get in the cage."

"Adam," says Magpie, somewhere behind him. "She's wearing fox."

"Cage the bird," insists Ada.

"Listen," says Magpie, so softly. "She's wearing *Fox*."

The trembling begins inside Adam's chest. It flutters there as if there's a butterfly trapped inside him. It makes its way from his chest, to his arms and his legs, and to the tips of his fingers where it makes the blood tingle through them. He feels his grip on the wrecking bar tighten.

"Look at me, Adam," commands Ada, and he does. She still has all the colours of sunset cascading across her fragile shoulders. Except, they're not her colours at all. They're Fox's colours. There, at her throat, is the white dash of Fox's chin.

Ada stands before Adam, small and unafraid and wreathed in stolen fur.

The first blow hits her square in the jaw, making a soft crunching noise. She folds to the floor, probably dead already, but Adam crouches and hammers at her with his fists until her skull is no more than fragments. The wrecking bar is superfluous; he casts it aside.

The murder takes mere moments, and when it is done, Adam carefully removes the bloodstained fur from Ada's lifeless shoulders.

When Adam stands, he notices that the rest of the party have fled. Magpie is also gone, but the Sinclairs' driver remains, rifle now trained on Adam. The driver's aim wavers, finger quivering at his trigger. His uncertainty does him credit, Adam thinks. For all his training, he still hesitates to shoot and potentially kill a man.

Adam approaches the driver, but he stands his ground. "Stop!" he cries. "Stop where you are!"

Pain blooms distantly through Adam as he is shot in the leg. His blood, a deep crimson, showers the grass. The next two shots hit him in quick succession, bursting through the same leg, but he doesn't stumble. Grabbing the end of the rifle, Adam slams it into the driver's chest. Then, tearing the gun free of the man's grip, he turns it on him, firing low. If the driver had enough respect to only shoot Adam in the leg, then he will return the favour. The driver falls backwards, blood pouring from the wound in his calf, crying out.

Adam pulls the bolt back on the rifle, loads another round.

On the wooden decking there lies a still-warm stack of clothes. Adam crouches, observing the silver crowns scattered across them. Perched atop the rose's bell jar is a large magpie with a crumpled beak, beady black eye glinting.

The magpie hops onto Adam's shoulder as he takes the bell jar, wrapping it in Fox's fur. The package is light, and he cradles it protectively against his chest, as if it's a child.

Apart from the moaning of the driver, the greenhouse is now very quiet. Ada's broken body cools nearby. Adam isn't sure why he pauses, but he does, observing the parody of paradise that surrounds him. It's like a bad dream, he thinks, where he knows that nothing is quite real. Only the magpie perched on his shoulder feels real. Only the matted fur between his fingers is real. Only the rose he carries feels real.

On his way back to the fake construction site, he stops at the shore of the greenhouse's artificial lake and throws the rifle into it. The gun splashes and sinks, still visible beneath the clear waters even as it comes to a rest among the pebbles at the lake's bed. Feeling light-headed, Adam clutches the bell jar between his hands, making certain that it will not tumble from his grip. He has left bloody handprints on the glass, and further matted Fox's fur, he notices. The bird on his shoulder chatters at him until he wakes from his hazy delirium; he continues, retracing his steps to the loosened pane of glass.

Crouching through, he emerges into the bright night.

Through the kingdom of greenhouses he stumbles, the magpie on his shoulder stretching its wings to keep its balance. Sometimes he looks down and notices how wet his leg is with blood. It's possible, he thinks, that one of the bullets struck an artery. Still he continues, turning only to see that the mansion is quiet. Curtains twitch, but nobody comes running out to try and stop him.

It feels like it takes years for him to cross the hills, eyes fixed on the stars as they slowly emerge in the dark. He mumbles constellations to himself – the constellations he once named, lying on the warm hills of Eden, in a language long forgotten. He remembers Eve's gentle laughter, her warm breath against his neck, the softness of her skin against his.

At last, he arrives at the abandoned petrol station.

When he stumbles against the car, he realises that he doesn't have the keys. He slides down with his back against it, vision wheeling; the soft moon is a blurred streak in the sky. He knows he should make efforts to remove the bullets and bind his leg, but he's feeling suddenly very tired, and he lets himself relax for a moment. He observes the long trail of blood he's left through the grasses in his wake, like a black river meandering down the hillside.

Placing the rose and fur on the concrete before him, he feels his eyelids trying to close. He doesn't put up much of a fight. A bit of rest would be good, he thinks. He can't remember the last time he went on holiday. But then, he can't remember much of anything, really.

The last thing Adam sees before unconsciousness takes him is the magpie with the crumpled beak. It perches resolutely atop a petrol pump, observing him with one glinting black eye, flashing the whites of its wings as it flicks them.

VI

A tree is a very difficult thing to kill. With a man, there are so many weaknesses that can be exploited: skin is easy to puncture, bones are easy to break, and organs are simple to smash. With a tree, though, a knife won't do. You can't kill a tree using your fists, and you can't kill a tree by shooting it, and you can't kill a tree by subjecting it to working conditions demeaning enough that it throws itself off a tall building. Killing a tree takes strength. It takes the application of an axe to its trunk, chipping away bit by bit until it topples. It takes great machines, with whirling saws. And even then, it might still survive. Even with its trunk gone, and its branches gone, and its leaves gone, its roots remain, buried deep in the earth, and the tree might live yet.

Eventually, Adam wakes.

He's laid out on a cold metal table, and there are bright lights aimed at his leg. Bowed over that leg is a middle-aged woman in sickly lime-green scrubs, digging around with some metal tools. Adam knows he should be in pain, but what pain there is seems distant, so he watches in fascination. She's using a pair of tweezers and a scalpel, and her hands are tremendously steady. The tweezers twitch and pull something free, and she exhales sharply, dropping the remains of a bullet onto the tray beside her. Satisfied, she lays out her tools and removes her gloves, searching around in drawers for a needle and some thread.

"Got a staple gun?"

Startled by the sound of his voice, she stares at him, lowering her mask.

"You shouldn't be conscious."

"A needle won't do it."

"I gave you enough sedation to keep a rhino under for a week."

There's a pause as she considers the needle.

"I do have a staple gun."

Pinching his flesh together, she applies the gun. There are sharp points of pain beneath his skin, but they feel far away, and he doesn't flinch. His leg is already covered in scars; this isn't the first time it's been put back together. Eventually, each bullet hole is sealed up. The woman cleans the wounds and wraps his leg with fresh white bandages. Then she wheels her chair back, and goes to wash her hands.

"I don't have any crutches," she says, "but I'll give you some antibiotics."

"I won't need them." He swings himself upright, and the room whirls unsteadily.

"Sure." She sighs. "I wouldn't walk on that leg for a while, though."

"I'll be fine."

Drying her hands on a towel, she frowns at him. "You were shot three times."

Putting pressure on his leg causes a needling beneath his skin, but it's no great discomfort. He takes a few steps to test it out and the staples hold; no red blooms through the white. He rolls his trouser down and stretches, rubbing the life back into his limbs. "Thanks," he says.

"Don't thank me. Thank your friend. He's paying off my mortgage."

"Where is he?"

"He said he was going to get some breakfast." She shrugs.

At the door, he turns and glances back at her. She's clearing away the bloody tools and disposing of the bullets. He supposes she was paid to not ask any questions, and that's fine. Adam's never been great at answering tricky questions. "Thanks," he says, again, and moves out into the bright world outside.

Edinburgh Zoo is mostly empty. A layer of frost covers it, and animals shiver beyond the bars of their enclosures, hiding from the cold. There's a drinking fountain beside the penguins, and Adam uses it to wash the blood from his hands. He finds a shard of skull embedded between two of his fingers, so he picks it out and lets it drop into the water, where it joins the red swirl and rattles away down the pipe. When the water runs clear, he uses it to splash his face, the shock of the cold sending a chill through him.

On his way to the dining area, he stops beside the tiger enclosure. One of them lopes over at the sight of him, breath steaming the window that separates them, and when Adam presses his hand against the reinforced glass the tiger rubs her flank across it. He can feel her voice vibrating the window as she chuffs in greeting, and he remembers other tigers, from another life. They were great, splendid cats, kept badly, and he recalls sneaking into their tent at night and letting them loose to wander, feeding them scraps of his dinner. He was the strongman at the circus, and just as exotic as they – forced to bend iron bars for audiences unused to the sight of dark skin. He remembers the death of a tiger so tired she could no longer perform, her execution by rifle, and he remembers taking her body from the rubbish heap and digging her a grave in the woods over the hill. He remembers shovelling earth over her and hiding her wonderful coat, and he remembers returning to the other tigers and mourning with them. They paced their small tent that night, searching the corners for their friend, and all Adam had to offer them was more scraps of food and useless comforting sounds.

It took Adam lifetimes to find all the pieces of Eden's Tiger. When they took her apart, they made her coat into a banner, and then a cloak. Her teeth they used for tools, making axes and saws, and then pieces of jewellery, necklaces and earrings. Her whiskers they made into a harp, winding them around lengths of strong cedar, the sad noises a mockery of her living voice. Her bones they whittled into idols and knives, things to worship and things to murder with. Her claws they kept as trophies. Look how fierce the thing we killed was. Look at us, such mighty men. By the time Adam had gathered as much as he could, the original hunters had all died of disease or old age, so he killed their children instead. The gathered remains, he buried in Siberia.

Rain starts to fall as Adam finds the dining area, where there is still no sign of Magpie.

He goes to the birdcages, as if they might present some clue. Their sharp eyes watch him pass, and some call out to him, hopping across and stretching their wings, but there are no magpies among them. So, he goes over to where there is a small petting zoo and sits on a bench to wait. Huddled in their shed, the keyhole eyes of the goats reflect the grey sky, and after a while they trot across and nuzzle at his hands. An alpaca stands beside him and snuffles at his shoulder, and a pink pig waddles across and chews at the edge of his shoe. Surrounded by the warmth of the animals, Adam raises his face to the sky and feels the rain on his cheeks; lets it run down his scars as if they are riverbeds; lets it wash away the worst of his memories.

On his way to the car park, he spots a large magpie with a crumpled beak devouring the corpse of a grey squirrel. The squirrel is splayed out beside a tree, and looks as if it's been dead for a while. "You took me to a zoo?" asks Adam, and the magpie pauses, tilting its head, glistening entrails dangling from its ruined beak. As if in answer, it immediately returns to devouring what remains of the squirrel. Adam leans against the tree and waits for it to finish.

* * *

The Edinburgh Fringe Festival is in full swing, and fire jugglers, and magicians, and masked men on stilts stride among the red and orange and yellow leaves. The rain has stopped, and the streets have dried so quickly that it's as if the sky never opened at all. The clouds overhead cast quick shifting shadows across all the performers and endless tourists. Adam makes his way down the long paths of the Meadows, carpeted in bright fallen leaflets promising marvels.

Perched on his shoulder is Magpie, who seems to be luxuriating in the attention he's being given. Despite his damaged beak, he is a magnificent specimen. There's something super-real about the quality of his feathers, and the sharpness of his claws, and the glint in his beady black eyes, and queues form around Adam and his bird as tourists demand pictures. For each, Magpie strikes a pose, spreading his wings, or puffing his white chest, or nimbly landing on an outstretched arm. Near the edge of the Meadows, Adam orders a cup of coffee, and by the time he reaches the Royal Mile his cup has been refilled with coins and notes.

Through a series of sharp pecks at Adam's shoulder, Magpie directs him to a richly decorated shopfront. Adam gives his cup of money to the homeless man sitting outside, and enters into the close gloom of the antiques dealership, which is filled from floor to ceiling with bits of furniture, paintings and cabinets of memorabilia.

"No dogs or guide dogs," says the man behind the counter, who has a moustache so magnificent that it's difficult to tell if his lips are moving when he speaks. The ends of his moustache have been waxed into points, and he wears a pair of braces over a white shirt and pinstripe waistcoat, as if he is an old-fashioned barber.

"He's a bird," says Adam. Magpie leans down and lifts a small piece of paper from Adam's breast pocket. Taking the paper, Adam hands it over to the antiques dealer. "I think this is for you."

Whatever doubts the dealer might have had melt away as he observes the paper. "Ah, of course. This way, sir." Shifting a glass table aside, he leads them through a pair of curtains and into a warm back room, which is filled with significantly more elegant pieces than the front of the shop. "I followed your client's instructions as best I can," says the man, "but if you'll excuse me a moment, I still have to finish wrapping the last article." And with that, he vanishes in a cloud of musty aftershave, leaving Adam surrounded by pieces of extraordinarily valuable and extraordinarily delicate memorabilia.

Magpie flaps across the room and lands behind an ancient wooden screen. Cracked vases and thin mirrors tremble in his wake. There's a rustling noise from behind the screen, but Adam pays it little attention; he distracts himself from all the valuable antiques he might accidentally break by glancing at the paintings on the walls. There are faded landscapes, and peeling portraits, and all manner of presumably extremely expensive pieces which Adam has no idea how to value.

One of the paintings startles him.

When Adam thinks about Eve, it's like trying to stare into a light that's too bright. It's impossible for him to contain the whole of her at once in his mind, so he has to think about a bit of her at a time. Sometimes, he thinks about her hands; the lines across her palms in patterns like roots, and the gentleness of her touch. Sometimes, he thinks about her lips; the fullness of them, and the softness of them against his skin. And sometimes he thinks about her eyes; the way they are the colour of earth after rain, and the way her pupils dilate almost imperceptibly when she looks at him.

There's a painting here featuring three washerwomen, wearing heavy, practical clothes, their hair wrapped up in long lengths of white cloth. They are of different ethnicities, and the artist has somehow managed to capture details in each that remind Adam of Eve. In the young girl, bent over a washboard and scrubbing, it's in the tension of her forearms. In the middle-aged woman wringing clothes out, it's in the curve of her neck, and the way the light plays across her collarbones. And in the grey-haired woman hanging up washing to dry, it's in the way her smile lines complement the sharpness of her jaw.

"What do you see in it?" asks Magpie, emerging from behind the wooden screen. Without his silver crowns, his smile seems to have been disarmed. The right side of his face is slightly sunken in, there is a spiderweb network of white scars across his cheek, and when he speaks he slurs his words slightly. He's wearing a dusty tweed suit, and straightening the collar.

"Reminds me of Eve."

Magpie pauses before the painting, and smiles a lopsided smile. "Yes. I can see it." He then stands before a long mirror and turns back and forth, brushing the dust from the shoulders and admiring his new suit. "What do you think?" he asks.

"I think it's tweed."

"What's wrong with tweed?"

"It's tweed."

"Well, I like it."

The dealer with the magnificent moustache returns, hefting a heavy package wrapped in brown paper. "This is for you," he says, handing it over to Adam. "Ah, and welcome back, sir," he says, to Magpie. "I didn't notice you come in. How does the suit fit?"

"Very well, thank you. My friend doesn't like it."

"Tweed is an acquired taste, I find."

"My friend has no taste."

The dealer observes Adam. "What happened to your bird?"

Adam turns the package over in his hands. There's something familiar about the weight of it, but it's neatly taped shut. "He flew away."

With the package under his arm, Adam follows Magpie back out into the festival, and the two of them elbow their way through the crowds. They stop at a pub filled from doorway to doorway with tourists listening to a comedian. The comedian isn't very good, and the room is quiet except for his rambling voice, nervous coughs, and crackle of the speakers. Adam finds a bench outside and Magpie smokes the latter half of a cigarette, recently abandoned and left to burn down in the table's ashtray. "Unwrap your present, then," he says.

Carefully peeling back the uppermost layer of the brown paper package, Adam reveals an antique gun. It's an old, well-decorated powder duelling pistol, and it fits well in his hand. Beneath it, he can see the shapes of the other seven guns, and their corresponding thick leather belts. "How did you find these?"

"I've set up alerts with most of the antique dealerships in the city. They let me know if anything unusual comes in. More than a few flags were raised for these. They belonged to a man named Captain Adam Carris, apparently. Ring any bells?"

Adam sighs. "I don't want them."

"You're going to need them."

Pulling back the firing hammer, Adam meets less resistance than he'd been expecting. "They've been disarmed," he says. "They're ornamental."

Magpie taps ash from the end of his cigarette. "You and I both know they can be repaired. And I'm working on getting you some gunpowder."

Placing the pistol back in the package with its fellows, Adam seals the paper shut. "What do I need them for?"

"I promised to show you what I've been spending all my brother's money on," says Magpie. "It's in Manchester. I'll drive. And when we get there, everything will start to become a lot clearer. You just hold on to those, for now."

"You could have just bought me a new gun."

"In Britain?" Magpie laughs. "You've been living in the USA too long, Adam. Besides, I took those old pistols showing up to be an omen."

They make their way back out of the pub. The terrible comedian has been replaced by a slightly better comedian, and the crowd are at least chuckling. "Tweed doesn't suit you," says Adam, as they emerge into Edinburgh. The problem, he thinks, is that the tweed suit makes Magpie look like a parody of a person. But then, maybe that's the point.

"Everything suits me," says Magpie, stamping out his stolen cigarette.

* * *

Manchester: like a piece of London has floated away, become an island, and rejected its heritage. Broad streets and eclectic architecture are wrapped in a layer of scaffolding and orange warning mesh, cars guided more by traffic cones and diversion signs than the marks on the roads. Construction cranes stand like flocks of yellow flamingos, looming over everything. Manchester: a sprawling, metropolitan, in-between place, neither north nor south; wholly itself, and wholly nothing of itself.

"Do you know," says Magpie, thoughtfully, "I saw Snake here, once."

"You did?" Adam can't remember the last time he saw Snake.

"Yes." Magpie weaves a clever route through the streets, dodging queues at temporary traffic lights. "He was working at a petrol station on the other side of town. I only noticed him when he started filling up my car."

"How was he?"

"Well enough, I suppose. Tired looking. Wearing overalls a size too big. I don't think he recognised me. The thing was, this was back when people were starting to get wary about smoking in petrol stations. A few explosions will regulate an industry like that. But all the while he was filling up my car, Snake had a lit cigarette at the corner of his mouth, limp between his lips. I was watching him in my wing-mirror, waiting for the cigarette to drop."

"Do you think he knew?"

"I'm not sure," says Magpie, carefully. "I don't think it was like that. I think he was just tired. He didn't even meet my eyes when I paid him. Just thanked me and moved on."

"Did you see him again?"

"Not after that. I went by the next week, and it was someone else filling up the cars. There was a new sign warning about smoking in the station. Maybe he got fired. Or maybe he did recognise me, and wanted to move on." Magpie shrugs. "Do you think about him much?"

Adam considers the question. "Not really." The truth is that Adam tries not to think about anything too hard, these days. The needling mass of thorns filling his skull makes it difficult.

Gradually, the orange warning signs recede, to be replaced by intermittent scrappy parks. Dog walkers keep tight grips on leashes as their pets snarl and growl and snap at each other, and exchange polite pleasantries above the contained violence. The edges of grasses poke beyond their fences, trying to find cracks in the concrete so they might burst free of their containment. Black birds hop among the piles of litter, dragging white plastic bags around until their rotting treasures spill out across the paths. The monolithic towers of central Manchester are being replaced by low, suburban houses, no longer terraces, but semi-detached.

Looming above the houses is a stadium.

It's an old, wooden place, marked by time, and the closer it gets, the more worn it seems. The weather has left scars across it, and some of its beams have rotted away, to be replaced by perilously balanced sections of scaffolding. The streets around it are composed of houses used to living beneath its shadow; sullen faces peer out from behind net curtains at the lone car as it passes down the empty streets. Then, when there are no more houses, there are the vast, weed-encrusted car parks surrounding the crumbling stadium, completely deserted, cracked white division lines being erased by years of rain.

Magpie parks somewhere near the back, steps out and takes a deep breath.

"Bracing, today," he says.

"What is this place?"

"I forget the name of the club. The team was terrible, though. Some upstart manager with too much money bought a few cheap footballers and had this place put together. They lasted three seasons before the money ran out. I got it *very* cheap at auction." Hauling open the boot of his car, Magpie rifles around until he finds an enormous set of keys. "So far as the council knows, I'm an eccentric millionaire using it as a private garden. I pay my taxes, contribute to various local organisations and charities, send the occasional hamper out to the surrounding houses, and everyone leaves it alone." When he gets close enough to the stadium's lowest extremities, he runs a hand across the peeling green paint. "No graffiti, and no tags. Football is a kind of religion in this area, from what I gather. The locals seem to think of this place as a sort of grave site, and that my bit of gardening is respectful."

Magpie retrieves the rose from the back seat of the car. It's still brilliant and perfect, contained in its bell jar; only marred by a crimson handprint across the glass. He hands it to Adam. Then he retrieves the fur shawl, running his fingers through it before handing it across. "I had it cleaned," he says. "There was a lot of blood on it."

The shawl is brighter in daylight. The grey sun brings out even more colours in it.

Together, they haul open the rusted doors leading inside.

There's an enormous trophy case in the dripping hallway, shadowed by the drooping, damp ceiling. At the very centre of the case is a tiny trophy, and Adam has to crouch down and squint to make out the writing engraved in it.

"FA Cup Participants," he reads.

"At least they tried."

Adam follows Magpie towards the bright white square of daylight at the end of the hall. The rose is light beneath his arm, but the fur shawl feels heavy, and when he looks at it, he can feel one of the thorns in his tangle of memories scratching at him. He realises it is a thorn of grief. So too was the thorn for his memory of Pike. Which means, conceivably, that every single thorn on every single branch twisted and knotted around in his skull is a single instance of grief.

How many has he mourned? How many are dead?

Adam clutches Fox's coat to his chest.

The stadium is full of life.

Everywhere Adam looks, something is growing. The pitch looks as if it's burst free, rolled over to the stands and devoured them completely, giving the effect of a broad, regular valley, all the way up to the distant heights of the stands. There are trees, and small fields of grass, and wild bushes, and patches of fungi, and even flowers. Protected on every side from the wind, the sight is tranquil, and the only movement is the burbling stream running in a channel through the centre of the stadium, and the hopping and gliding of the birds as they dart from tree to decaying wooden bench. The sight of the stadium is dazzling.

This is a good place, Adam thinks. A good place to lay Fox to rest.

"You find somewhere for the rose," says Magpie, hauling a bag of compost from a stack. "I'll find somewhere for Fox."

Together, they move through the huge garden, crunching across frosted swathes of grass.

Near a beech tree, Adam spies a place where the rose will be in light most of the day in summer. There's a patch of empty soil not taken up by grass, so he kneels down and scoops out a deep enough hole. Then he carefully lifts the glass bell jar, and gently removes the rose from its temporary prison. The thorns of it snag at his fingers as he dusts down its exposed roots. Placing it reverently in the ditch, he takes handfuls of compost and, filling it in, pats it down. Magpie hands over a watering can, and Adam sprinkles a little across it. Satisfied, he sits back on the grass and rubs his hands together to remove the dirt. He's surprised to find red among the bits of soil; there are small cuts in his fingers. The rose's thorns are sharp enough to pierce his skin – sharp enough that its roots will taste his blood.

Magpie, meanwhile, has been digging at the roots of an alder tree with a shovel. It's a well-chosen place, Adam thinks – the hole Magpie excavates resembles the entrance to a burrow. When enough earth has been cleared, he reverently places the shawl inside. Then, he carefully closes it up. Adam wanders across, and he and Magpie spend a few moments in quiet contemplation, listening to the light breeze rustle the trees.

Fox, in the snow.

The earth is white and the sky is white and everything in between is white – trees and river and breeze, snowflakes tumbling – but there are all the colours of Eden's twilight, captured in her coat. She waits in the shadow of a branch, where her eyes gleam like the first stars of evening, fixed on the hare in the clearing. And when she leaps, the movement is fluid and silent, eclipsing the hare in her shadow.

"So what do you think?" Magpie asks.

"What do I think about what?"

"About all this."

"The stadium? I like it."

Magpie chuckles. "You haven't worked it out yet, have you?"

"Worked what out?"

"Tell me what's wrong with my garden."

Emerging from his reminiscences, Adam examines the stadium. It's a stunning array of species – not exactly exotic, but not mundane either. It's the kind of thing he'd expect from a city's botanic gardens. There doesn't seem to be anything wrong with it. If Adam had any criticism, it would be that the garden's contents don't quite seem to fit together. It's like Magpie's tried to put together a jigsaw puzzle by cramming the pieces in any old way. There are exposed bits of soil here and there, and no real paths leading through it, so that the whole thing feels patchwork. It's no crime, though; it's just the telltale mark of an inexperienced gardener. With time, Adam thinks he could make this garden really something to behold. For a start, he'd do something about the arrangement of the flowers.

The flowers...

Beneath the stadium's broken-glass boxes, there's a single sunflower, still in bloom, which doesn't make any sense. In fact, there are flowers here, there and everywhere, arranged erratically. The problem is that this is late autumn, and there shouldn't be any flowers. In fact, the leaves on the trees shouldn't be green. And neither should the trees be fruiting. Over among a set of benches, there's a tree still blossoming, and only a few steps away from Adam is a chilli plant, bright red chillies dangling beneath its rich green leaves. There's an apple tree with fresh, rosy apples hanging from its branches, and a pear tree, burdened by the weight of its fruit, and everything here is so superbly, ridiculously healthy, as if the season here is the perfect season for each individual plant.

Everything here is like the rose: a super-real specimen. Of course, he should have noticed it the instant he stepped into the stadium. The thatch of thorns in his head must have kept him from realising the strange truth of the place – making it all seem mundane.

Silently, Adam wanders among the plants. At the centre of the stadium, a thought occurs to him, and he removes his shoes and socks. Squirming his scarred feet in a patch of grass, he wriggles his toes and feels the blades between them. Then he looks up at the distant sun, which is a cold silver coin behind the cloud cover. There's an idea forming in his head. It's the seed of an idea, which needs nurturing – which needs light, and earth, and water to grow. Kneeling beside the canal through the centre of the stadium, Adam cups handfuls of cold water and sips at them, making his teeth chatter. Then he returns to the chilli plant and plucks a fresh, red chilli from it. The heat of it is like fire down his throat, and it makes his eyes water and nose run, and it makes him laugh; the taste of it is so familiar. It's a flavour he never thought he'd find again. Pressing his nose into flowers, he breathes in their heady, intoxicating scents, and he goes from tree to tree, pressing his ear against each and listening to the life there – the low creaking and groaning – and feeling the hard bark beneath his rough fingers.

Of course.

"Everything here is from Eden."

"Yes," says Magpie, and his smile broadens, revealing his remaining teeth.

Adam feels breathless. He can hear his bloom rushing around beneath his ribs, and he turns around and around, feeling the chilli still burning his throat. He tries to take in every bit of the hidden garden, every last piece of paradise, gathered here upon the pitch and benches, gathered here in secret, where they might be hidden away from the world. "It's more than just the rose. So much more. You're collecting pieces of Eden," he says, and he can feel the tears rolling down his cheeks, blurring his vision, and he can feel the laughter rising from deep within him – the fully formed idea blooming. Collapsing to his knees, Adam bunches the grass between his fingers, and he knows that it will never wither, and it will never die. Nothing here will. It was all made before death, just like he was.

VII

Adam remembers through touch. It's in the snagging of brambles at his fingers, the cut of the grass across his wrists, and the lines and curls of gnarled bark he traces as if they are a topography of paradise. The artificial river running through the middle of the stadium isn't from Eden – Adam imagines the futility of using a sieve on the ocean, to try and reclaim every last perfect drop of water – but that doesn't matter, because when Adam places his hands in the stream between the high reeds and lets the waving weeds on the riverbed curl and uncurl wetly around his fingers, he remembers anyway. When it starts raining, he takes shelter beneath the trees and remembers by listening; the droplets rushing and rustling the leaves draw him into himself and return him to a time when his whole world was a garden.

Eventually, he falls asleep, propped up against a broken goalpost. When he wakes the rain has stopped, and he's not sure if it's a new day or the same day. There's no sign of Magpie, but he can hear voices echoing in the entrance tunnel, and all at once a stream of children appear. There are ten of them – half of them dressed in blue, and half dressed in red – and one of them has a ball, which he kicks from foot to foot. The children in blue run across the grass and make a set of goalposts using their jumpers, while the children in red do the same on the other side of the green stretch.

"Are you allowed to be here?" asks Adam, emerging into the sunlight.

One of the children in blue stops, foot paused on the ball, and studies Adam with an interrogative expression, as if he is the intruder. "Do you work for Mister Corvid?" The rest of the group gather around him, hands in pockets, arms folded.

Adam considers the question. "I'm the gardener," he tells them.

"Mister Corvid says it's okay if we practise here," says one.

"So long as our parents don't come," says another.

"And your parents are okay with that?"

The child with his foot on the ball shrugs. "My dad says that Mister Corvid is a 'good bloke' for keeping the grounds."

"Well *my* dad says he's a bit strange."

"My mum says she wants to know if there's a Missus Corvid."

"I like his teeth. I want silver teeth."

There's a murmur of agreement among the children.

"Do you want to be our goalie?" asks one of the children in red. There are immediate protests from the children in blue.

"Sorry. I've got work to do," says Adam.

The children go about their game, five to a side. Adam is hesitant about letting them run across the grass in their spiked boots, but he quickly realises that he's being too protective. The grass is tougher than the children are; as they grow up, become teenagers, become adults, become middle-aged, become old, wither and eventually die, the grass will remain green, and sharp, and live on. The grass has lasted this long in the bitter ruination of the world outside paradise, and a few kids running around on it aren't going to do much to damage it.

Eventually Magpie returns, and the children pause to cheer as he emerges from the tunnel. He beams at them, and half his teeth are silver; his dangerous smile has been repaired. He's wearing a dark coat over a white shirt, and seems to be in good spirits. "I see you've met the locals," he says, sitting with Adam on one of the stadium's stained plastic bucket seats.

"You got new teeth."

"I got new teeth a couple of days ago."

"Oh," says Adam, rubbing at the back of his head. "Sorry. I didn't notice. I think I've been pretty distracted."

They watch the ball as it rushes through the grass, propelled from one end of the uneven field to the other. At one point it goes wide and rolls into the canal, and one of the children splashes across to reclaim it from the reeds. Adam hasn't been keeping track of the score, but neither have the children. It doesn't seem to matter.

"Ready to go yet?" asks Magpie.

Adam realises that he had assumed this place was an ending of some kind. As if he might just be able to stay here and put down roots, like one of the trees. The idea that there is even a world outside the stadium bothers him; he's not sure he wants to experience it again. He imagines it will be like going back to watching television on a black-and-white set after experiencing full colour high definition. "Go where?" he asks.

"First, we need to do a bit of shopping. Then, we're going to Crow's funeral."

* * *

Central Manchester is bustling with people. Magpie queues for coffee and orders one for Adam, who sips at it reluctantly. Wherever Adam looks – sky, building or pavement – the world seems dull, as if someone's turned the colour saturation down. Slowly, though, and with the help of the coffee, he begins to feel himself waking from the dream of Magpie's stadium garden. People rush around him, and it's there that he notices the bright colours he thought were missing: a purple mackintosh coat; a sunshine yellow baseball cap; the neon whirling of phone screens and billboard advertisements. There are pigeons among the people, and flecked in their grey feathers are iridescent blues and purples and aquamarines.

Beyond wire railings, and between high buildings that reflect the grey sky, waits the canal, and Magpie navigates the thin walkways around it, through private courtyards and empty brick alleyways. Here, Manchester is intermittently bright and dark, following no pattern, so that Adam finds himself dazzled by the constant shifting. The people they pass are hurried men and women with grey faces and stern expressions.

Up a spiral of wooden steps they emerge into a bustling open-air market, where the coarse voices of the sellers mingle with the coarse voices of the crows that hop among the litter. Adam steps around discarded banana peels and plastic bags, through corridors of tents, from which a melee of scents, sweet and sour, contend for his attention. The sky here is blue and grey in patches, and Adam tries to focus on it, ignoring the calls from the vendors trying to sell him phone cases, and imitation watches, and discount cabbages.

At a tall tent filled from top to bottom with threadbare T-shirts and trousers, Magpie enquires after their largest sizes and manages to find a few specimens that might actually fit Adam. And at a bench beside a stall selling fruit, from which the vendor's voice is a constant stream of wordless noise that Adam is unable to interpret, Magpie tries on a pair of the trousers for fun, pulling them up around his skinny legs and strutting to and fro. He laughs so hard that Adam thinks it's a wonder his crowns don't come spilling out of his mouth.

"What do I need these for, anyway?" Adam asks.

"You smell like a man who's spent a week sleeping under a tree."

Further along, there is a stall selling particularly ripe looking fruits individually wrapped in vacuum-sealed plastic. Magpie hands an envelope brimming with cash to the grey-haired saleswoman, who loads a plastic bag with a choice of fruits from all across her selection – pears, and strawberries, and peaches. The worst are the bananas and the oranges, Adam thinks: the way that the plastic oozes around them like a second superfluous skin.

They stop for lunch at a stall selling steaming noodles. Adam devours his, surprised at his hunger, but then, he can't remember the last time he ate. Maybe he really has spent the last week in

Magpie's stadium. Noodles squirm around Magpie's chopsticks, and when he slurps at them Adam thinks they look like worms wriggling between his lips.

"Tell me what you think of these," says Magpie, between mouthfuls. He pushes the bag of fruit across, so that it spills its contents. One of the bananas falls from the edge of the table, and when Adam reaches down to recover it he notices the bruise now marking it despite its protective packaging. There's something uncomfortable about handling the plastic-wrapped fruits; the textures are all wrong, and lights gleams across them in strange ways.

"Open one," says Magpie.

Setting the rest aside, Adam unwraps an orange. The plastic comes free easily. He continues to unwrap it, peeling apart its skin with his fingers, and then parting its segments. The sharp sting of citrus rises from the fruit, and he plucks the seeds from its flesh, weighing them in his hand. There doesn't seem to be anything special about the orange. "It's an orange," he says.

Magpie laughs. "It is an orange. But it's an orange that costs twice as much as any other orange here. It comes from a special farm, where oranges are grown all year round and wrapped in their own little packages. Of course, you and I know that the packaging does nothing. It's all an aesthetic to say: look at how much we care about our fruits. The superior quality of them is evident in the way we protect them, each in their own sheath. They must taste better than any of our rivals' fruits. Devilish, really."

"It's just an orange, though."

"Exactly. That's what makes it so brilliant."

"Why did you buy these?"

Magpie shrugs. "Know thy enemy. These are from the Sinclairs' orchards. From what I can gather, Frank Sinclair still has at least one more piece of Eden. And once we're done at Crow's funeral, we're going to take it from him. How does that sound?"

Adam munches at a segment of orange. "I've been thinking," he says.

"Have you, now?"

"Your collection. What's it for?"

"What do you mean?"

"I mean – the stadium. The garden. What are you gonna do with it once you've finished gathering up all the bits?"

Magpie shrugs. "I haven't really thought that far ahead."

"Seriously?"

"I am but a humble curator, Adam. It's not my place to assign meaning to the art."

"Sure." Adam pops another segment into his mouth.

"Tell me, then."

"Tell you what?"

"Your idea. There's obviously something happening in that big skull of yours."

"I mean…" Adam pauses, before eating another piece of orange. He turns the segment over in his hand, studying the network of veins through it; they resemble the lines of his palm, he thinks. The last time he ate an orange, he was in jail, and that feels like whole lifetimes ago. "So many are dead."

"You're going to have to elaborate for me."

"Fox, I mean. And Pike. And Tiger."

"And all the rest. Yes, Adam. I know how many are dead. I helped Rook build his firm, remember. I've seen the files."

"Well. What if there was a safe place for them? Those still alive, I mean."

"You want to offer them my stadium?"

Adam shrugs. "Why not?"

Magpie's face is perfectly expressionless for a moment. Then his smile emerges, slow as sunrise. "Tell you what," he says. "You agree to help me rid Frank Sinclair of his last pieces of paradise, and we can present your idea to Rook. He'll be at the funeral."

There's a warm glow in Adam's stomach that might be the orange, or maybe something else. "That sounds good," he says.

After lunch they head deeper into the market, to the indoor section, where the roof closes in on them and the noise becomes an echoing crescendo. There is no escape from the stalls and scents in here, and all the flashing lights, and the bloodshot whites of wide eyes, leave Adam feeling claustrophobic. At a stall selling war memorabilia, Magpie hands another enormous envelope to the vendor, while Adam glances through the medals in the display cabinet. He recognises some of those symbols, and he wonders if he ever earned any of them for himself. The vendor rolls a large, sealed barrel out from under his table, and he and Magpie shake hands. "There you are," says Magpie to Adam, rapping his knuckles across the waxed wood.

"What is it?"

"Gunpowder."

"You bought a barrel of gunpowder?"

"I promised I would. For your guns. You're going to have to carry it, though."

Adam crouches beside it and checks the seals. The barrel seems watertight. He's still hesitant about hauling a barrel filled with explosive powder through a busy city centre, though. "This is a bad idea."

"Don't worry. We'll be fine."

"Where are we taking it?"

"There's a gym a few streets over."

"Why are we taking a barrel of gunpowder to a gym?"

"So you can have a shower, Adam. You stink."

The barrel is heavy, and has the acrid, metallic smell of explosives that Adam hates. It conjures dark images in his thoughts: images of the dead and dying, lying across bloodied fields, and all the birds landing and feasting on them, their wings disturbing the haze left by the guns and cannons. The whimpering and weeping and wordless crying out of the dying never affected him, he knows; the worst was always the screaming of the horses. It's strange, he thinks, the way that he doesn't mind thousands of his own children going to war, but the thought of a single horse dying on a battlefield affects him so much: the rolling eyes, the frothing at the mouth, and the simple, clear pain, felt without understanding. There was a time, Adam remembers, that he did care about his children, but he's not sure when or why that changed. The answer lies somewhere in depths of the thorns wreathed around the inside of his skull: some forgotten memory at root of his grief.

"Here," says Magpie, handing Adam a white plastic card.

"You have a gym membership?"

"Of course I have a gym membership."

Magpie has a stick-figure body, Adam observes. "Why do you have a gym membership?"

"It's a bit like a zoo, don't you think?" Magpie grins. "Leave the barrel with me."

The showers are too hot, but Adam doesn't mind. He bows his head and lets the water cascade over him, pooling in his scars and running like rivers down his bare flesh. The clods of earth clinging to him are washed away, revealing yet more scars. Around him, men with red faces and muscles like slabs tremble in the heat, washing away sweat and exchanging envious glances with each other. Adam closes his eyes and idly traces his scars – all those slashes and swirls marking his skin – until his hands reach the heart beating in his chest, and there they pause, feeling the steady thump of it against his ribs. It's Eve's heart, and he spends a while listening to it, hidden there so deep inside him, safe beneath all his layers of flesh and muscle and bone. His body is its armour, he thinks – dented, and worn, and bashed, but still strong enough to protect it, even after all this time.

Once Magpie's garden is complete, he will show it to Eve, he thinks, and maybe they could stay there for a while, and remember how things were together.

"You all right, there?" A man has been trying to speak to Adam for a while, it seems. This man has particularly bulbous muscles, and his thighs are so broad that they chafe as he wanders across, clenching and unclenching his swollen fists so that his biceps flex. "I was just asking, how much do you bench?"

"Sorry?"

"Bench. How much do you bench? You must dead-lift, right?"

"No, sorry."

"Look, mate. Between you and me. What are you taking, for results like that?"

"Taking?"

"You need to put me in touch with your trainer. With your dealer."

"You've lost me."

The man draws himself up close. "Steroids," he hisses. "What are you taking?"

"I'm not."

"Nah, mate." The man's face reddens further. "Don't fuck me around. Look at you. You can't get results like that without some serious help."

Adam turns off his shower. "I was made this way."

Sifting through the new clothes, Adam finds a combination that feels comfortable enough. The rest he bins, along with his old clothes, noting the earth and blood encrusted into the fabric. It was probably a good idea to change, after all. He spends a while unwinding the bandages from around his leg, and plucking the remaining staples from his flesh. The gunshot wounds have healed well, and in a couple more weeks they should scar up nicely. The scars will be white whorls, and they will join the white lines struck across his shin. Sometimes he thinks that his scars are like the night sky, and that he might name some of the constellations marking him.

Before he leaves the gym, he scrubs at his old military coat until the worst of the blood and dirt has been removed from it. It's a good coat, he thinks, and it would be a waste to throw it away. It sits comfortably across his shoulders.

Outside, Magpie is sitting on the barrel of gunpowder and drumming at it with his hands and the backs of his feet. A gathering of tourists are watching him, and taking flash pictures, and clapping along. He drums a clever crescendo, and leaps from the barrel with a bow, before cupping his hands out to them. Coins and notes flutter from wallets and purses, and he pockets handfuls of cash, thanking them and thanking them.

"You look refreshed," he says, when he notices Adam.

Carefully hauling the barrel of explosive powder, Adam does not reply. He doesn't think he could string together any kind of sentence that would instil caution in Magpie. And besides, if Magpie has somehow survived this long, he must be doing something right. It is possible, Adam concedes, that every risk Magpie takes is carefully calculated, no matter how unlikely that seems.

* * *

Adam's pretty sure that time doesn't move at the same speed everywhere. In Manchester, a lot of the buildings look as if they're straight out of a science fiction book – as if the city exists in a temporal valley, and time has run from the surrounding country to quicken the pace of progress there. Out in the Lake

District, though, it doesn't look as if much time ever passes. The trees could be the same trees as centuries ago; the mountains casting the same shadows; the rivers winding the same routes. Only the motor of Magpie's car feels out of place here, rumbling and groaning down the rocky lanes, a futuristic chimera intruding upon a place where everything else is ancient and wild.

The barrel of gunpowder rolls across the back seats, jarred by every pothole.

Through an open wooden gate, Magpie drives alongside a meandering river, beyond which is a huge, yellowing forest. Peering at the map across his lap, he taps the paper triumphantly. From between the trees, they emerge into a muddy clearing, where the road ends and a small footpath begins. There are dozens of other cars parked here, shiny and black and gleaming. "This looks right," he says, folding his map. "The service should be at the end of the track."

Outside, the wind curls and uncurls the edges of Adam's coat.

"You go on ahead," says Magpie, leaning against his car.

"You're not coming?"

"My brother has a way of droning on."

"You need to talk to him."

"I'll be along soon. Don't worry, Adam. I'm just not very good at funerals."

Flicking through his phone, Magpie hums a song to himself.

Making his way up the track, Adam tramples crisp brown and orange and yellow leaves, which gust around his legs and skitter across the hard earth. Above the trees, the peaks of mountains are visible, with white tips scratching the open sky. The forest drips leaves of every autumn colour, and sat upon a branch among them is the shape of a large bird, watching over the winding path like a sentry. Owl flicks his wings as Adam passes, the great bird's head slowly revolving to follow his progress.

Among the leaves and trees, there are petals. They are red, and yellow, and blue, and purple, and orange, and white, and they flutter across the muddy track. There are benches arranged in the clearing ahead in rows like pews, and they are filled with mourning figures dressed in black – all manner of people who must have known Crow from her life in America. Adam emerges into the wide clearing, which is set up beside the rocky bank of the river. This appears to be the very base of the valley.

At the head of the congregation is a small wooden stage, upon which is a large portrait of Crow smiling, wearing a silver dress and holding a glass of champagne. Beside the portrait stands Rook, delivering a speech from a lectern as if he is a lecturer at a university, with the white sun reflecting from his rounded spectacles. Among the pews, and stands, and mourners, are dozens and dozens of colourful flower arrangements in bunches and vases, with their loose petals drifting out in every direction, landing on the dark shoulders of the mourners, sticking to the portrait of Crow, and drifting out in a great stream across the frothing river.

There is a spare section on a bench near the back, and Adam claims it, brushing petals from the plastic surface. Sat beside him is the enormous figure of Pig, his black jacket struggling to contain his meaty limbs. Pig doesn't notice Adam, because he is snoozing peacefully, with his chins resting against his barrel chest. On the other side of Pig is Butterfly, who is wearing a colourful summer dress beneath a red jacket, and has her hair braided in a rainbow coil. She leans across, whispering so as to not interrupt Rook's speech. "Do you like the flowers?"

"They're the best bit."

"My idea." Butterfly beams and leans back.

Adam tries to listen to Rook's speech, but it seems fairly generic – words that might be said at any funeral – and he's sat so far back that it's drowned out by the rushing of the river and the weeping of the mourners anyway. So, he leans back and listens to the gentle snoring of Pig instead, watching the rise and fall of that prodigious chest.

Adam hasn't had a funeral in a while, because he's been living a lot of inconsequential lives. He's been enjoying the idea of being the man in the background of the book: the one-line character who fixes the car, or shoes the horse, for the protagonist. In that way he has slipped between lives with barely a whisper for a long time now, moving on to his next name and destination with no fuss. When he leaves his lives, his neighbours and colleagues sometimes give him a card wishing him luck, but little else, and he prefers it that way. He allows himself to fade from their lives and be forgotten as he moves on, so that the sensation of letting one life end and another begin is no more upsetting than throwing away an old pair of jeans and putting on a new pair.

It wasn't always that way, of course. Adam used to live a lot of lives that he was proud of, and reluctant to leave behind. He and Eve lived almost too long in Thebes, for instance –

working in the Valley of Kings. The passing of pharaohs and nobles kept them both busy. It was Eve's pleasure to work as an embalmer, part of the hallowed team tasked with preparing the bodies for entombment, and she spent her days steadily growing familiar with the interior anatomy of the human body: finding all its weaknesses, and ruminating on ways of repairing it better. Meanwhile, it was Adam's pleasure to bring life to the arid valley: finding ways to nurture greenery in the spaces between the ever-expanding array of tombs, all while hauling skins heavy with water up from the river for the masons. Adam liked the idea that both her work and his work were devoted to life, in a place devoted to death. Sometimes, at night, Eve would show Adam sketches she had made of the arrangements of the organs inside the people she was helping to embalm, and Adam would wonder at it all, and flex his fingers just to see his tendons moving through the skin across the back of his hand.

Adam flexes his fingers now, making his scars stretch.

On the wind, he catches the sound of dogs barking.

Eventually, Rook's speech comes to an end, and a queue forms to shake his hand. Adam and Butterfly join the queue together, and leave Pig where he is. The queue is slow to move, and Adam takes the time to study the portrait of Crow. The portrait is a photograph, taken candidly at a party, and the photographer has managed to capture a rare moment with her; Crow's smile is unguarded and genuine, and Adam finds himself absorbed in her moment.

"Owl tells me that you've found my brother," says Rook, when Adam comes to the front of the queue. His hand is small, but his grip is firm.

"He's waiting with the cars."

"Ah, yes. He's never been very good at funerals. Thank you for bringing him."

"We should talk."

"We can catch up at the wake. Magpie does enjoy a good canapé, and I am looking forward to finding out where all my money has been going." Rook smiles, wryly.

As Butterfly moves up to kiss Rook's cheek, Adam catches another sound on the wind: the distant noise of what sounds like a hunting horn. The dogs didn't sound out of place when he heard them – he imagines there's no end of dog walkers out here – but the horn is unusual. Adam moves away from the river, to the edge of the pews, and peers into the dripping forest, listening for more. The wind drifts across him, changing direction from moment to moment, and it brings him no further noises. But there is something else, a familiar sensation – a sort of trembling stillness, as if the forest has taken a deep breath.

Crouching, Adam presses his hand against the ground. It's shivering.

The horn sounds again. Closer now. And the noise of the dogs is rising.

Turning back to the funeral, Adam wants to shout at them, to warn them that every instinct he has is telling him something is coming. But the scene is so tranquil – the drifting petals and leaves, and the mourners in delicate dresses and suits, and the plastic pews and the winding river – that it seems impossible anything should happen to disturb the peace cultivated here.

Pig has awoken. Still in his chair, he seems to be the only

other funeral attendee to have noticed the noises coming from the woods. Adam meets his eye, and they both turn to watch the trees, branches twitching in the breeze, leaves falling in gusts. There is movement among them, now, a churning kind of shifting in the shadows, as if there is a wave rolling through the forest. The dogs are barking and snarling.

"Get to the river!" yells Pig.

A tide of dogs crashes through the undergrowth. Their eyes are wide and wild, and froth drips from their snarling mouths; a terrible, tormented kind of hunger makes their limbs shudder.

The dogs rush and leap, jaws snapping. Adam throws the first away, but the next two bite into his arms, and then a third into his leg. Tearing them from his limbs, Adam glimpses the chaos behind him: the dogs smashing into the milling mourners; chairs tumbling aside; the screaming as people are ripped into. And there is Pig, standing before Butterfly, bashing dogs away with a chair.

The hunting horn sounds again.

Beyond the frenzy of falling leaves, and whirling petals, and snapping jaws, more shapes smash through the trees. Horses stamping hard, their riders wearing red coats and black caps, carrying hunting rifles. The one with the horn sounds it again and again, signalling the charge, and the terrified hunting dogs surge and snarl, more frightened by the thundering of the hooves at their backs than by any quarry at the funeral.

At the head of the hunting party, his terrier teeth bared in a snarl, wisps of white hair sticking out from his red scalp, is Frank Sinclair, and hanging from the end of his rifle is a tail the colours of sunset, tipped with white. Fox's brush swishes with the movement of Frank's horse, and he yells at the top of his lungs.

"You murdered my wife!"

Knuckles white, he brings his rifle to bear. The shot skims Adam's neck, and he is sent tumbling, knocked aside by a horse. More dogs rush to snap at him, and he bashes them away, trying to roll himself upright.

Petals and leaves mask the sky, but there is a shape up there, the silhouette of something huge with wings. Above the horn, and the stampeding horses, and gunshots, and screaming, there is an avian screech. With a wet crunch, Owl scythes through a horse, carrying it and its rider bodily for several yards before dropping them dead. When he lands, he sends petals and leaves scattering, clearing space with his colossal copper and bronze wings.

The charge breaks; horses and riders lose their momentum, made uncertain by the monster among them. Owl takes flight, screeching, and dogs scatter before him. Shots ring out as red-coat hunters turn, and there are red bursts from between his feathers.

Throwing dogs aside, Adam hauls himself to his knees.

Before the riders can regroup, an enormous shape smashes through the pews towards them. Covered in bristling coarse black hair, Pig squeals – a primal, animal warning. The dogs find a new fear and scatter before him, falling over each other in their efforts to flee. The horses roll their eyes, desperate to avoid him, but they are not quick enough. Pig gores into the flank of the first and it shrieks, throwing its red-coat rider. He crashes through, trampling both, unstoppable with momentum. More fall, bloody and ragged, sliced apart upon his mighty tusks.

The last of the dogs rush away from Adam, and he stands. Nearby, a fallen rider squirms beneath his horse, and Adam takes the rifle from him.

Adam takes aim. The rifle bucks. A rider falls from his horse.

Pull the bolt back. Load the next round.

Among the petals and leaves, a black bird is visible, flapping in the faces of the horses and making them buck precariously.

Adam takes aim. The rifle bucks. A dog dies.

Pull the bolt back. Load the next round.

Overhead, avoiding the fight, caught in a beam of sunlight, a butterfly flutters, its wings the colours of summer.

Adam takes aim. The rifle bucks. A rider dies.

Pull the bolt back. Load the next round.

There, at the edge of the forest, his teeth open in a snarl of futile defiance, Frank Sinclair turns about. He knows he is being routed. Yet he still raises his rifle up, towards the enormous silhouette of Owl. The rifle cracks, and Owl falls.

Adam takes aim. The rifle bucks. Frank Sinclair's horse rears and the shot goes wide.

Pull the bolt back. Load the next round.

Frank's horse bolts, taking him back into the trees along with the survivors of the hunting party. Injured dogs mill in their wake. Adam takes aim. The rifle bucks. But he isn't quick enough. The shot hits a tree, and Frank Sinclair is gone. The rest of his hunting party is gone. There are only a few dogs still moving, and Pig charging at them, ripping them apart with his gleaming, bloody tusks.

Adam lowers the rifle.

There, among the dying mourners and dying riders and dying horses, is Owl in the shape of a man. Rook is beside him, naked, trying to stop the flow of blood. Striding across, Adam helps. It looks as if Owl has been shot several times, mostly through his arms, but there is one shot through his gut: Frank Sinclair's bullet, punching a horrible hole through his flesh. Owl's eyes roll; he is delirious. Adam and Rook staunch the bleeding as best they can, together.

When there is nothing else for Adam to do, he stands and takes his rifle.

Mourners are helping other mourners, weeping and frightened. Among them lies Pig, still in his native shape, exhausted and covered from tusk to tail in blood, his chest rising and falling. Yet he seems uninjured. None of that blood is his own. As Adam examines him, Butterfly lands on Pig's nose, her bright wings fluttering as if she is a collection of petals come to life. Pig grunts gently, his wet nose snuffling, his dark eye fixed upon her.

There is a horse with two broken legs, whinnying, panicking and still trying to move. Adam loads his rifle and shoots it dead. Nearby is another horse, its guts spilled from its open belly, gored and dying, whimpering in pain. Adam loads his rifle, and puts it out of its misery. And further along, trapped beneath the weight of a dead horse, a red-coat rider lays weeping. "Please," he begs. "Adam, please. I implore you. I can tell you anything. I can pay you. Please." Adam pulls the bolt back on the rifle, but the magazine is empty. So he staves the man's head in with the butt of it.

"You need to leave." Rook is taking charge at last, shouting at Adam. "You need to leave before the ambulances arrive. You can't be here. The authorities can't see you."

"What about Owl?"

Rook clenches and unclenches his bloody hands. "I think he'll live."

Throwing his rifle aside, Adam makes his way over to the edge of the forest – the place he saw Frank Sinclair go. There are deep hoofprints everywhere, but he has hunted men through worse. Adam plunges into the dripping yellow forest, chasing after the remains of Frank Sinclair's hunting party.

VIII

Back when state lines were mere suggestions, and towns were sprouting up like weeds across North America, a dying marshal promoted Adam to the rank of deputy so that he might pursue a man in the name of the law. The man's name was Randy Turnbull, and he had shot the marshal during a confrontation outside the bank of the town where Adam had found work as a blacksmith. The bank's new safe had not yet arrived, and the bankers had made the questionable decision to keep the miners' wages inside a locked drawer, so Turnbull had decided to rob them. Adam was of the belief that Turnbull would have robbed them even if they did have a safe – there was a kind of wild desperation in his eyes, as if all the good steel in the state couldn't keep him away from that cash.

Turnbull fled south on horseback, and Adam followed on foot, because he could find no horse strong enough to bear him. Across valleys and through mountain passes Turnbull went, pushing his horse harder than a horse should be pushed, until, at the end of the first week, Adam came across Turnbull's steed, dead and abandoned at the edge of a shallow river. Turnbull had taken it upon himself to haul his stolen cash himself, making his tracks deep and his stride slow. Still he continued, displaying an almost supernatural turn of grit, through dusty plains and rocky valleys where the sun baked the ground and the warm winds swept away his tracks.

From time to time, Adam lost the trail, but it was plain enough where Turnbull was headed: south, and further south still, towards Mexico. It was at a town in what would soon officially be called New Mexico that Adam finally caught up with him, almost a month into the chase. The man was known to be taking a drink at one of the taverns. Yet, instead of simply striding inside and shooting Turnbull dead, Adam chose to ask the local sheriff for help.

This proved to be a vital mistake. The sheriff – a gruff man with drooping moustaches – was of the belief that Adam was a "no-good Negro" who had stolen a badge and was impersonating the role of deputy. Adam was promptly arrested at gunpoint, and only managed to avoid an immediate lynching because of the sheriff's belief that a marshal should oversee it. By the time that marshal arrived – two weeks later – to confirm Adam's legitimacy, Turnbull was long gone into Mexico. Adam carried on tracking him, without so much as an apology from the sheriff, who spat in the dust of Adam's wake. But he would never catch up with Turnbull. The man had successfully vanished.

*　*　*

As Adam tracks Frank Sinclair and the remains of his hunting party through the autumn forest, his wounds start to insist on making themselves known. The bites in his arms and legs sting as he strides, and the gunshot wound in his shoulder is spreading a liquid warmth across him. Adam can feel the bullet lodged there, grating up against his collarbone with every jarring step.

The forest is filled with tracks. There are hoofprints and pawprints crossing the damp earth in every direction, and it's difficult to tell where Frank Sinclair went. Blood marks the ground, splattered crimson across yellow leaves and thick dark roots.

There is movement ahead, and Adam follows it through the dripping yellow trees to where a pack of ragged dogs are tearing into the remains of a fallen hunter. There are long scars across their backs, and their ribs are protruding; they are a circle of teeth, devouring one of their torturers. Adam advances, and the dogs part to let him through. He crouches beside the fallen hunter, and recognises him as one of the naked people from the Sinclairs' greenhouse. Retrieving the dead hunter's rifle, he moves on, and behind him the circle of teeth closes.

Adam follows the tracks up a slope at the edge of the forest, and through a muddy pass between two high hills. Beyond the pass is a wide valley, filled with dying wild flowers. The flowers are purple, and deep orange, and white, and red, and the tangled mess of them sweeps away ahead of him, the mass of colours broken by the trail of muddy hoofprints trampled through them. Adam can see a dozen red-coat riders on horseback in the far distance, crossing the stream at the centre of the valley, one of which is small, and has wispy white hair. Kneeling among the wild flowers, which are so frosted that they crackle beneath him, Adam raises his rifle, pulls the bolt back, and takes aim across the iron sights.

Then, after a long pause, he lowers it.

The problem is the horses. At this distance, Adam knows that his aim will be too flawed. The rifle's calibre is weak enough that the wind will make the bullet drift, and even if he were to compensate, he would still be more likely to hit a horse than a rider. Adam has already had to execute two horses today, and he has witnessed the bloody end of more. Those horses have done nothing to warrant more pain and panic than they have already endured.

Adam makes his way down into the valley, following the trail trampled through the flowers. Soon, there are only the colours of the flowers and the dazzling bright light from the sun, shadows shifting across the frosted ground as clouds drift quickly with the chill winds.

By the time he reaches the river, he can no longer see the riders. The waters froth white, and caught up in the current are colourful petals and yellow leaves. Adam kneels beside the water and lets it rush around his fingers, considering where to go from here. It took him a while to walk down to the river, and it will take him longer still to cross it. The hunting party already had a significant head start when he entered the valley, and they're likely to have a whole fleet of horseboxes waiting somewhere ahead, to whisk them all away, back to Scotland. There is little hope of him catching them now, he knows. So, frustrated, he turns, and makes his way back to the autumn forest. Maybe he can still get back in time to help with the wounded.

As he goes, he dismantles the rifle. Each piece he sows, as if the gun is composed of seeds. He wonders what kind of plant would grow from a gun seed. It would be a grim, twisted tree, he thinks, and from its branches would hang silver bullets, which would chime in the wind. When only the rifle's bullets remain, he rolls them around in his palm, and at the edge of the valley he scatters them, watching them flash and tumble and fall among the bright flowers. And then he turns, and leaves the vale of dying wild flowers behind.

* * *

On his return to the autumn forest, Adam spies red and blue lights flashing beside the river clearing where the ruins of the funeral lie. There are men and women in uniform spread out and scouring the woodland floor with spiked sticks, taking a census of the dead, and cataloguing evidence. Adam knows that he will be spotted if he ventures any further into the valley, so he turns to leave, but as he does he spots a small wooden shack neatly camouflaged in a yellowing copse nearby. Something glints in one of the shack's dark slotted windows: a lens, trained across the trees. Somebody is watching the progress of the police.

There is a rack of binoculars hung up on the back of the shack, and Adam grabs a pair, figuring he can use them as a sort of makeshift club. But when he opens the door, there is only Magpie inside, wearing a brown duffle coat and flat cap, and for all the world looking exactly like a birdwatcher. He flashes Adam a silver smile, and raises a finger to his lips, motioning for him to remain quiet. Then, he pats the empty stool beside him.

The warped wooden stool creaks as Adam sits.

"Any luck?" whispers Magpie.

"I lost the riders."

"Ah, well." Magpie lowers his binoculars, draws a packet of gummy worms from one of his pockets, and pops it open. He chews on a bright green worm, thoughtfully. "Nothing to worry about. Frank Sinclair and his pastoral fetishist fan club have threatened Rook, and he will ruin them for it, mark my words. Did you ever visit Rook's cottage?"

Adam can remember a few of Rook's homes – the house in Merrion Square, the villa beside the Vatican, and the apartment overlooking Central Park – but he can't picture any cottages. A cottage seems too small for Rook, somehow. "I'm not sure I did."

"Well. My dear brother built a cottage up on the east coast of Scotland a couple of centuries back. He spent ages finding the perfect location, and settled on a windswept heath above a cliff edge just north of Berwick – it even had access to a cove with a rocky beach. He spent months hauling rocks up from that beach, and piling them together into a sort of cottage-shaped heap, and not content to simply buy furniture and roofing, he even went as far as to learn a whole selection of trades, and make everything inside by hand. I'm still not sure what drove him to do it, but it turned into a real labour of love; that cottage was a retreat for the summer months, where he would go away from the world for a while and fly along the coast. And I must say, the result was impressive. Say what you like about Rook, but he has impeccable taste. I'm hardly ashamed to say that I stayed in that cottage myself from time to time – my brother has a policy of always leaving a window open wherever he goes, for any errant birds that might need a little shelter for a day or two. That cottage stood the test of time for almost two centuries, weathering the weather and the approaching crumbling cliff edge. In fact, I think Rook was looking forward to that cliff eroding enough that his cottage would fall from the edge. Some symbol of the passing of time, maybe. But he had no such luck, in the end.

"A couple of decades ago, when he showed up for his usual summer retreat, the cottage was gone, and in its place was a golf course. I don't think I've ever seen my brother angrier. Normally, when he's annoyed at you, he won't shut up. But this time, he just went very quiet and got to work. The golf course's owner was some wealthy American developer who figured that the cottage's owner wouldn't have enough money to challenge him in court. Rook didn't bother challenging him in court. Instead, he put each case and client running through Corvid & Corvid on hold for a month, and devoted every resource available to him into ruining that man. He went for the man's money, and by the end of the month had every penny of it. The fool even showed up at Rook's office, begging on his knees for his money back. And do you know what Rook told him? That he could have it back, if he rebuilt the ruined cottage. From what I understand, he actually gave it a go. Without any money, the best he could do was go to the beach and do what Rook did in the first place: haul rocks up, one by one. They found him cold on a sand bar after a week, a heavy rock clutched between his bloodied hands, dead from a heart attack. Beautiful, really. And I feel as if a similar fate is in store for Frank Sinclair and his friends. Mark my words: they'll all be dead or begging on the streets by the end of the year."

Adam feels a little of the tension gripping him loosen. "Good," he says. And when Frank Sinclair is dead, he will go and find Fox's tail, and bring it back to the stadium to reunite it with her coat.

Adam raises his binoculars and focuses them on the funeral. The river is a rushing silver sliver, making for a kinetic backdrop to the chaotic and colourful remains of the ruined gathering. Pieces of chairs, and vases, and trampled flowers lie in splinters everywhere, and though the dead have mostly been removed, there are plenty of white-clad forensic officers still struggling with some of the heavier corpses. A few horses are being towed on trolleys along the track. The scene is a muddled rainbow of destruction, with petals still coating everything, but the dominant colour is a vibrant shade of scarlet. Near the stage, Adam spots the portrait of Crow, smashed into a crumpled canvas heap.

Such a waste.

"Worm?" Magpie offers his selection.

Accepting the packet, Adam fishes out a blue specimen, but when he places it in his mouth it's strangely gritty. He checks the sell-by date. "These went off a decade ago."

"Did they?" Magpie raises his binoculars. "I should really empty my pockets more often."

Adam hauls himself to his feet and checks over his wounds. Most have stopped bleeding, but the gunshot wound in his shoulder is still seeping red. "We should head to the hospital and check on Owl. He got hit pretty bad."

Magpie shakes his head. "No time. We need to get back to work. We only have a window of a few days in which to steal another piece of Eden from Frank Sinclair." Upending the packet of worms into his mouth, he grinds his jaw around to chew at the gelatine mass. Then, sliding his sleeve back, he checks his watch. "I still need to show you it. And if we leave now, we can get in before closing."

"We should really check on Owl."

"And do what, Adam?" Magpie fastens his coat. "Did you ever learn medicine?"

"No. That was Eve."

Magpie sighs, and his expression softens. "Look. Owl's in the best possible hands. Rook will see to that. So how about you and I finish what we started? Then, when we're done, we can show Owl my little collection. Surely that would be a better use of our time than pacing hospital corridors?"

Adam remembers how good it felt to see the stadium for the first time. To realise what it all was. And besides, Magpie is right. All Adam's good for is his strength. He never had Eve's gift for healing. "All right," he says, at last.

Outside, the winds have picked up, and there's a sharp chill in the air, rustling the trees and sending yellow leaves spinning. Adam follows Magpie along a thin and winding track, away from the ruined funeral. As they go, he catches sight of creatures moving among the shifting branches: squirrels, and foxes, and crows. And as they exit the valley, he spies an especially large black bird high up in an orange oak, observing them with its beady black eye. When it takes flight, he notices that it only has one leg.

* * *

Adam appreciates London from afar. The city is a jigsaw puzzle made up of pieces from dozens of different jigsaws, where no two pieces quite fit together comfortably, and at a distance it has a colourful charm. Up close, however, the city makes him feel lost, and he thinks that its people seem lost as well, as if their lives have taken on that flawed jigsaw feel, and their identities have become as fractured as their city.

Magpie has managed to navigate the car to Piccadilly, where they have become wedged between two tall red buses in the middle of a traffic jam. The traffic lights ahead keep changing from red to orange to green to orange to red, but nobody is moving. Crowds flow around the car and buses, and the noise of the city is almost suffocating as it rushes in through Magpie's open window. Magpie himself has fallen asleep, with one hand still curled around the wheel of his idling car. On the back seat is the barrel full of gunpowder, which has been rolling precariously from side to side the entire journey south, and Adam has been kept wide awake by it – waiting for an errant spark to ignite it and turn his world bright.

With a start, Magpie wakes up. The bus in front of them is moving. With a few clever manoeuvres, which jostle the barrel, he steers the car through gaps in the crowds and down to Pall Mall.

The apartments here are all tall, and composed of exquisitely maintained architecture, with glittering chandeliers visible beyond the net curtains of the high windows. Shining, sleek cars are parked everywhere, and men and women in expensive clothes are helped out by doormen in well-tailored suits. Adam has never liked the strutting of the wealthy; he has spent a great many of his lives being summarily dismissed, or treated like property, by the kind of people who live here.

Pulling up beside one of the apartments, Magpie is helped out of his car by a doorman. Hefting the barrel out of the back seat, Adam follows them up the marble steps and into a lavishly lit reception. "You have a place here?"

"Mostly for the parking," says Magpie.

Even the light fittings are gilded, Adam observes. "Why are you spending Rook's money if you can afford this?"

"I have a little put away," concedes Magpie, "but buying stadiums and transporting pieces of Eden halfway across the world is slightly beyond what I can afford. Trust me: Rook won't miss the money."

"He sent me to find you."

"Of course. But I imagine he did that out of curiosity – not genuine concern about his pockets being emptied. Let me put it to you this way, Adam. In this country, if you counted all of my assets, I would be considered a millionaire. If you did the same for my brother, he would be considered a billionaire."

The difference between those two statuses feels meaningless to Adam, because both are beyond his ability to fathom. Adam knows how much it costs to buy a loaf of bread, or a bus ticket, or a packet of pumpkin seeds, but he's always struggled when it comes to thinking about things like economics. The problem is numbers, he thinks. When something is reduced to a number – like a fortune, a length of years, or a death toll – then it becomes compressed; reduced to a simple figure that does not truly account for awesome amounts of money accumulated, or time having passed, or lives being lost. Maybe only billionaires can afford things like stadiums, he supposes.

The entrance hallway of Magpie's London apartment is filled from wall to wall with boxes and crates. Some have been opened, revealing unusual pieces of art, or intricate bits of equipment, but most are unopened and have gathered dust. "Leave the barrel and go clean yourself up," he instructs, exchanging his brown duffel coat for what seems to Adam to be an identical black coat.

Magpie's bathroom is grand, and tiled in white and gold. Adam removes his clothes and inspects the damage done to him. There are still some dog teeth embedded in his arms and legs, so he plucks them out and makes a pile of them, running water over the wounds until the blood stops seeping. The gunshot wound in his shoulder has stopped bleeding, and though he can still feel the bullet lodged in his shoulder, he doesn't think he'll bother removing it. There are already enough shards of shrapnel, and slivers of glass, and bullet fragments buried under his skin that the addition of one more isn't going to make much of a difference.

"Here." Magpie appears with an armful of clothes. "Hopefully these should fit."

Sifting through them, Adam finds a tunic and a pair of breeches that seem large enough, and pulls them on. He can't remember the last time he wore an outfit like this, but it must have been a long, long time ago, during a life he's forgotten. "Why do you have these?"

"Costume pieces. I put on a production of *Othello* a few years back, and one of our actors was enormous. Tremendous actor, though."

"Did you direct?"

"I starred, naturally." Tilting his head back dramatically, Magpie's silver teeth gleam in the white bathroom lights. "There's something delicious about being a bird pretending to be a man pretending to be a man."

There are a few tears in Adam's coat, but with the worst of the blood washed away it seems salvageable. He pulls it on and inspects himself in the mirror. With the coat, and tunic, and breeches, he looks like a man from a dozen different eras. Which is close to the truth, he supposes. He splashes water on his face for good measure, and dries himself on one of Magpie's impeccably white towels, turning it crimson. "Ready," he says.

"Wonderful. Follow me."

Back in Piccadilly, Magpie navigates the crowds through to the Royal Academy of Arts. The Academy is situated in a set of galleries beyond a courtyard, where the tourists are so thick that Adam feels as if he's wading through people. In the centre of the courtyard is a kinetic sculpture made of metal, which moves in a tentacle-like fashion, its tall tendrils casting strange shadows across the people taking endless flash photographs. And at the far end of the courtyard is a bright banner, declaring that the Royal Academy is hosting a special exhibition called The Jewel of Paradise, which the public are invited to view, for a price.

The queue to see The Jewel of Paradise is lengthy, and winds through the art-filled corridors of the Academy, so Adam takes his time absorbing the other exhibits. He knows that his experience with fine art is a little out of touch; he is too used to art as a function of the wealthy, used to catalogue themselves, their ancestors and their lands. The art on display here seems to be interrogative of that function, in ways that challenge him, and as they slowly make their way through the halls he finds himself fascinated by the peculiar sculptures, and strange portraits, and bizarre photographs, made of materials and using methods that he is totally unfamiliar with. In fact, as they venture deeper and deeper into the winding corridors of the Royal Academy of Arts, Adam finds himself enjoying the sensation of trying to interpret the pieces of art here. There is even a certain joy to be found in his lack of understanding; the art feels as if it's interrogating him, as much as he's trying to interrogate it.

Through a door where their tickets are checked, they are let into a wide conservatory at the centre of the Academy, which is bursting with fake greenery. The room is circular, and has a reinforced misted-glass dome roof, so that daylight filters through. The noise of all the visitors mostly drowns out the gentle rushing of the water running beneath the floor, visible through a thick black metal mesh. The greenery is on every side, separated from the visitors by a black railing, and seems composed of plastic potted plants with large flowers coloured blue and red and yellow. At the centre of the room is a fake cherry tree, simultaneously blossoming and fruiting, pink and red, and situated beneath that tree, at the far end of the circling crowds, is the Jewel of Paradise itself.

Eventually, they come to the display box.

The Jewel of Paradise is far less impressive than Adam thought it would be. It is indeed a jewel, or a gem: a lump of red and green, shaped like an apple. The apple is crystalline, and reflects the light of the sky across its multitude of polished surfaces. As Adam leans closer, he notices that the crystal sculpture has a delicate jade leaf, and a crescent bite through it. Struggling to see what's so special about it, he reads the explanatory notice: "The Jewel of Paradise, sculpted by Edith Sinclair in the late thirties, is the prize of the Sinclair collection, on display for the first time in nearly fifty years. The Royal Academy would like to thank the Sinclair Foundation for their generous loan of the piece."

"I don't get it," says Adam.

"We're not here for the Jewel."

"What are we here for?"

"That." Magpie nods at the tree.

The fake tree at the centre of the conservatory has mostly been ignored by its visitors. Separated by another black railing, its dark and tangled roots have become the resting place for discarded receipts and ticket stubs. Its blossoming pink canopy casts intricate shadows over everything, and by all accounts it should be the focus of the room, were it not for the Jewel.

The tree, at a glance, is nothing more than a piece of decoration, so Adam peers closer, observing the quality of its petals and small, red fruits. And as he follows the gnarls and twists of its branches, he realises that he recognises it. He knows those roots, because he sat among them once, in the bright sunshine of Eden. He knows those fruits because he used to pluck them, and savour them, and spit the hard stones at the centre of each. And he knows those branches because he remembers the birds perched upon them: all those brilliant birds of paradise, preening among the pink petals and calling to each other in joyous conversation.

The tree is not fake, after all. In fact, it is perhaps the most genuine object in the room. Its pink petals, which from time to time drop and spiral and join the rubbish at its roots, blossom eternally, and its sweet, waxy red fruits are tiny temptations, still as sweet as they ever were in Eden. There is a sign attached to the railing surrounding the tree, which reads: DO NOT TOUCH.

"Why is this here?" Adam frowns.

"Hubris," says Magpie. "I expect the Sinclairs and their friends love the idea of strangers ogling at a piece of glass in a cabinet while a genuine piece of paradise stands ignored and unseen before them. I imagine them standing around, sipping champagne, patting each other on the back and laughing with each other about how clever they are. How *enlightened* they must be." Magpie sneers. "Thankfully, that hubris has made them stupid. This tree being here gives us a brilliant opportunity."

"You want to steal a tree?"

Magpie's dagger-smile gleams in the gloom. "Absolutely."

Adam raises his hand to catch a petal as it falls from the tree, and it comes to rest on his palm, as gentle as a whisper. When he closes his hand around it, he feels the silken texture of it fold easily into the recesses of his scarred skin, and tries to remember the taste of the tree's cherries.

IX

Magpie's apartment is palatial, but specifically in the sense that it feels as if the contents of an entire palace have been crushed into it. There are Fabergé eggs in the fridge, and oil paintings of castles stacked up against the walls, and wherever Adam goes he finds himself tripping over rolled-up rugs and tapestries. Magpie himself is spending the evening pacing around his dining room, chattering excitedly into his phone. After a while watching Magpie accidentally sweep ornaments from the dining table, and mantelpiece, and cabinets with the edge of his gilded robe, Adam decides to explore the rest of the apartment, in search of something to pass the time.

Soon, he knows, they will steal Eden's cherry tree.

At the rear of the apartment is a door half hidden behind a tall stack of unopened crates, and beyond that door is an office crammed, from wall to wall, with papers and journals and leather-bound books. Adam idly sifts through it, and discovers that most of the papers bear the Corvid & Corvid letterhead. The books are filled with grossly outdated statutes and case-law, and the deeper Adam explores, the older they get. He manages to shift enough paperwork to clear the chair behind the desk, and sits there in the warm light of a dim lamp, flicking through Magpie's old work journals before settling in to reading one.

The journal he chooses is a ledger of belongings written by Magpie on behalf of Corvid & Corvid in an attempt to catalogue the estate of an heirless millionaire. It's fairly banal legal work, but as Adam reads the listings, he slowly becomes absorbed in the client's life. There are all the hallmarks of wealth – the statues, the portraits, the exotic rugs, enormous mirrors and custom pieces of golfing equipment. But there are signs of life, as well: dog collars, and endless spare tennis balls; stacks of discarded typewriters and computers; heaps of unfinished manuscripts and newspapers from bygone eras. The man had too many coats, and stashed in some of the pockets were dusty wads of cash. At the bottom of a drawer filled with screws and bits of string, rested an out-of-date passport, still pristine, with no stamps or visas.

As Adam continues reading, he grows familiar with the belongings, and the walls of the great house rise around him, enclosing him like the walls of a prison. He is helplessly lonely, crippled by an anxiety that makes him unable to go out into the world for fear of rejection, and unable to complete any of his manuscripts for fear of inadequacy. Sometimes he will go to the golf club and golf alone, celebrating good days with expensive cognac and bad days with expensive wine. His four dogs are his ceaseless companions, and the reason he doesn't end his life. Some days he will stand beneath his apple tree with a length of rope, and on others he will pluck the apples from that tree and pick the seeds out with his fingers so that he can enjoy the crisp fruits without worry of cyanide poisoning.

Adam is startled awake by a prolonged crash from elsewhere in the apartment. Sunlight is leaking in through the small section of the office window not buried in books. He hadn't noticed himself falling asleep, but the ledger is still open on his lap, filled with Magpie's florid handwriting. Stretching his limbs, Adam rises and goes in search of the source of the noise.

Magpie is caught up in a tangle of bicycles fallen from an overfilled cupboard. Today he is dressed from head to toe in high-visibility cycling gear, and, to Adam, looks like a stick figure drawn in yellow highlighter.

"Going cycling?"

"Good morning, Adam! In London, you have three choices. You can either idle in traffic, get shot through the earth in a cramped tube, or cycle and choke on fumes. Personally," says Magpie, as he wrestles a bicycle free, "I choose the fumes."

"You could walk."

"Nonsense. I'd never arrive on time for anything."

Adam watches Magpie cram the tangle of bicycles back into the cupboard. "What's the plan?"

"We steal the cherry tree at noon sharp." Magpie straps his helmet on. "As such, I need to go and finalise certain arrangements. I'll be back in a few hours."

"What should I do?"

"I need you to go to Brighton and deliver your pistols to a fellow there. He'll have them fixed by the end of the month. I've packed them up for you, and written the address on a piece of paper. It's all in the kitchen." Propping the front door of the apartment open with his foot, Magpie, hopping, manoeuvres his bicycle into the richly carpeted hallway. "I wouldn't drink from the metal flask," he says, with a wink. "I've filled it with gunpowder instead of coffee. Might give you a bit of a kick, but probably the wrong kind."

"Sure. I can do that."

"Marvellous." Magpie straps his helmet on. "I'll meet you back here for some lunch, then we'll go and steal the tree. Don't be late!" There is more clattering as he wheels away down the hallway, and then he is gone.

Alone, Adam spends a few moments disentangling his thoughts from his dream of the ledger. He can still taste the acidic apple, and it feels as if there's bits of it stuck in his teeth. Then, stumbling over stacks of packages and wrapped-up treasures, he goes in search of the apartment's kitchen. He'll have to catch a train down to Brighton, he thinks.

* * *

St Pancras Station is different than Adam remembers. It's just as cavernous as it's always been, but the echo has changed. So many people create such a clamour of feet and voices, intermingling with the announcements and noise of all the trains, that he's not as able to hear the pigeons. Worse, when he studies the high rafters, he notices that spikes have been installed to prevent any birds from roosting. Gradually, Adam makes his way through the station's labyrinthine layout, searching for the train he needs and searching for stray feathers on the floor.

As he descends deeper into the building, he hears snatches of a song in its echo. It sounds as if someone's playing a piano, and the tune is familiar. The song draws him into itself, and he feels as if he is navigating not through people but through the low waves of a gentle sea. It's a very old song, he knows: older than any of the people he passes, and older than the station it echoes in, and older than the very idea of railways.

As Adam approaches the musician, he begins to hear the words accompanying the piano. The singer's voice sounds as if it's rising from the depths of an ocean. It's not a musical voice at all – it's more of a seismic rumble – and the words being sung are in a language Adam knows he's long forgotten. He doesn't remember what each word means, but he does remember the sentiment behind them. The shanty is bidding the winds to rise – to tense the ship's sails and make it fly across the waves like a bird. There is a circle of people ahead, gathered around the piano chained to the wall at the station's heart, and sat at it is a broad figure, singing with abandon, as if he might make the trains of St Pancras fly from their rails.

Adam emerges from the circle, and feels the words rise from his own throat. His voice sounds as deep as the depths of the sky at night, and though he doesn't remember the language well enough to speak it, he knows the song just as well as his skin knows its scars.

The man at the piano turns, but doesn't stop playing. He looks like a roughly hewn statue: his dark eyes are embedded deep in his craggy features, and his thick fingers are calloused where they emerge from the sleeves of his beaten blue overcoat. He wears a flat cap, with white wisps of hair emerging at its edges

173

like white clouds through a grey sky, and his thick grey brows look like thunderheads, shadowing his coarse cheeks. His rocky face breaks into a grin of recognition, a grin that makes him look as if he has a mouth full of pebbles.

Together, they finish the song. There is a smattering of applause from the audience.

"Well, ain't this a surprise," rumbles the musician as he rises, first shaking Adam's hand with a crushingly tight grip, then pulling him into a crushingly tight embrace. "The first man, come to sing old songs with me." Hauling a heavy looking pack across his back, he looks Adam up and down. "Why, you ain't changed a bit. A few more scars, a bit less hair."

"How are you, Crab?"

"I'm well enough, lad. Well enough. What brings you this way?"

"Gotta go to Brighton. What about you?"

"Just heading home." Crab flaps his pack open, revealing a large chunk of veined white marble, carved with curls. "Been working as a mason these past few decades. Client in Sheffield looking for someone to carve him a marble fireplace, wanted to see a sample up close. What you headed to Brighton for?"

Adam reveals the contents of his satchel. "Getting my guns fixed."

Crab's stormy brows rise. "Well, now. Last time I saw you wearing these, you were heading to France, coat covered in shiny brass buttons. War with Napoleon," he rumbles, thoughtfully. "Half a century of death and gunpowder. And now there's a bloody great tunnel, and you can hop on a train and be in Paris in a couple of hours." Reaching into the satchel, Crab turns the first gun over in his hands. "Funny how things turn out, ain't it?"

Adam admires the sleek trains, idling on their platforms.

"What do you need your guns for?" asks Crab.

Adam considers the question, but he's not entirely sure how to answer. He settles on: "I've been doing some gardening, and I've run into something of a pest problem."

Crab raises a brow. "Must be a hell of a pest."

"It's an invasive species."

Crab chuckles, which makes him sound as if he's gargling marbles. "Tell you what, lad," he says. "I'll save you a trip. You just leave these with me and I'll restore 'em. I worked for the Queen's own armoury while you were away fighting the French. There ain't no powder pistol in Britain I couldn't improve." Replacing the gun in Adam's pack, Crab takes it and hauls it over his free shoulder. "So long as you ain't in a hurry? Might take me a few days."

"No hurry."

"Grand." Crab slaps Adam's arm. "Got a workshop in Lambeth, down by the canal. Come visit me next week and I'll have some old vases we can test 'em on."

Together, they wander out of the station and back into the bright light of King's Cross.

"Thanks, Crab," says Adam.

"It's a pleasure, lad. Good to see you."

"Good to see you, too."

As Crab departs, a broad shape shuffling through the crowds that swirl between St Pancras and King's Cross, Adam pauses, noticing the rainbows. There appears to be an awful lot of rainbows in London, today. Everyone is wearing bright colours, and the coffee shops are advertising rainbow-themed drinks, and every visible flagpole has a rainbow flag hanging from it. There are more rainbows in the haze left by the street cleaners, and in the oil slick oozing into the drains, and in the chrome exhausts of the cars that idle along the busy road. Only the open blue sky lacks rainbows, though Adam is careful to search every corner of it. As he starts walking back to Piccadilly, he wonders what they're all for.

* * *

Adam pauses outside the British Museum. He has some time to kill and figures it might be nice to look at some relics and reminisce of Londons past. Today, there's a queue of people lining up to go through a security checkpoint at the gates – they are searching bags, and running metal detectors over everyone, before allowing them inside. There doesn't seem to be any particular reason for all the heightened security, but then, there are extra layers of security everywhere, these days: the product of a paranoid age, Adam thinks. He also thinks that all the bits of metal embedded in him would undoubtedly set off those metal detectors, so he goes to a bookshop instead.

In the front window is a display for a book called *My Friend the Murderer* by Cassandra Coleman, and the cover is a highly embellished version of Adam's mugshot. It doesn't look much like him any more, he thinks – the artist has drawn so much attention to the scars across his face that he looks like a patchwork of different people. He steps inside and flicks through a copy, only to find a complete stranger described in the pages. The book claims that Adam was often violent, involved with the cartels, and ran a dog-fighting ring out of his own backyard. Adam is depicted as a villain, and Cassandra is depicted as a survivor. Adam places it back on the shelf and wonders how many other books he appears in – how many fictional versions of himself exist. Quite a few, he imagines, some of which are being sold here. There is a whole rack of Bibles in the Religion section, and he knows that the version of him contained in them varies quite heavily from translation to translation.

The bookshop is large, and well stocked. Adam considers his options and, inspired by the museum, wanders over to the History section. Adam has something of a strange relationship with history books. The problem is that he's lived through a lot of the history being described, and whenever an obvious inaccuracy occurs, he finds it jarring. Nevertheless, he settles on an ethnography of the villages of West India, and finds a comfortable chair to sit in, flicking through and letting the words pass into him. The ethnography is dry, and describes everyday village life in exhausting detail, but in that detail Adam recognises echoes of Indias past.

The shelves of books around him, and the gentle muttering of the shoppers, and the repetitive, formal language of the ethnography bring Adam back to a time he had almost forgotten, when he and Eve lived at the Mahavihara in Nalanda. The Mahavihara's library was enormous, and required a lot of maintenance, which Eve was happy to help supply while Adam worked on the gardens outside. In the evenings, he would go among the books and read and read until darkness gripped the library, and there he would sleep until dawn, and continue reading by that first light. He remembers the shuffling of the scholars among the shelves, and the distant mutterings of the Buddhist temples, and the rich parchment smell of all those books.

Whenever a monk or a teacher or a visiting scholar died, it was Eve's honour to shelve their books. Death by death, the library grew, and death by death, Adam's knowledge of the world beyond the walls of the Mahavihara expanded. Yet what he remembers most fondly is the way Eve would sometimes come and sit next to him in the darkness of the library at night, and there recite some of the poetry she had memorised. To Eve, poetry was the finest of her children's inventions – the height of their art. Her recitals were gentle, intimate things, as if she were sharing not words with Adam, but kisses, each flavoured by the taste of the verse she told.

When Adam leaves the bookshop, and resumes his walk back towards Piccadilly, he notices a great many couples in the streets, heading in the same direction as he is. They are dressed brightly, in the same rainbow of colours as the flags hanging from the shops everywhere, and they share kisses with each other openly, hands entwined. They are sharing poetry with each other, Adam thinks. He gets caught up in their affection, and his memory of Eve in the library at Nalanda, and he realises that the thorns embedded in his thoughts feel a little less sharp today.

*   *   *

Piccadilly has been cordoned off.

Police loiter at the cordons, wafting themselves with flyers against the heat of the bright day and sharing smiles with each other, with the crowds. A group of mounted officers stand together, idly chatting with each other, and none of them pause to watch Adam pass.

Beyond the barriers is a parade. It's an unusual parade, Adam thinks, because everyone seems to be a part of it. Nobody's waiting at the side of the street to wave the floats and marching bands along; instead, the crowds flow with the parade, making the floats look like rafts buoyed along by a river of people. There are double-decker buses crammed full, bedecked with rainbow flags and blasting noisy, tinny beats at the streets, and there are fabulous, bright marching bands with mismatched outfits playing music to wholly different rhythms, and there's even a float with a grand piano attached to the back, being played by two different people simultaneously, creating a catastrophe of competing noises. Everybody is dressed in bright colours, and there is an abundance of glitter, as if bare patches of skin are real estate that needs to be occupied by shimmering colours. Cannons shower glimmering rain over the thickest patches of people, and everybody seems to be dancing. In the buses they shuffle their shoulders, and on the road they twirl and laugh, and nobody is judging anyone for the quality of their moves; Adam watches a girl in a wheelchair whirling about on two wheels.

"What is all this?"

Magpie has wrapped himself in a rainbow flag. "Pride, Adam."

It seems so obvious, now. Adam has never attended a Gay Pride event before, but he has read about them. Mostly, the outrage over them. The newspapers in America have never been very kind to Pride, and paint them as pathetic, confrontational events, more about causing controversy than giving a minority space to celebrate. But now that he's here, all those articles he read seem pathetic in turn: as if they were written by snooty men and women, sneering from behind net curtains. All he can see here is joy.

Magpie makes his way through the parade with elegance – somehow finding a rhythm to every step, so that he dances as he goes. On the other hand, Adam feels large and clumsy, tripping over himself and other people, and getting smeared with glitter. Only, he is delighted to find that nobody seems to mind his clumsiness; they buoy him along and through, helping him to go where he needs to go; hands keep him upright and guide him past pockets of celebration, making him feel welcome.

At the entrance to the Royal Academy of Arts courtyard, Adam pauses. He would have liked to have spent longer with the parade. Magpie removes the rainbow flag from his shoulders and hands it to a passing couple, and they drape it over themselves like a blanket. Beneath, he is wearing a black jacket, which he dusts down and adjusts.

"Your jacket's inside out," says Adam.

"I know," says Magpie, with a wink.

The courtyard is sparsely populated. The same metal, tentacled kinetic sculpture as before eels, but there are few tourists snapping pictures of it today. Instead, the courtyard is being used as overflow for the parade: a quiet space for folk to take a break from the celebrations. In bright outfits, they loiter at the edges and on the steps, open faces to the open blue sky, and Magpie nods and bows and laughs as he skirts around them, sharing in their celebration and encouraging them. "Brush some of that off," he says, motioning at the glitter coating Adam's arms, and Adam does as he's told, leaving a trail of silver and purple in his wake.

Inside the Royal Academy are a few tourists, waiting out the parade. They peer through the windows, cameras held hesitantly, unsure if Pride is something to be photographed. The Academy's security seem bored; sitting at desks and on stools, some watching the remnants of the parade outside with a longing while others flick through their phones. Magpie's demeanour immediately shifts as he enters the Academy, changing from celebratory and flittering to irritated and sober. He pays for two tickets to the Jewel of Paradise exhibition, and the girl behind the desk barely glances at him.

Through the Royal Academy Magpie goes, taking his time and studying exhibits with an apparent interest. The hallways are so sparsely populated that his footsteps echo, as do Adam's. Only, instead of leading straight to the Jewel of Paradise exhibition, Magpie takes Adam on a winding route through room after room, before mounting a set of steps leading up to the galleries above. Adam tries to take in the art, but he is distracted, unsure of Magpie's intentions here. He feels as if he would quite like to go back to the Pride parade and join in the celebrations.

Through an archway is the upper gallery surrounding the

Jewel of Paradise. The reinforced glass dome above is bright today, filling the room with light and making all the greenery gleam; and there, at the centre of it all, is the brilliant cherry tree, which is a remarkable shade of pink against the pale walls and floor. Its eternally blossoming petals flutter, caught in some errant air-conditioning breeze. There are tourists admiring the Jewel in its glass case, but there is no queue for it today, and only a couple of guards on duty. Magpie makes a point of ignoring the view of the tree below, and goes from portrait to portrait hung up along the upper gallery, admiring each as if he is a buyer in the market for good art.

"What's the plan?" asks Adam.

"We're going to steal the tree," says Magpie.

"Yeah, I get that. But how?"

"In about…" Sliding back the sleeve of his jacket, Magpie checks his watch. "…a quarter of an hour, you're going to pick it up and walk out with it."

Leaning over the balcony, Adam studies the black railing at the base of the tree, and then at the bulk of it. Its cherries gleam like rubies among its pink petals, and its trunk is a gnarled weave of wood. "It looks pretty heavy."

"You're going to have help."

"From who?"

Magpie's semi-silver smile shines in the bright daylight beaming down through the roof. "Everybody," he says, as he comes to the corner of the upper gallery. There, he reaches up and twitches the cable running into the security camera attached to the wall. It doesn't dangle free, but it does come loose, and the little red light at the front of the camera fades. "Timing is important," he says. "Do what I say, when I say it. Okay?"

"Sure," says Adam, uncertainly.

"Wonderful," says Magpie, with absolute confidence. "Then let's begin."

Back downstairs, Magpie makes his way through the Royal Academy with greater purpose. He winds a route between strange, contemporary sculptures, and into a room with unusual, blurry photographs of trees, all the while chatting to Adam about nothing at all. The guards pay him no attention, and nor do the attendants. In a broad hallway with two sets of enormous double doors to either side, Magpie glances about to make certain that nobody is watching, before entering the set marked Staff Only.

This room is a large storage space, lit by weak fingers of light from the slotted, barred windows on the far wall. "They got the tree in through three sets of double doors," he says, stepping around empty crates and sculptures wrapped in bubble wrap. "And we're going to take it out the same way."

The double doors at the back are chained shut. Beyond them, there is the roar of the crowds, and through the slotted windows Adam can see the bright colours of their banners and clothes. The bass beat of their music vibrates the stone floor and up through Adam's feet, and all he wants is to throw these doors open and go out there among his children. Magpie removes his black jacket and pulls the sleeves through so that it's no longer inside out, revealing it to not be a black jacket at all, but a silver sequinned jacket, which twinkles brightly even in the gloom of the storage space.

Watching his watch, Magpie counts down beneath his breath. There is a loud knocking at the doors.

"Answer that," says Magpie, his eyes agleam, "if you'd be so kind."

The chains are thick and new. Adam twists them until they break, and slides the remains free. Then he hauls the doors back. The noise of the parade is immediate, and a push of people rushes into the room, making the heart in Adam's chest beat quicker. At their head is a team of fabulously dressed folk carrying DJ equipment: a heavy-looking set of speakers, along with turntables and cases of records. Light spills into the dark space along with them, and their smiles and laughter seem as bright as the blue sky as they unroll long rainbow banners and start setting up, throwing the switches on in the storage chamber so that it's abruptly filled with a glow.

The rush of people setting up is so great that Adam is unsure how to react; he is still stood with the broken chains in hand, even as the banners are hauled high above the doors. PRIDE PARTY AT THE ACADEMY, they read, and just as Adam manages to catch sight of the words, the pounding of loud music begins.

There is a cheer from the crowds outside, and they begin to flow into the Royal Academy.

"The next door!" cries Magpie. "Quickly, Adam!"

Pushing his way clumsily through the people rushing into the room and filling it as if the party is a liquid, Adam manages to make his way across to the double doors marked Staff Only and hauls them both back. The party immediately pushes further in. There are people with water pistols, spraying each other and laughing, and there are rainbow flags being draped across sculptures, and there are the Academy's guards, awake and unsure how to process the overwhelming rush of people flowing into the building, mumbling into radios and doing little to prevent the party as it spreads.

Magpie seems to be everywhere, his sequinned jacket shimmering silver along with his smile, and wherever he goes he spreads cheer and celebration, filling the corners of the corridor so tightly with dancing people that there is no room for any of the Academy's staff to move even if they wanted to. "The last doors, Adam!" he cries, over the thudding music. "Now!"

Forcing his way through, Adam pushes at the last set of double doors leading to the Jewel of Paradise, and they refuse to give way. The crowds crash across his back like a wave, pushing him against the rough wood, but they stay shut. Bracing himself against the tiled floor, Adam presses both palms against the doors, and with a great, splintering crash, they smash inwards, the remains of the barred lock twisted and broken. There is a great cheer, and all the people of the Pride party flow around Adam and into the bright chamber with the tree at its centre. With them comes the music, the speakers and DJ dragged into the room, so that the great dancing noise trembles the leaves of the fake foliage at the edges.

The party is in full swing. It surrounds Eden's cherry tree.

Instead of trying to control the party, the tired and overwhelmed guards give up. Some stand hesitantly at the edges, along with tourists snapping pictures, but Adam spots one among the people, dancing, his white shirt stained with glitter. Managing to keep his feet, Adam slowly advances on the tree. He notices movement up on the high balcony, and there is Magpie, carrying a silver cannon. Magpie aims the cannon over the room and it spurts silver confetti in a shower. There is a cheer so loud that it almost drowns out the music, as confetti shimmers and drifts and fills the air, fluttering like the petals of the tree.

There is no stopping the party now.

"The tree, Adam!" Magpie's voice is barely audible.

Stepping over the railing, Adam presses his hands against Eden's cherry tree. The rush of familiarity makes him dizzy, makes the room whirl around him. Dropping to his knees, he shakes his head to clear it, and then runs his hands over the black gratings covering the roots. There is running water beneath the grating, and an enormous clump of earth, kept permanently damp by it. They must have dug deep into the floor to be able to house the tree in here. Throwing back the bolts keeping the mesh in place, he pulls the gratings away and fully reveals the mass of earthen roots there; those roots, like tremendous worms, buried in a huge clump of muddy soil. The roots are a huge network, bigger still than the branches of the cherry tree, and as Adam buries his fingers in the mud, he is almost overcome by a great wave of memories.

The voices bring him back.

There is a megaphone, crackling louder still than the rhythm of the party, and through it Magpie is chanting: "Raise the tree! Raise the tree!" And caught up in the chant is the party, the voices of those celebrating rising along with his. Maybe they understand what Magpie is trying to do, or maybe they are simply going with the flow, but it doesn't matter. Crouching on one knee, Adam can feel the force of their combined voices urging him on; urging him to take hold of the strongest knots of roots at the base of the tree; urging him to grip tight. And with his shoulders straining, and his back straining, and his neck straining, and his legs straining, he hauls.

The tree slowly ascends, gratings falling aside, clumps of loose earth crumbling from its exposed roots.

"Raise the tree!" continues the chant. "Raise the tree!"

His every muscle burning, Adam rises to his feet, holding the tree high.

The cheering reaches a crescendo, vibrating through him and clattering at the thick metal gratings, but Adam knows he can't hold the tree for much longer. The weight of it is too much; he can barely keep his grip, and his muscles are shaking with the effort of staying upright. Pink petals and silver pieces of confetti drift around him.

Hands reach out to help.

The crowds converge, and all come together to carry the tree. The pride parade takes hold of the cherry tree's roots, and its trunk, and its branches, and all together they keep it aloft. The tree rolls around, so that it rests at an angle across Adam's shoulder, and his view is entirely engulfed by its branches; all those branches, bursting with pink petals and red cherries like jewels; all those branches with hands gently holding them and taking the weight of them. Together, they hold the tree high.

There is more chanting, more instructions led by Magpie, but Adam can no longer hear them. He is buoyed along by the crowds. He takes one shaky first step, and then another, gaining slow momentum. The crowds don't walk with him – instead, they remain around him and pass the tree among them as Adam walks, their hands and combined strength keeping it aloft across his shoulder. Slowly, so slowly, with the rhythm of the celebration running through him, Adam walks. Beyond the gratings he goes, and over the tiles of the Jewel chamber, and through the hallway, and into the storage space, Adam retains his momentum – one step at a time, taking the tree from the Academy.

Everyone is caught up in the movement. The cheering is loud in his ears.

With Eden's cherry tree over his shoulder, Adam walks out of the Royal Academy of Arts and into the bright light of day.

* * *

The crowds seem to have swelled. The noise rises and falls like the crashing of ocean waves against a cliff, and everyone is moved along helplessly, caught up in the currents swirling around the parade. With Eden's cherry tree over his shoulder, Adam is buoyed further along; hands of every shade reach out to help him carry it, one hard step at a time, inevitably deeper into the mass of people. Yet Adam doesn't stumble. The heat running through him is immense, as if the heart in his chest is a furnace and his veins are a network of pipes, delivering white-hot blood to every part of him.

There is the parade, ahead, barely visible through the great branches of the tree, and all the blossom and crystalline cherries in between. And among the buses brimming with people, and the dancers each dancing to different songs, and the lovers marching hand in hand, there are floats, and the back of the nearest float, approaching slowly, is empty. A destination, Adam thinks.

Adam's thoughts are coming slow; he knows he must keep his concentration on maintaining his grip. Hands are reaching out to him as well as the tree, smearing his skin with glitter; and there are faces, as well, lips pressed to his arms and his back and leaving lipstick stains, as if the crowds might urge him along with the tenderness of kisses. And it's working, Adam knows. Better than all the hands helping him carry the tree are those who choose to cheer him, lending him strength with every yell and touch.

The float approaches slowly, and Adam is drawn to it.

There are muscular men waiting aboard the float, and the worst of the weight of the tree is lifted from Adam's shoulder as, together, they haul it upwards. Blossom whirls around Adam as the tree rises, and he glimpses the brightly dressed bodies helping from below, the girls and boys and women and men and so many others dripping with glitter, blowing on whistles and dancing as they pass the roots of the tree up. The bright sun is behind the branches now, glinting as the last of the weight is lifted from Adam, leaving him numb and helpless, all his strength put into carrying the tree this far. Now, he stumbles. Bustled about by the crowd, he falls to one knee, his blood pounding in his ears. Adam breathes deep of the damp air, the stink of all the bodies and thick perfumes and fumes from the floats making him dizzy.

There are people above on the float, locking the tree down; passing great straps through its tangled roots to keep it anchored.

Then there are people helping to lift Adam instead. They come to him, strong and weak together, and raise him just like they raised the tree, and suddenly he is above the crowds, on his back, with all their hands beneath him. He can feel them trembling with the weight of him, but he feels weightless, with only the blue sky above him and the tree beside him, as if he is back in Eden and floating in the river. The hands pass him along, not far, only to the float, where he is placed gently down among the roots of the tree.

They pass him bottled water, and a man in a high-visibility jacket asks him if he's okay, and then he is left alone, exhausted and sat among the roots of Eden's cherry tree, watching the crowds in a kind of stunned stupor. People blow him kisses as the float passes by. Some climb aboard and dance around the tree, and the streets of London are so bright, with rainbow flags and rainbow people, hands joined, celebrating themselves.

As Adam's heart slows, and feeling gradually returns to his limbs, he clambers to his feet and, clinging hold of the tree, waves at those below. He feels the slow smile across his face as it emerges, like a hesitant sun from behind thick clouds.

When the parade comes to a junction, Adam notices that it's Magpie driving the float; he leans out from the cab, and his sequinned jacket sparkles in the sunlight. He waves up at Adam, and honks the horn with a rhythm that the crowds clap along to. Adam isn't sure what kind of destination Magpie has in mind, but he thinks that it doesn't matter yet: they are being borne along by the parade, and there's no escaping it for a while. The police at the cordons are paying the tree no particular attention, so he decides to relax.

Reaching up into the branches of Eden's cherry tree, Adam plucks a fruit. With delicacy, he places it into his mouth and tastes it. The flavour is brilliant: every bit as brilliant as he expected it to be, as if every morsel he's tasted since Eden has been ashes on his tongue by comparison. Adam wipes the tears from his cheeks with the back of a hand, and notices the way that they mingle with the glitter staining his skin. Then he spits the cherry's stone into his palm, and considers it. The stone has a weight to it, he thinks – a weight not found on Earth.

Once, maybe, Adam would have gorged himself on cherries. He would have snatched them down from the branches of the tree and spat stone after stone onto the hard earth, consumed by greed. But today one cherry is enough. The gift of this tree is something that the people here deserve, for all their help, as unwitting as it might have been. So, he takes handfuls of cherries – plucking them carefully so that their departure does not damage the tree – and scatters them among the crowds.

Bright red jewels, glinting as they fly.

Hands reach out to grab them, and there are cheers. Blossom falls, and cherries rain, and faces are raised to the sun, laughing. The crowds spit stones across the pavements and streets, but some throw their stones over walls and into gardens, finding bare patches of hard, grassy earth. And maybe, Adam thinks, just maybe there will be an epidemic of mortal cherry trees in years to come, along the route the parade took today. Adam is not greedy, he does not deplete the tree of its current crop; there are enough handfuls for plenty to have a taste, and he feels as if he's sowing the cherries like seeds across a field of brightly dressed bodies.

When he has thrown enough cherries, Adam sits back against the trunk, exhausted. This would be a good time to die, he thinks. Not being shot at, or drowning, but here, beneath Eden's cherry tree, surrounded by his children, joined together in celebration. And with that thought comes a realisation: that he has been waiting to die for a long time. For entire lifetimes, in fact. Centuries, wandering the Earth in search of a good place to die. Adam closes his eyes, feeling Eve's heart beat in his chest, half expecting it to stop. But it doesn't. When he opens his eyes again, her heart is still beating. That's okay, though, he thinks. Today, he doesn't mind living a bit longer.

X

One of Adam's favourite lives was the life he lived as a postman in Dorset. He had a cottage between two small farming villages, and was responsible for the mail of both. In the morning he would walk from one village to the other, his satchel heavy with packages and letters to deliver, and in the afternoon visitors would arrive at his cottage with mail for the delivery van, and more often than not those visitors would stay for a cup of tea and to enquire after his garden.

Adam's garden was the talk of both villages. It was twice the size of his modest cottage, and he took care of it year round, cultivating it with a careful eye. On his days off he would take trains to flower shows across Britain and abroad, seeking out the finest complementary shades and shapes to improve his garden; and when at home he would peruse newspapers and gardening journals for the rarest seeds and the means of making them grow in such a county as Dorset. Adam's garden was a place of wonder, no matter the time of year. Even in the depths of winter, the shape of it was remarkable, and the potential of it was overwhelmingly apparent – the majesty of what it would be come spring. As the years progressed, Adam's garden grew taller and ever more brilliant, featuring exotic flowers otherwise unseen in Britain, and it became bright with birds and insects.

Then, Adam was drafted. It was a sudden thing. He was aware of the formal letters he was delivering to the men of the villages, which he knew had something to do with the European tensions disrupting his supply of rare seeds, and he knew that those men were leaving for the towns and cities, but the full realisation of the draft and the war only reached him when he received one of those letters for himself. Adam was to fight, he was told, for the good of the country, leaving him in a precarious position.

Usually, Adam preferred to avoid war where possible. Usually, he would simply retreat; vanish to a corner of the world free of conflict. This time, however, he was not ready to leave his current life behind. He had put too much time and effort and love into his cottage garden. If he ignored the draft and stayed, it would not take long for the authorities to notice and forcefully dislocate him from his life anyway. Which left him with one option: go along with the draft, play the good soldier, wait out the war, and come back afterwards.

Given no more than a handful of days before he must go, Adam did his best for his garden, leaving it in such a state that the girls and the old men of the villages could maintain it, given simple instruction.

Then, reluctantly, he left for war.

The trains were full of men like himself: men not entirely sure what they were fighting for. The newspapers were all loud with patriotism. Adam's uniform had to be custom made to fit him, his rifle was small in his hands, and he was never entirely comfortable in his new boots, which fit too tightly. He was ferried to France, there to join a unit of men drafted like himself, and the country was much changed from his last visit. Everyone seemed frightened, and the streets and the fields seemed darker. Only the sky was still bright, and even then never quite often enough. Adam's unit was shuffled from deployment to deployment: from city to town to field to trench. Sometimes he spoke with the locals, and they laughed at his archaic French, and corrected him, and taught him the new words. Men died around him – shot and stabbed and diseased – and as Adam fought, he filled his pockets with seeds: all the flowers of France for his Dorset garden.

More men died. Sometimes Adam killed them with his rifle, and sometimes Adam killed them with his hands, and he was never certain who he was killing them for, or why. Then his last day at war came, stood in a trench so sodden that the mud came up to his ankles. There was a profound silence as a yellow cloud drifted along the trench and the men around him died. Adam choked, of course, and his eyes watered, but the gas had little other effect on him. He sat down in the mud and watched the men of his unit die, sifting through the seeds in his pocket and wondering at his own indifference. And when the gas dispersed he returned, alone, to the medical tents far behind the front lines. The doctor in charge checked Adam over despite his apparent fortitude, and when it was found that Adam had been shot no less than six times, his wounds in varying states of decay, it was decided, at last, that he should be sent home.

The ferries and trains were filled with wheezing men missing limbs, their eyes wide and glassy. By the time Adam made it back to Dorset, he was told that the war had come to an end. With his pockets still full of seeds, Adam returned to his cottage, eager to resume the life he had left behind. There were stacks of mail for him to deliver, his cottage was thick with vines, and one of the local farm cats was there to greet him along with her new kittens. All seemed pleasant enough until Adam came to his garden. It was utterly transformed. Gone were all the plants he had cultivated: the unusual and exotic and complementary species he had brought together. Gone were the birds and insects giving it so much movement and sound. In their place lay dark furrowed rows of earth, sprouting the green leaves of root vegetables. Adam's garden had been ploughed over, made into a place for food to be grown. For a while he simply sat among the ruins of his garden. Then Adam left, in search of a new life elsewhere.

* * *

Magpie leaves a trail of pink petals as he drives down the M1. His window is rolled down, and the breeze coming through it shivers the sequins of his jacket. Adam turns to see the stolen cherry tree through the back window of the van's cab. Its branches tremble in the wind, and its cherries gleam like jewels as they swing.

The motorway is mostly empty, and it only takes a few hours to reach Manchester. Magpie weaves a route through the busy streets, and the rainbow banners attached to the van stream in its wake. The bright colours attract the attention of pedestrians and drivers alike; they wave in delight, or honk in disgust, and everybody seems caught up in the politics of the rainbows instead of the spectacle of the tree being transported. It looks as if there was a Pride celebration in Manchester today, as well as London; there are pockets of people wearing rainbow face paints, who wave small rainbow flags enthusiastically at the van as it passes them by.

At the stadium, Magpie backs the van through a gate.

The hidden garden is vivid in the sunshine, and for Adam returning to it feels like coming home. He spends a while sat in the shade of the trees and listening to the late insects buzzing, enjoying the feel of the place and recuperating from his time away. Eventually, he makes his way over to the van to check the stolen cherry tree. It seems to have weathered its turbulent journey north well enough, even if it has lost the majority of its petals. Those petals will return, he knows. The tree will recover, and within weeks it will be in full bloom again. He loosens the straps holding it down, and rubs at the clods of earth gripping its roots to keep them compact a little longer.

Magpie joins him, admiring the tree. He has changed out of his sequinned jacket, and is wearing a long black coat. "I'm sorry that I'm not going to be around to help you plant it," he says, reaching up to pluck a cherry from a low branch.

"You're not?"

"I have a flight to catch in..." Magpie checks his watch as he munches. "...a few hours."

"Where are you going?"

"Beijing." Spitting the stone into his hand, Magpie throws it among the long grasses. "Frankly, I'm not a fan of Beijing.

The markets are shameful. Kittens in hamster cages, and turtles in keyrings. I'm hoping to be back before the new year, if I can manage it."

"Why Beijing?"

"One of Eden's orchids has shown up, and I need to get hold of it before anybody realises that it doesn't die." Plucking a few more cherries from the tree, he pockets them. "My work never ends," he says.

"How many more pieces are out there?"

"I'm not sure, Adam. Eden was a big place."

Eden was a big place, Adam remembers. Bigger than this small stadium. Bigger than Manchester. "How often do pieces show up?"

"Regularly enough to keep me busy. There are plenty of rumours to follow up on. And sometimes I get lucky. You see this carnation?" Magpie crouches, and runs his fingers across its delicate scarlet petals. "I was in Paris for Fashion Week, idling away some time at a show, when a gentleman in a sumptuous sea-green suit strode onto the catwalk with it in his lapel."

Adam glances around at all the gathered pieces of the garden. Each with their own small story. There must be hundreds, here. "What should I do?"

"Plant the tree. And then whatever you like, really." Magpie shrugs. "Stay a while. Do some gardening. Relax. You've earned it."

Adam peers up into the network of the tree's branches. He knows that it will take him days to plant it alone, but he finds himself relishing the work. This is something that he knows how to do. Better yet is the prospect of remaining here and working. Right now, it resembles a patchwork collection of plants instead of a garden, with its flowers and trees and grasses arranged haphazardly. But he knows, given time, he can rearrange it into something cohesive; something even better than the sum of its parts. He can restore some of the lost majesty of Eden to this place. And then, when he's ready, he'll tell Rook about it: about his idea to offer it as a kind of sanctuary to Eden's scattered animals. And then, last of all, and best of all, he'll show the hidden garden to Eve. "Okay," he says. "I can do that."

Rubbing remnants of dirt from his hands, Adam gets to work.

It takes a while to haul the tree down from the bed of the truck. Its roots are clenched like a fist, and its branches scratch at his skin. The sun rises to its zenith, and then starts to sink, and by the time Adam has the tree propped up at the edge of the stadium garden, he realises that he is alone. Magpie is gone. The only remnant of him is his silver jacket, which he has left draped over the back of a plastic chair. In the last light of day, it shimmers like the surface of a river.

Adam retrieves it and, using a spar of wood, plants it like a flag at the edge of the garden.

* * *

Adam goes to a flower show.

The flower show is in the middle of Derbyshire, and is set up on the grounds of a regal estate. An enormous mansion overlooks the tents and show gardens, nestled among the green and yellow mixed evergreen and deciduous trees of the surrounding woodlands, and its windows are framed with gold. Adam's not sure why the gilded windows bother him so much. They are a symbol of grotesque excess, perhaps, as if the sheer grandiosity of the architecture isn't enough to convey the wealth of its owners. The house has been roped off, to prevent any stray gardeners from muddying its opulence with their filthy hands.

It's planting season, so the flower show is as much devoted to gardeners purchasing seeds and bulbs for the next season as it is about showing off the last flowers of the year. There are display boxes where expert gardeners have miniature arrangements on show, and Adam is fascinated as much by the biographies beneath each as he is the gardening. The display boxes are splendid things, each carefully cultivated and aesthetically pleasing, and the biographies of those who planted them include multiple academic achievements. Adam is vaguely aware that schools of gardening exist, but confronted by these awards, he wonders what it takes to become a master or a doctor of gardening. There is plenty to learn, he has to concede.

Deeper into the show, there are enormous tents filled with out-of-season displays, and Adam goes from one to the next, pausing at each to absorb the sights. There are artfully arranged cacti, and he runs his fingers gently across their bristles. At a pool so crammed with lilies that there is no water visible, he kneels down and admires the colours of the dragonflies humming above the white and yellow flowers. And where there are bunches of roses, each placed into vases and arranged by colour, Adam spends time inhaling the heady scents until he is made dizzy by them.

It's a good job that he already has a garden to attend to, he thinks, else he would be tempted to take home so many bulbs and seeds.

Adam eventually stumbles across Crow, who is swinging in a designer hammock on sale at a stall. An expanse of purple orchids are reflected in her oversized sunglasses, and she is chewing thoughtfully at a piece of toffee. She is wearing a denim skirt, and a denim jacket over a white T-shirt.

"Double denim?" asks Adam.

"Rachel Jackson likes retro clothes," says Crow. "Rachel Jackson especially likes wandering around the vintage shops of Leeds in search of bargains. Crow, however, doesn't like being Rachel Jackson, and can't stand Leeds. Crow thinks that Leeds has all the hallmarks of a city, without enough personality to set it apart in any meaningful way. In fact, Crow thinks she would much rather be living literally anywhere else." She peers at Adam over the top of her sunglasses. "Since when were you such a fashion expert, anyway?"

Adam looks over the hammocks, but none of them look quite strong enough to hold him. "One of my clients in LA had a lot of subscriptions to fashion magazines."

"And you read them?"

"You get a lot of time to kill in the security business."

Crow unwraps the last of her toffee, and offers him a square. "I was thinking," she says.

"What were you thinking?"

"Do you remember when we went to Naples?"

Adam tries to recall a trip to Naples with Crow, and is surprised to find that he can. The tangle of thorns knotting his memories has loosened enough to allow him glimpses of moments he thought forgotten. "There were flowers," he says.

"That's right. You wanted to tour the graves of your favourite poets, so we went to Naples to see Virgil's tomb, and by the time we got there it was the middle of summer." She motions at the display of orchids. "It was a ruin, even back then, but the whole place was covered in tiny lilac flowers. They were growing out of the cracks in the walls, and on the roof, and all the way across the surrounding fields. I don't think I've ever seen you so impressed by anything. You looked as if you'd have happily laid down next to Virgil and died right there." Crow rolls a piece of toffee around between her fingers, making them sticky. "I was thinking. A whole bunch of poets have died since then. Maybe we should go on another tour, now we're both stuck in Europe."

"Where do you reckon they buried Burns?"

"Scotland, I'd imagine."

Adam tries his toffee. It tastes too sweet, and clings to his teeth.

"How did you find me?" he asks.

"I was a private investigator in another life."

"What are you now?"

"Rachel Jackson is meant to be a student of fine art. I'm not very good at it, though. I don't really have the knack. But I am looking forward to the crippling debt. What about you?"

"I've been doing some gardening."

"Thought it'd be something like that. You look a bit more like yourself again." Using the stub of a pencil, she scribbles a series of digits onto the back of the toffee wrapper. "Here. Give me a call when you fancy a holiday. We can find Burns, and Wordsworth, and all the rest."

"Sounds good."

"Say, did you ever find out what Magpie's been spending Rook's money on?"

"I did." Adam tries to find the right sequence of words to tell her about the stadium garden, but here and now he thinks he understands why Magpie showed it to him instead of trying to sum it up in words. Language does not do the hidden garden justice. Adam finds himself imagining Crow discovering the garden for herself – perching once again among the branches of Eden's gracious trees.

"What are you smiling about?"

"It's best if I show you. Are you free?"

Crow checks her watch. "I need to start heading back up north in an hour. How about next weekend?"

Adam brandishes the toffee wrapper. "I'll call you."

"See that you do." Crow stretches her arms and stands. "Tempted to stretch my wings. Things are usually a lot clearer up above. Down here all you get is mud on your shoes."

Adam inspects the soles of his boots. They are indeed caked in mud.

* * *

Adam is astonished by how many Manchesters there are.

He has grown so used to the singular cities of America that the plurality takes him by surprise. He observes dozens of

Manchesters occupying the same space, like a photograph taken using multiple exposures. The city wears its eras all together at once, and everywhere Adam goes he is confronted by dead ends and ruins muddled with brand-new blocks of buildings. There are so many Manchesters that he finds himself getting lost, not only in the labyrinth of constant deconstruction and reconstruction, but in his own memories of Manchesters past.

By contrast, the stadium garden is a place fixed in time. Around it, the city clamours: gulls roost and cry, planes groan low overhead, and passing trains rattle its plastic bucket seats constantly. Adam is often awoken by sirens. But the patchwork garden is a jewel that reflects itself in its brilliant facets. As Adam tends to the garden, he finds himself lost in it, but in an entirely different way to his disorientation in the city. In the hidden garden, Adam loses himself to precious, tender memories. He's never entirely certain about the authenticity of the memories, and often identifies the flaws and impossibilities in them, but he enjoys them nonetheless: remembering Eden through its remnants.

One day, Adam decides to dig a shallow canal from the river through the garden, in order to irrigate the eastern reaches better. It begins to rain as he digs, so that he finds himself hauling up clumps of mud, but he doesn't mind. He likes the sound of the rain on the leaves of Eden's trees, and the way that droplets splash across the back of his neck, keeping him cool, and he especially likes the way that the pigeons roosting in the trees coo gently, and rustle their feathers as they huddle together. Later, he thinks, he will go and buy some seeds, and feed those pigeons, and maybe they will fly over Manchester and sow them in high places, and in years to come the city will be ever so slightly greener than it was before.

There is the crunching of footsteps falling across the grasses.

Adam rises to see men approaching through the rain. They are wearing hunting gear in shattered green-and-brown patterns, and carrying old rifles with bayonets, which they raise as he turns to face them.

The rain is making the black streaks they have painted across their faces run, and their hair is clinging to their scalps, but Adam recognises them. They are from the garden party at the Sinclair's house; the same men who he last saw on horseback, stampeding across Crow's funeral.

The whites of their eyes are bright in the gloom.

One of them underestimates the length of Adam's reach. The strike is quick enough that none of them react; their eyes simply turn, in horror, to the man who has had his throat gouged through with the blade of Adam's shovel. That man drops his rifle and grips his ruined neck with both hands, gurgling as blood pours through his fingers.

His blood will be absorbed by the soil, Adam thinks. It will feed the roots of Eden's trees.

The bayonets waver. Adam grips his shovel in both hands, watching for the next opportunity.

The next man to approach is Frank Sinclair, who is almost a head shorter than his friends. White strands of hair cling wetly to his pockmarked head. He is carrying an especially large antique rifle, and emitting a low growl as he advances, with Eden's tall grasses almost up to his shoulders.

There is the crack of a shot, and Adam is thrown backwards.

He comes to a rest at the base of a tree, his vision reeling and focusing only on the pigeons as they take flight in a startled flock. This is the moment before the pain, Adam knows; the moment he has to respond before he is immobilised. Only, he finds he has no strength to stand. In fact, he realises he is unable to draw breath. Focusing on his chest, he notices that it is a bloody ruin, and that two of his ribs have been exposed. The cage keeping Eve's heart safe has been broken.

There is a loud ringing in his ears. The shovel is too slippery for him to keep his grip on.

Frank Sinclair's rain-streaked face comes into view, and the pain of the shot hits Adam all at once. It is a fiery agony, pouring outwards from his chest and making his limbs shudder. "You're even more of a fool than I thought," he says. "My cherry tree has a tracking device embedded in it."

Frank Sinclair crouches. "This belonged to my grandfather," he says, showing Adam his rifle. "He used it to hunt elephants in India. Their heads are still hung in my house, you know. Beautiful even after all this time."

The other riflemen have dispersed, their shapes fleeting. There is a rumbling, audible beneath the rain, and Adam spies the blurred red and white lights of trucks being backed into the stadium. "Don't worry about all that," says Frank. "Concentrate on me. I'm telling you about my grandfather."

Adam tries to raise his shovel, but his arms won't obey him.

"My grandfather was cursed," continues the small man. "From the time he was a boy, everything went wrong in his life. At school, he was ridiculed for breaking slates and wearing ragged clothes. His every childish secret found its way into the hands of his enemies. His progress was slow, and what few friends he had were driven away from him. And as a young man, he fared no better. Girls would shun him, his fellows would mock him, and his teachers would punish him constantly for wrongdoings falsely attributed to him. The curse followed him beyond his schooling, as well. In society, he was an outcast. Rumours went abroad of terrible secrets having nothing to do with him. His relatives began to disinherit him, and soon, he had nothing. No friends and no happiness. Misfortune followed him even into the gutter, where he was trodden upon, spat upon by the lowest of the low for his supposed depravity. Lesser men would have ended their life. Lesser men than my grandfather would have given in.

"But my grandfather went into hiding instead. He changed his name, and with the last of his money went to the Americas. There, at last, he escaped his curse. He prospered. He erected great orchards, and made a new fortune. He married, and his wife gave birth to my father. Then, only then, did he realise that the curse of his early life was not incorporeal. When he cast his memory back upon it, it was possible to see the malicious pattern of it. That there must have been an agent behind his systematic ruin. So, my grandfather decided to investigate. He sent private agents back through the ruins of his early life, to examine all the evidence and attribute it to somebody. Searching for the source of his supposed curse.

"And do you know what my grandfather found? He found a man. Or something pretending to be a man. It had been Martin

Corvid haunting him, and deliberately causing him his every pain. Martin Corvid, spreading all the rumours, and causing all the mischief that was wrongly attributed to him, and turning everyone against him. So, my grandfather had Martin Corvid followed. And the reports were strange. Very strange. Because my grandfather's agents all agreed that this Martin fellow was not entirely of the human race. That while outwardly he walked and talked like any man, he was in private a winged thing. A bird. And one of the lowliest among them. A wretched magpie.

"The mystery deepened when my grandfather returned to England and set careful watches on Martin Corvid. He saw that the bird who had haunted him so maliciously was busy, tremendously busy, with machinations involving strange and beautiful evergreen plants. That he was a collector, and that he was collecting a rare breed of undying flora. Fascinated by this revelation, my grandfather hired yet more investigators: forensic legal experts, to covertly examine the source of all of Martin Corvid's funding, the prestigious Corvid & Corvid legal firm. And that's where he found all the rest of them, hidden in Corvid & Corvid's labyrinthine filing system. So many beasts of the earth and birds of the sky and fish of the sea, walking around, pretending to be people. A whole damned zoo of them. Then, at last, in the correspondence between two fowl, came the decisive clue to explain it all. They were reminiscing with each other about an ancient, lost place, you see. The place where they once lived. A biblical place. They even called it Eden.

"My grandfather, being the pious fellow that he was, realised what Martin Corvid was doing. He realised he was witnessing one of Eden's wretched creatures trying to gather together the scattered pieces of its lost paradise."

Frank Sinclair's eyes widen. "That was when my grandfather decided to make his own collection. One not belonging to a mere scrabbling animal, but to a man. A man descended from you, Adam, and rightfully deserving of paradise. He went out to the depths of the Sahara following rumours of an immortal flower, and there found the rose. Eden's rose. The rose you and your fowl stole from me."

Frank Sinclair sighs, and leans back on his haunches in the mud. "But, I digress. You're wondering why Martin Corvid haunted my grandfather. What my grandfather could have possibly done to deserve such a terrible curse. It took him a long time to realise. To remember that fateful day. Because it was such a slight thing. A childish, boyish act. My grandfather was at play in his garden, you see. Chasing cats with sticks. Flicking seeds at the chickens. Throwing rocks at the birds in the trees. And he remembered that he struck a magpie, that day. Hard enough that it fell from its perch. Hard enough that he ran away, in tears and repentance, convinced he had accidentally killed the thing. Hard enough that he prayed for that bird for a week afterwards. So small an act, Adam. So natural a thing for a boy at play to do. But I suppose it was portentous that such an unremarkable thing should eventually lead to such a remarkable discovery as my grandfather eventually made.

"Anyway. I should explain why I'm here." He runs a hand through his rain-slicked hair, as if to casually style it. "I want you to see. I want you to watch as I take every last piece of Eden from you and your fowl. For the sake of what you did to my wife.

"Ada was such a timid girl, when I met her. Weighed down by her doubts. I remember the first day I saw her, in church. The pastor was making an extraordinary, impassioned speech, and she caught my eye because she was paying him no attention at all – she was staring instead at the sky through the window. I remember the way the sunshine fell on her, as if God himself were shining a spotlight on her. We spoke, afterwards. She believed in God, of course, but she had so many doubts in Him. She could never hear His voice through the sermons of the preachers, or even in the very words of His good book. When I showed her the rose, and told her what it was, it transformed her. Ada fell in love with Eden. And even when I told her my grandfather's story, she didn't want Magnus Corvid mounted on a wall – she wanted him caged, instead, so that she could admire him. She was always gentle, that way.

"Do you know how delighted she was, the day she found out that the first man was still alive? I still have an agent in Corvid & Corvid, you know. Monitoring the activity of that salacious firm. And when he brought us news that Adam himself was still wandering the Earth, we drank ourselves merry, and laughed deep into the night. I think Ada fell in love with you, that day. I think she loved you more than she ever loved me. Of course, she was ecstatic when our contact informed us that you were flying to Scotland. Ada insisted on being the one to collect you. She even called me, panicked, at the airport because she couldn't find you. It took her the better part of the afternoon to trace your footsteps.

"What you did to her…" The butt of the elephant gun ignites new pain through Adam as Frank Sinclair presses it against Adam's bloodied chest. "She was wrong to love you. And I was wrong to admire you. You are no man, Adam. You are as much an animal as Magnus, or any of the others. Just another beast pretending to be human." Frank twists the rifle, heightening Adam's agony. "My grandfather's gun isn't always immediately fatal. I've seen an elephant stumble around for hours before bleeding out. I suppose the same will apply to you. Hopefully, you'll remain alive long enough to see this stadium when it's empty. While your corpse rots, I will build a new paradise, in Ada's honour. In God's honour. And then I will hunt down all those beasts and fish and fowl pretending to be men, and make them remember what they really are."

When Frank Sinclair walks away, he reveals the trucks filling the stadium, and the men working around them. They operate pneumatic arms and winches, and mechanical drills and shovels, and dig up all corners of the hidden garden. They pull trees, roots and all, from the earth, and they cut the grasses into squares and place those squares onto flat-beds, and they pull flowers up in clumps and secure them in jars, and Adam is helpless, pinned up against his tree until that, too, is torn up. He watches as the world whirls around him, shifting as he is rolled into an earthen pit, with the rain soaking through him and muddying him from head to toe.

Adam can feel his blood leaving him as it runs into the soil. But there, with his cheek against the cold earth, he can no longer see the garden as it is dismantled. He can only hear the whine of machinery, barely audible over the rain. Clenching his fists, he tries to breathe. Squeezing his eyelids shut, and gritting his teeth, Adam tries to stay alive just a little bit longer.

It takes an age for them to leave. Adam drags pained breaths through himself, concentrating on remaining conscious. And when there is only the rain rattling over the rafters, and the rumbling of the trucks has faded away, Adam inhales and exhales sharply, agonisingly, feeling his throat rattle. He is weak from blood loss, but he thinks, he hopes, that his lying prone here means that the earth has packed tight enough around his ruined chest to stop the worst of the bleeding.

Eve's heart still beats inside him. Keeping him alive.

Slowly, so slowly, he draws himself up to his knees, keeping his arms folded across himself. Slower still, he stands in the ruins of the garden and blinks the rain from his eyes.

They have taken everything. The stadium is an empty earthen basin.

Dragging his legs, Adam takes steps towards the exit. He can feel his blood rolling warmly down his stomach and dripping across his legs, mingling with the chilled rain. Hauling himself one foot after another from the barren earth, he falls against the wall of the exit, waiting there for a wave of nausea and dizziness to dissipate. Just a little further, he thinks. Just outside the stadium is the place he needs.

Forcing himself onwards, he trudges unsteadily down the long corridor, past the trophy case and back out into the rains splashing the cracked tarmac of the stadium's car park. Rolling himself through the broken turnstile at the entrance, he turns into the empty street beyond, where yellowing grasses stick up from gaps in the cracked pavement. Nobody drives up here any more. Nobody bothers coming this close to the stadium except for the children, and the rains have driven them away.

But there, on the corner, is the shattered box he needs.

Glass hangs in shards from its every broken window, and it is so covered in bright graffiti that it seems to glow in Adam's vision. He shoulders the door open and stumbles inside, leaning heavily against the wet metal frame and raising the receiver to his ear. Somehow, the ruined handset still has a dial tone.

Fumbling through the pockets of his coat, he manages to locate the toffee wrapper. The number swims in his vision, so he grits his teeth and breathes until the pain focuses him, and unsteadily dials the number as it sharpens.

The phone buzzes at him. A faint voice tells him that he must insert coins into the dented machine. Adam grips the base of the metal box and wrenches at it until it comes free, spilling a silvery stream of money. Most tumbles through his bloodied wet fingers, but he manages to catch a few pieces; enough that when he feeds them into the slot, the handset against his ear starts to ring.

Adam slides down to the floor of the shattered phone box, crunching among the broken pieces of glass and ripped-up advertisements. The grey sky swirls unsteadily overhead, and the trills of the phone are minutes or hours apart. The sky is darkening as he watches it, but he soon realises that it's unconsciousness trying to claim him, so he grips hold of a handful of glass until the pain startles the sky back into brightness. Just a few moments more, he thinks. Just a few moments more, and then it will be okay to die.

A click. A voice. "Hello?"

Adam opens his mouth, but no sound comes out. He tries again, but when he manages a croaked word, he realises that it's useless because he has dropped the handset. It lies there on the sodden ground before him, with burbled crackling emanating from it, and he has no more strength left to pick it up. He has no more strength for anything. Even the glass cutting into his palm seems distant now, and even his pained breaths are unable to startle him back into focus. The world outside the phone box darkens, then the phone box itself, until there is only the vague glow of the stained brown lamp overhead.

Then there is only the faint beating of Eve's heart, getting weaker.

There, in the broken phone box, the first man lets himself fade away.

XI

Eden's ants were like droplets of sap come to life. Adam would spend days at a time following them, and studying them, and enjoying the way that sunlight passed through their tiny, amber bodies. He would peer as closely as he could into the entrances of their nest, trying to discover the hidden hierarchy inside the underground architecture, and he would admire the way they carefully cut into leaves with their strong jaws, and easily carried sections that seemed far too large for them to move, always with purpose, and often walking in strictly organised lines. Sometimes, Adam would copy the ants, and usher his children into queues, and they would stride across Eden, cutting down huge palm leaves, and marching triumphantly with them held over their heads to present them to Eve, their queen, by laying them at her feet. And sometimes, Adam would lie perfectly still near the ants' nest, with his arm outstretched across the forest floor, just to feel the tickle of their tiny feet as they crawled across him.

In Cologne, Adam helped build the cathedral. The first few years involved a lot of digging, for the foundations, and Adam stole as much displaced foliage as he could to replant in the forests.

The forests were wonderful, providing shade in the hot summers, and shelter in the mild winters, and Adam would spend a lot of his time when not at work watching the ants that inhabited it. They were a long way removed from Eden's ants, but they were still fascinating to Adam, especially when it came to the politics between the different nests and species. Eve, meanwhile, served at the cathedral's construction, providing food to the builders, and stonecutters, and labourers. And in that way, she learned architecture. This cathedral was to be special, she told Adam; its spires would scratch the sky. And at night, she would show him the sketches she had copied: marvellous cross-sections of the enormous structure. Adam especially enjoyed the way she would liken the design to the human body. The pillars and arches were like ribs, she told him; the transepts like outstretched arms.

One day a year, every year, the ants in Cologne's forests would fly. Their backs would split to reveal delicate wings, and they would fill the rich space between the roots and branches of the trees with their clumsy flights. Adam and Eve would take the day off from their work, and together they would walk the forest paths and enjoy the feeling of the bright sunshine and all the flitting, tiny bodies bringing such joyful movement to the place. There was a glade not far from their home where they would stop, and Eve would dance in the sunshine there, and laugh as they crawled up her legs and ribs and launched themselves from her outstretched arms, and Adam would lie back among the grasses and admire her. The ants were her congregation, he thought, and her body was their cathedral.

Adam wakes to the sight of machines and flowers.

The machines surround his bed on every side. Some of them beep, and some of them hum, and some of them flash. They are tethered to various parts of him using brightly coloured cables and clear tubes dripping liquids of various hues. Adam has no idea what any of the machines are for, so he doesn't detach himself in case they are doing something important. Instead, he turns his wrists over and inspects the cannulas feeding him the fluids. His skin is slightly scratched from the multiple attempts they must have made to penetrate it, and he briefly entertains the idea that they might have ended up using a hammer and chisel to puncture him.

The flowers are balanced on the machines. There are bunches of every species imaginable, held in plastic vases and paper cups and rolls of newspaper. Some of them look store bought, and some of them look freshly picked, and the thick perfume of them masks any possible medicinal scent. Adam spends a while simply lying there, waiting to fully awaken and admiring all the flowers. There are curtains, so that the machines and flowers are all he can see, but that's okay. He feels as if he has spent a very long time trying to walk along a tightrope, and he needs a few moments to regain his balance.

There is a rattling as the curtains part, and a woman wearing a white coat enters, flicking through a thick clipboard of medical charts. "Awake at last," she says, when she notices that Adam's eyes are open. "Our miracle man. You were in surgery for a full day, which is a new record for this facility. Congratulations." She checks some of the machines. "You also set what we believe to be the country-wide record for the amount of shrapnel pulled from a man. We were digging metal out of you for a few hours, and some of it was quite old. You must have a lot of fun going through metal detectors." Adjusting two of the drips, she turns to him. "Don't move too much. Your chest is currently being held together with a whole reel of wire, and from what I'm told it was an absolute nightmare threading it through you. Apparently, your bones are as tough as ivory, and your skin is like hard leather. Apart from your other records, you may have the record for the highest number of surgeons baffled. Luckily for you, it's not a statistic we keep track of." She pulls away the curtains surrounding his bed. "I'll be back in a while to make sure you're still alive. Remember: keep still and let yourself heal."

The room is now bright with sunlight, and Adam blinks through it as his doctor strides away. There is another bed opposite Adam's, and laying within it is Owl. Even prone, wearing a plastic breathing mask, and hooked up to rows of machines, Owl looks mythological. It's in the way that his sinewy physique is still tense, even while he is unconscious, as if he is ready to leap into action at any moment. His muscular arms are spread wide and strapped to long boards, and there are long metal pins penetrating his bronze flesh at various angles, no doubt to help his bones set. To Adam, he looks like a fearsome facsimile of the crucifixion. Owl's bed is also surrounded with beeping and whirring machines, upon which are perched dozens more bunches of flowers, almost hiding him from view.

There is soft laughter, and Adam turns his head to see Crow, who is perched on one of the room's long windowsills. She is wearing a polka-dot dress the same red as her lips and heart-shaped sunglasses, and the light of the sky gushes into the room around her. Today, her prosthetic leg is black, and she swings it idly as she continues her conversation on her phone. Adam doesn't interrupt her. He is content to lie where he is. The grey sky behind her whirls with quick clouds, but time seems slow here. There is no pain in Adam's chest, but it does feel like there is a weight upon it, as if somebody is stood on top of him and keeping him pinned down.

Eventually, Crow concludes her phone call and wanders across.

"You're a lucky man," she tells him, finding a seat at the end of his bed.

"So I'm told."

Adam voice is hoarse, so she offers him a little water.

"When I found you," she says, "there was a hole in your chest big enough to nest in. And I'm told that they dug more than one bullet out of you. I don't know what you're made of, Adam, but it's tough stuff."

"Dust."

She laughs.

"Who are the flowers from?"

"Butterfly. She's been replacing Owl's whenever they start to wilt, so I'm sure she'll do the same for you. That was her on the phone, actually."

"How is she?"

"Did you know that Pig owns a canal boat? The two of them are sailing it through Glasgow right now. I imagine that it's this old, rickety, peeling thing, but Butterfly has a wonderful way of describing everything. She makes it sound as if it's a great, gleaming galleon, and that Glasgow's canals are treacherous waters thick with pirates. The best bit is the way she makes it sound as if Pig is a mighty captain, commanding an eager crew and bedecked with medallions. Apparently, he even has a special sailing hat." She raises her heart-shaped glasses to her forehead. "I can see why he dotes on her so much. I think the world's a brighter place with her in it."

"Especially in winter."

"Especially in winter," she agrees.

"What about Owl?"

"Oh, he's fine. Or rather, he will be when his bones set. He keeps struggling whenever he wakes up, so we're keeping him under most of the time. You wouldn't believe the amount of sedatives it takes to keep him drowsy. Thankfully, this place is very discreet. The wonders of private care, I suppose. How are you feeling?"

"A bit sore."

"I should imagine." She shuffles up and runs her fingers across the thick bandages binding his chest, making his skin tingle with needles of pain. "Rook is on his way. He's been busy in London, working to ruin the men who ruined my funeral. He'll be wanting to know who did this to you. Do you remember what happened?"

In this warm and bright place, Adam's past seems dark and cold. He tries to piece together the moments before he woke, but there are only splinters of moments – memories like slivers of shrapnel embedded in his mind. "Bits and pieces," he says. The phone box is the most vivid: that ruined place he was sure was going to be his coffin.

"Well, get some rest. My brother will be here soon, and you can tell him all about it." Crow lowers her heart-shaped sunglasses and wanders over to the wide windows, throwing them open and making the curtains billow. Droplets of rain drift through. "We're out on the Yorkshire moors here," she tells him, "so the air is always fresh. No city noise, and no light pollution. The stars come out at night, like they used to. I'll see about getting you a wheelchair, and maybe, when it stops raining, we can go outside and see them."

* * *

It continues to rain. For a while, the rain is no more than dots and dashes down the windows. Adam watches it from the comfort of his bed – the way it soaks the curtains. Within hours, the sky begins to darken, and the rain becomes violent. There is a constant rumbling, accompanied by lightning, and as tired as Adam is he remains awake, admiring the storm as it develops. A nurse arrives to fasten the windows, and the curtains cease their dramatic billowing, but the drumming of heavy droplets on the rooftop continues: the heavens smashing at the tiles of the hospital. Crow returns with a wheelchair and a bounty of snacks gathered from various vending machines, and she helps Adam to sit up and slide out of bed. The windows are only a few steps away, so there's no need to untangle himself from all of his wires and tubes; they are draped behind him like a cloak.

Crow perches on the windowsill, and Adam sits back in his chair, and they munch through packets of crisps and watch the storm together: the way the hills light up every time lightning strikes. In the pauses, the darkness is so complete that all Adam can see in the windows is his own reflection – a stooped giant, wrapped in white bandages.

For days, Adam wakes to yet more rain. Then, one day, the rain stops and the world outside is water. There is a dull dawn of great grey clouds, low over the murky brown flood that has consumed the landscape. All outside is still, and the hospital room is quiet, and Adam feels as if he has awoken to a moment outside of time. It takes him a while to realise that the power is out – that all his machines are still, and the lights are off. Slowly, he disentangles himself from his cloak of cables, pulling needles from his arms, and unpeeling the stickers attaching monitors to him. He gently presses at the architecture of wires keeping his chest closed beneath his bandages; they scratch and scrape at his ribs, and there is a reparative needling, but no pain.

A black silhouette in the sky breaks the peace, the blur of its blades whirling the clouds. A helicopter is coming.

Crow arrives surrounded by staff: nurses, and orderlies, and doctors. She looks tired, and is wearing the same clothes as yesterday. The group gather around Owl's bed, and needles flash as they are thrust into him; he is punctured and filled with sedatives. Carefully, they free him of the machines, place the wilting flowers of his collection aside, and prepare a route. They start to roll his bed away, towards the open doorway.

"Where are they taking him?" Adam asks.

Crow wipes at her eyes with the back of her wrist. "A different hospital. One with power. The floods got a lot worse last night. How are you feeling?"

"I'm okay."

"Good. Our own transport should be here soon." Crow lies on Adam's bed with a sigh, resting among the fallen petals of flowers.

Adam peers out. "All that water," he says. "Like the sea's swallowed the world."

"Worse every year," says Crow. "There won't be much land left at this rate."

"Plenty of sky, though."

She smiles. "I'm going to go fetch a few things."

Adam watches Owl's helicopter depart, becoming a distant dot, and when it has vanished into the far horizon the grey clouds begin to clear, revealing patches of blue. A boat appears in the distance, with froth writhing in its wake.

"I found your coat," says Crow, when she returns. The coat is beaten and worn and full of holes, but somebody has thought to wash it – there is no mud or blood staining it. Adam gratefully shrugs it on. "And that," she says, peering out at the boat, "should be for us." She gives Adam a backpack, and covers him with a few more blankets. "For the journey."

The hospital is dark and mostly deserted, but for a few remaining members of staff. The lower floor is completely flooded, and bits of medical equipment bob in the murky waters. Crow helps Adam roll through to the grand central staircase, and there she sits at the edge, making a tower of playing cards while she waits. By the time she crowns it, the waters are lapping at the step on which it stands. "This is the first time it's stopped raining in a week," she says. "It's like a monsoon season." She leans back and watches the flood as it curls towards the base of her tower.

All at once, the tower collapses. Cards float away: kings and queens, aces and hearts. Adam watches them drift and bob and remembers the rains that struck him back in Manchester. It feels a lot longer than a week ago. The insect buzz of the boat's motor fills the hall as it sweeps through the hospital doors. It's no more than a small motorised tub, but it's nimble, and being directed by a broad-shouldered figure in a yellow mackintosh coat. The boat's brightly dressed captain brings it around to the foot of the steps. "How you both doing?" he rumbles, merrily.

"Hi, Crab."

With one foot on the steps, and one foot in his boat, Crab keeps it steady so that Adam can stumble aboard. He is surprised by how weak his legs are; it is as if all his strength leaked out of the hole in his chest. The boat rocks, and Adam seats himself as centrally as he can, while Crow situates herself at the tub's fore.

"All good?" rumbles Crab.

"Let's get going," says Crow.

"Right you are." Seating himself back at the boat's motor, Crab beckons it into life. He leans forward, and pats Adam on the knee. "Back into the bright wide world, eh lad?"

The world is indeed bright, and Adam watches as the dark bulk of the remote hospital slowly recedes. There are still staff up on its roof, and they wave at the boat as it departs, and Adam raises his hand in return: a thanks that feels insufficient. Ahead, the endless waters are broken only by the tips of the rolling hills that emerge from the flood, and Adam finds it difficult to imagine there is any dry land left. It feels as if the waters have swallowed the world; have washed away the worst of it, perhaps.

*   *   *

Yorkshire feels like it's gone.

The highest hills of the moors rise from the flood, with trees clinging on to them as if they are themselves marooned. The currents that pour and swirl around them are treacherous and ever-changing, and sometimes Adam spots a distant dinghy or raft trying to navigate the watery labyrinth. Crab directs his little motorboat through it all, finding passages beneath skeletal canopies and across improbable shelves of frothing surf. The murky water is rich with debris that bumps against the boat – branches, mostly, but bits of rubbish as well. Crow dangles her arms in the water and pushes the worst away, until the long night finally catches up with her. She draws blankets from her bag, and nestles up beneath them at the motorboat's fore. Sometimes, when the boat lurches across waves, the spray makes rainbows over her, haloing her while she sleeps.

Crab is following a burst river to the sea. They must be sailing across a floodplain. Adam leans over the edge of the boat, and tries to see the country beneath it.

There are the shapes of fences down there, and shale walls, and paved roads, and they pass over the wrecks of sunken cars and caravans, which have aerials that scrape across the boat's base. In the distance, between the hills, Adam spies the spire of a church, and before long he can see the silhouettes of entire buildings under water.

The little boat sails across the car park of a supermarket, surrounded by the skeletons of shopping trolleys, and the water is filled with bobbing crisp packets and ready-meals. Adam fishes out a curry meal for one, and some smoked bacon, and a bag of fresh lettuce. It's funny, he thinks, how it's only the stuff wrapped in plastic that floats.

Adam pops the bag of lettuce and tentatively munches on a leaf, only to find that it's perfectly preserved. He offers the bag to Crab.

"No thanks, lad." Crab has donned a bright yellow hat that matches his coat, and looks, to Adam, like a cartoon of a sailor. He steers with one hand, and keeps his other locked tight around the edge of his boat, as if he might be sailing by feeling the currents that wash across her. "Got you a present," he rumbles, and pats the boat's stowage box.

Releasing the catch, Adam reveals his gun belts, the pistols shiny and polished.

"There's a bag of ball bearings in there," says Crab. "Fly a lot better than a shot. And a flask of powder, too. I took that dusty stuff you brought me and mixed it with some other things. My own special recipe. Should make a big bang."

Adam's arms ache as he hefts the pistols, turning them over. They look as good as new. "Thanks, Crab. I guess I owe you one." Fastening the stowage box shut, Adam turns back to the water.

The rooftops of houses rise from the waters here, and the detritus of many lives has bobbed to the surface around them. A set of colourful balloons glides past, along with the sodden shapes of party hats and paper plates. An entire platter of sausage rolls breaks apart against the hull of the boat, before sinking. The severed heads of sunflowers float upright, parting with the currents.

The sky brightens with the shifting of clouds, and the waters sparkle at the edges.

Beside the church spire, the boat's engine sputters and grinds to a halt. Adam leans over the edge while Crab hauls at the little engine's pulley and spies the multicoloured bunting that has wound itself around the engine's rotor. The bunting seems to have been hung up between the village's lamps for some autumnal celebration, but is now holding the boat firmly in place. Adam reaches in as far as he is able, with his chest needling in protest, but he is unable to reach any of the tiny string flags. "You might have to go down," he says.

Crab eyes the tangle. "Reckon you're right," he says. Unfastening his mackintosh, and removing his boots, he strips down to his trousers, revealing a chest that looks like a map of a mountain range. "Shan't be long," he rumbles. Placing his yellow hat on Adam's head, he winks, and jumps without hesitation into the flood. The murky waters splash as if he is a boulder fallen into them, and there is a long stream of bubbles before the surface calms. Then Crab is no more than a dark shape, swimming beneath the boat and working at the knotted bunting.

Munching at lettuce, Adam enjoys the moment of calm; the distant sound of birds calling. There are quite a few birds using the village rooftops to perch upon. Adam can see a pair of herons watching the waters from the vantage of a petrol station; every now and then one of them strikes at the water, without any success. A roost of pigeons coos up in the rafters of the church spire, huddled together beneath its bell, and there seem to be multiple families of ducks and moorhens, bobbing on the currents between the buildings and preening at themselves. Adam watches a gaggle of geese paddle down the main road, honking conversationally as they go, and wonders how long it will be until they fly south. It must be soon, he thinks.

"What is that?"

Crow has awoken, and is sitting up, rubbing the sleep from her eyes.

"Adam, what *is* that?"

"What is what?"

"Those birds…"

The distant calls he heard earlier are indeed drawing closer. A cawing chorus, noisy in the quiet. Adam searches the sky as Crow stands, unsteadily, straightening her dress.

"Where are they…?"

Finally, Adam spots them. An untidy flock of black birds, feathers falling as they quarrel with each other. They stream out in an arrow, chasing something small at the arrow's point. Adam shades his eyes against the sun, and tries to see what it is that's being so desperately hunted. Whatever it is, it has bright wings with shifting colours, and it tumbles like a leaf through the blue and white sky, barely evading the frantic beaks of its pursuers.

Crow's breath catches in her throat. "Oh, *shit*." There is a whirl of feathers and limbs and wings as she changes shape, launching from her clothes, sharp beak shining. Her prosthetic leg thumps as it falls. Glossy black wings wide, she flaps and soars high, cutting through the air to intercept the quarrelling flock. Hands clenching and unclenching, Adam is helpless, only able to watch as she bursts through them, shrieking and tearing with her single claw. The bright-winged insect at the flock's head tumbles unsteadily, the tips of its wings ragged. A few black-feathered bodies fall away, cawing their coarse anger at Crow as she beats them back, but enough are still chasing Butterfly. All it would take is the strike of a single beak to kill her, Adam knows.

Hauling the stowage box open, Adam grabs a pistol.

It's a glinting wood-and-metal affair, ornately carved and finely tempered. His hand knows the curve of its hilt, and his finger knows the press of its trigger. He lets himself load it, watching as his fingers find the powder and bearings, and use the gun's ramrod to push them into place. He feels himself strike the duellist's pose, chest burning as he straightens, free hand at the small of his back, gun hand outstretched. He sights along the barrel, and though Crow is up there, and though Butterfly is up there, he knows with absolute clarity that he will hit neither; his body is too long learned in the art of gunfire, his aim too perfect. Adam pulls the hammer back with his thumb.

Then, a moment of indecision. Adam does not want to kill any of those birds.

He raises the pistol at the sky. There is a sound like thunder, and the gun bucks.

The flock scatters. Every bird in the village takes flight all at once: the pigeons, and herons, and ducks, feathers falling as they rush away from the sound. Adam lowers the gun, hating the smell of the powder, and the ringing in his ears, and the dull ache in his arm from the power of the blast. He chucks the spent pistol back into the stowage box, kicks it shut and raises his hands to receive the ragged insect that falls gently towards him.

There are brilliant colours as she shifts. Then Adam is holding Butterfly in the shape of a girl. She is small, and cold, and her skin is covered in scratches and cuts. Adam holds her close as she sobs, throwing her arms around his neck. "I found you," she whispers, breathless. "I didn't think I would. I flew for so long with the wind. Like a kite. I've never flown so far before."

"You're safe," says Adam, because it seems like the right thing to say.

"I had to find you."

Another thump as Crow lands, perched upon the boat's fore. Limbs shift as she too changes, naked and unafraid, with the blood of birds still wet upon her foot. "Give her your coat, Adam. She'll freeze." Before pulling any of her clothes back on, she grabs her prosthetic leg and fastens it into place, rubbing at her stump. "That was a very stupid thing to do, Butterfly."

"I had to find you," she repeats. Shrugging his heavy coat from his shoulders, Adam wraps her in it and sits her down. She nestles into his side, sipping at a plastic bottle of water. "You don't understand. They took him. They took Pig."

Crow rinses the blood from her toes. "Who took Pig?"

"I don't know." Butterfly tugs at strands of her rainbow hair, running them behind her ears. Her eyes are wide, and she is still breathless from her flight. "I told you we went sailing along the canal, in his boat. We weren't expecting the rains to be as bad as they were, so we shored up for a few days, tying ourselves to a little jetty while the canal became a lake. It just kept coming down. I couldn't believe it. But it was fine, because he was there. He was wearing his hat – you know, that special hat he has, the peaked cap with the anchor on it – and he was in control, and everything was fine. We had plenty of supplies, so we sat inside and ate tins of beans and drank glasses of wine while the rain thumped at the roof of the long boat. We were going to weather it out."

Crow pulls her dress down over herself. "What happened?"

"We were up on the roof. It was silly, really. We had a picnic in the rain, because it didn't matter if we got wet because it was warm inside, and we had towels. We sat there and snacked on bits and pieces and watched as the waters slowly rose higher and higher. It's pretty, the way that water is so chaotic in heavy rain. All those droplets smashing and breaking the surface. We both got completely soaked through, and it was heavy enough that you could tilt your face to the sky and drink from it, but we just laughed and laughed at each other. And maybe that's what got their attention. Maybe that's how they found us."

"Who found you?" Crow rolls her sock back on.

"Remember I told you that the canal was a lake? It's really bad up there. As bad as it is down here. There's just water, everywhere. Enough water for bigger boats. They had a yacht. I couldn't believe it at first. To see that great big shiny white yacht cutting through the water towards us was surreal. It was all lit up and warm, and there were people up on the foredeck, and I stood up and waved at them, thinking they were friendly and just coming over to say hello."

"A yacht?" says Adam.

"I swear, I'm telling the truth. It was a yacht in the canal, which wasn't really even a canal any more. There was shouting. I remember the shouting. And there was a sound like a firework going off. But it wasn't a firework. Pig jerked back. And there was blood. Then there were more firework sounds, and I realised that the people in the yacht were shooting at us." Butterfly clings to Adam's shirt. "I didn't know what to do. What are you meant to do in a situation like that? Pig almost fell off the top of his boat. But he stood strong, even when there were more shots, and he bore his tusks at them, and when the yacht drew up close, he pushed me backwards, pushed me from the edge of the boat so that I had no choice. I flew. The rain was heavy, and hard, and it thumped at me so strong I thought I would sink, but I flew as best I could through it, searching for cover. There were the canopies of trees nearby, and I used them for shelter. I found a branch lower down, where I could still see our boat. There were men on it. I could make out their silhouettes. And I could see Pig, too. He was fighting them. Trying to spear them on his tusks. But the men had sticks that flashed with electricity. Cattle prods, I thought. And they struck at him again and again until he stopped moving." Her words slowly turn to heaving sobs. "And then they dragged him onto their yacht, and sailed away with him."

"Did you follow them?" asks Crow.

"I couldn't." Butterfly weeps. "The rain was too heavy. I couldn't fly, and I didn't know how to sail Pig's boat. I had to wait so long for it to stop raining. It took hours and hours. And when I got back onto the boat, I couldn't call anyone because the phone lines were dead. I waited and I waited, not sure what to do, until the rains cleared up enough and I could come and find you. I'm sorry. I'm really sorry. I didn't know what else to do."

Crow rifles through her bag and retrieves her phone, jabbing at it and scowling at the lack of reception. The birds that scattered at the sound of the gunshot are already beginning to return to the village. They flap from the heights of the sky and come to rest on rooftops. Adam watches them, letting his mind turn over.

The boat rocks slightly as Crab pulls himself back aboard, grinning triumphantly. The bunting that had been bound around the boat's motor is now bound around him instead, tiny colourful flags hanging from his weathered limbs. His stony smile fades as he takes in the boat's new occupant. "What did I miss?"

"We've got to go north," says Adam.

"What's happened?"

"Someone's taken Pig," says Adam, remembering, so clearly, the yacht parked outside the Sinclairs' house, casting its shadow and blocking out the sun: a memory so stark in his mind that it surprises him with its clarity. "I know who took him. And I know where they've taken him."

XII

There was once a flood so bad that Adam and Eve had to build a boat.

They were living up in the Atlas mountains at the time, and the heavy rainfall took them both by surprise. The country they were living in was not known for such storms. Yet the rains kept coming, and the waters kept rising, and before long Adam and his children were dragging as much timber as they could into the higher reaches of the mountains, where Eve and villagers from all across the local area began to build. Eventually, the waters rose high enough that they covered the forests, and Adam was reduced to paddling over to uprooted trunks and guiding them back to the steadily ascending shoreline. All manner of creatures, great and small, emerged from the lowlands and retreated up the mountainsides, and among them were some of Eden's creatures, dispossessed of the garden but still as striking as the day they were made. Eve's construction grew larger and larger, until it was big enough to accommodate all the villagers, and all of their children, and all of Eden's creatures, and even some of the local animals. A great ramp was left open in the base of the boat, and everyone walked, and crawled, and slithered on board, in a great stream of living things that continued until the floods grew too high. Then Adam and Eve sealed the ship, and all inside sat tight, waiting for the rains to stop. They had to stop eventually, after all.

Outside the sky was always dark, as if night would never end, and rain drummed constantly against the roof of the boat. But inside there was warmth, and community, and though quarrels inevitably arose, and living things consumed each other as they were wont to do, the quarrels were brief, and what few deaths there were never seemed gratuitous. The boat was heaved from its scaffolding, and floated across the furious floods, and Adam and Eve did their very best to make sure that everyone inside was comfortable and secure.

During the worst days of the storm, when Adam started to lose track of the passing of time, and everyone on board the boat was stricken with fear, he began to hear laughter outside. The laughter was intermittent, and chattering, and he would wander the hull and press his ear against it, trying to determine the source. The rains drummed their endless rhythm across the roof, and the muttering of all the people and creatures inside the boat was constant, and the laughter continued, drifting in from different parts of the boat. On the worst day of all, when the boat rocked deliriously from side to side, and the laughter coming from outside seemed endless, Adam unsealed the door and went out on deck, gripping hold of the sodden ropes he and Eve had secured all around the ship. The storm raged at him, and thunder rolled, and lightning shattered the waves that surrounded the boat, and he stumbled, slipping and sliding across the deck, in search of the laughter.

All around the ship, there was nothing but water and waves. And in a flash of lightning, Adam finally saw the source of the laughter. It was a bird, perched on the railing at the edge of the ship, splaying its black-and-white wings for balance, its claws buried deep in the splintering wood. Of course, Adam knew who it was. He should have recognised the croaking. It was Magpie; Eden's own Magpie, flicking his wings at the furious heavens and laughing at the drowned world.

* * *

Crab steers his little motorboat east, through the flooded ruins of Yorkshire. In the distance is dry ground where higher land emerges, and there are islands everywhere, and from time to time he navigates around sections of railway or motorway protruding from the water. There are a lot of people on the high ground – camps in the hills, and parties huddled in tents, and queues of cars going nowhere. The people often wave, and call out to Crab's boat for aid.

Butterfly rummages around in the boat's lockbox, and retrieves an ancient binder of maps. The maps are yellow and brown, and the lines across them, meant to denote rivers and hills and roads, look, to Adam, more like folds of skin. Extracting maps from the binder, one by one, Butterfly makes them into paper boats. Each time she completes one she sets it in the water, giving it a little push towards the shore, leaving a steady trail of paper boats in their wake.

"What are you doing?" asks Crow, after a while.

"Sending them help."

"They can help themselves well enough," rumbles Crab, and indeed, helicopters hum overhead, and all manner of boats weave back and forth. Adam even spots a swan-shaped pedal boat going south, with a Union Jack dangling from its neck. None of this seems to deter Butterfly, however; she folds a whole armada of paper boats for the refugees, and when she runs out of maps, she uses whatever other bits of paper she can find: receipts, and bookmarks, and banknotes, retrieved from pockets and wallets.

Sometimes there are bodies in the water. They bob lifelessly, bloated and staring at the great blue sky with wide white eyes, and Adam finds himself watching them and searching for some kind of connection. Yet every time he thinks he comes close to sympathy – at the sight of a lone child, or a family trapped in a car beneath the waterline – the thorns growing through his thoughts tighten, and he remains as indifferent as the floods that killed them.

When Crab's motor runs low on fuel, he steers to a sunken petrol station and dives down with an empty red canister. Beneath the water he is nimble – a dark shape moving as easily as a quick darting fish – and Adam observes him grabbing chocolate bars and cans of drinks from the petrol station shop. Crab slides a ruined credit card through the broken till's slot, and laughs so hard that streams of bubbles rise from his nostrils. He returns with a rocky grin and a full canister, and Adam is given to believe that Crab would be perfectly happy were the country to remain submerged.

At night, the sky is so clear that the stars are dazzling. Butterfly watches them with wide eyes, wrapped up in Crab's mackintosh and huddled against Crow for warmth. When a shooting star streaks overhead, she mumbles beneath her breath. "I know it's probably a piece of a satellite burning up in the atmosphere," she says, afterwards, "but I made a wish anyway."

Crow has been checking her phone hourly, with the glow of it gleaming in her tired eyes. "We've got to get reception eventually, surely?" But as the boat churns steadily across a broad lake of flooding, glinting with stars, she flings it into the water. "Out of battery." Removing her prosthetic leg, she rubs at her stump. "I'm going to fly south and find Rook. Somebody needs to tell him what's happening."

"I'll come with you," says Butterfly, stretching her arms. "I'll just get in the way here."

"You can barely fly."

"I can fly fine. The sky is clear, and you'll be with me."

Crow removes her dress and folds it neatly. "Fine. Will you be okay, Adam?"

"I'll be okay."

"I'll look after him," rumbles Crab, with a wink.

"I'll fly fast, and we'll bring help." There is a shift, and Crow's limbs become wings. She grips hold of the boat's fore with her single claw, and croaks hoarsely.

Butterfly unfastens Crab's coat and shivers in the chill night air. "You need to look after Pig when you find him," she says. "He's lost without me." There is a whirl of colour, and her wings shimmer in the moonlight – all the shifting shades of summer captured in them. Butterfly lands on Adam's outstretched hand. Her tiny legs tickle at his skin, and her long tongue unspools, tasting the salt flecked across him, and her bright red antennae twitch. She takes flight, drifting upwards and into the open sky. There is the rustling of feathers as Crow joins her, and then they fly away south: a great dark bird with a vividly coloured insect fluttering beneath her wing, vanishing into the night.

By the time the sun begins to rise, Crab has finally steered into the sea, where he brings his boat to speed. The nose of the little tub skims the waves, and white flecks of water splash across Adam, and Crab holds onto his yellow hat with one hand to stop it from flying away with the wind, grinning a grin so wide it almost splits his head in two. Before long, England becomes Scotland. The rocky edges of the cliffs rush by, and so do various river mouths, until Crab finds the right one, whereupon he slows the boat and navigates upstream, fighting against the churning brown current inland. "Nearly there," he says. "How you doing, lad? Maybe you should try and get a few winks of sleep before we arrive."

"I don't think I could sleep if I wanted to."

"That's fair enough."

Crab steers his boat deeper inland, and gently around the ruins of a cottage, where the waters are thick with yellow leaves. The branches of drowned trees scratch at the tub's hull. Ahead, the hills form a yellow crown around a broad glen, encrusted with forests.

"Not long now," he rumbles. "What's your plan?"

Unfastening the boat's stowage box, Adam hauls his gun belts onto his lap. "We're going to find Pig," he says, and with a scrap of rag and a ramrod, he cleans the pistol he fired earlier.

* * *

With his pistols strapped across his chest, and the smell of gunpowder fresh on his fingers, Adam's memories are stirred. The waters are full of dead horses, and their bloated corpses bounce from the boat, and Adam knows there was another time, another life, when he was surrounded by dead horses with his pistols heavy across his shoulders. There was the booming of cannons, and there were men with golden buttons sewn into their heavy red coats, and there was a burning flag. He remembers the burning flag clearest of all – the way the wind made the embers dance at the edge of it. Many died that day, he knows. Many by his own hand.

Sometimes, Adam wonders how many of his descendants he's killed.

There was a time when he knew all of his children by name, he thinks – when he could describe their personalities, their desires and dreams and fears. Then there was a time when his children became strangers to him, sons and daughters of sons and daughters branching out across the world over generations. But even then, he cared for them and about them. He took pains to learn their names, and help them where he could. Nowadays, he finds it difficult to connect with any of his children. He is consumed by apathy. The binding around his thoughts, each barb a prickle of grief, is to blame. Soon, he thinks, he will have to confront whatever lies at the heart of that tangled growth. He can't be apathetic forever.

The Sinclair estate is partially submerged. Fruit risen from the shattered remains of sunken orchards bobs with the currents, bright and engorged in the dark eddies, which are infused with effluence. Oil has also risen from the sump pools, making the waters shimmer as they rush around the hills. Sinclair House itself is half drowned, and the windows of its upper floors glare across the devastation while the windows of its lowest floor siphon the tides. Only the tremendous glass structure up on the rise to its rear emerges mostly clear from the waters, a splendid gemstone reflecting the sky with its uneven shatter-shard facets, while the flood licks hungrily at its base.

"What on Earth is that?" rumbles Crab.

"It's a greenhouse," Adam tells him.

Navigating through the ruined estate, Crab comes alongside the enormous crystalline structure and cuts the engine. He peers through the partially submerged glass at the bright garden inside. While black effluence is splashed across everything outside the greenhouse, everything is clean and uncorrupted within: the greens are greener, and the whites are whiter, and the mirrors meant to cast sunlight across it seem to be reflecting a brighter sky. "Hell of a thing," he rumbles, scratching at his chin. "You reckon they've got Pig in there?"

Adam takes stock of the greenhouse garden. Before him is a small meadow, surrounded on all sides with wild shrubbery bursting with berries: luscious greens punctuated with ripe reds and blues. As Adam takes his census of the contents, he notices that a few specimens stand out. There is a birch up on a hillside with particularly silvery bark, and there is a rich creeping vine gripping hold of the glass in a familiar pattern. There are pieces of Eden planted here, he realises – pieces stolen from the stadium garden. No doubt the rest is further inside.

"I think so," says Adam. "Somewhere inside."

"Right you are." Crab taps experimentally at the glass. Then he hits it with his fist. The pane does not so much as tremble at the strike. "Ain't never seen glass like this before," he rumbles. "If I had some tools, maybe I could get through. You know a way in?"

"There's an airlock."

"An airlock?" Crab squints across. "What kind of greenhouse has an airlock?"

"It's not just a greenhouse. It's a vault."

"A greenhouse vault. Right." He runs his coarse fingers down a section of the thin metal frame between the panes. "Well, if there's gonna be any weakness, it'll be along one of these. How's about you go try your airlock, while I take a tour of the place, see what I can see?"

"Sounds like a good idea, Crab."

Part of the hillside the greenhouse is set upon rises from the waters nearby, and Adam disembarks, unsteady on the spongy grass. He tightens his pistols across his chest, feeling the sting of the wound still healing beneath the crossed belts. The little boat churns steadily away through the dark waters with Crab at its helm, buttoned up in his bright yellow mackintosh. He hums as he goes, and his dark eyes, embedded in the thick folds of his face, interrogate the superstructure. Adam watches the boat until it turns out of sight, and then he draws two of his pistols, preparing to face whatever lies ahead.

The yacht is moored beside Sinclair House, its white flanks stained by the floods. Shattering one of the first-floor windows of the house, Adam ducks inside. The interior stinks of damp and rot, and water splashes against Adam's boots. He wades through, listening for any signs of life, but he hears nothing except the groaning of the old manor house as it slowly disintegrates. Pieces of damp art peer down at him from the walls, black mould already thickening across the bright colours. To the rear of the mansion, the airlock glows at the end of a gloomy, dripping corridor, and it is shut against the floods.

Adam holsters his pistols.

Beyond the glass airlock, the vault is resplendent. Mirrors reflect the pale sky upon the rolling hills, which are covered in long grasses. Adam recognises those grasses because they are from Eden, and planted at their edges, and among them, are more pieces of paradise: vividly coloured flowers and small trees gushing with rich leaves. A small stream sparkles as it meanders among the hills, and a few figures wade in the clear waters. They are the elderly people Adam met the last time he was here, naked except for the tiny silver crucifixes around their necks, and as Adam peers at them, some of them notice him. A muffled cry is raised, and they mill about. Yet it is the tree at the fore of the magnificent view that draws Adam's attention. Standing at the height of the tallest hill is Eden's cherry tree, and its petals drift in the artificial breeze running through the garden. They are a pink veil that partially obscures the creature at the tree's trunk.

Pig has been chained to the cherry tree.

Chains are wrapped around his limbs and his neck, so that his bloodied belly protrudes. His clothes have been torn to rags, and his skin has been cut and bruised so badly that every inch of exposed flesh is red and black. He dangles helplessly from his chains, and his head is drooped, his pale tusks gleaming as they arc from his torn lips. The only sign that he is still alive is the laboured rise and fall of his chest, and the occasional twitch of his heavy limbs.

The garden's occupants gather.

Some are carrying hunting rifles, and others are empty-handed, but all of them are naked. Their wrinkled, pale flesh quivers as they approach the airlock, and at their head is Frank Sinclair. The small man is grinning, or maybe snarling, and his little teeth are white against his ruddy flesh. The party comes to a halt before the airlock, glaring through the multiple layers of reinforced glass as if their contempt alone might murder Adam where he stands.

Frank's voice crackles through a hidden speaker.

"I killed you," he hisses. "I watched you die."

Adam notices Pig try to raise his head. The flesh around his right eye has swelled so badly that he is only able to see out of his left eye, and he blinks away the crust of blood holding it closed. When he catches sight of Adam he coughs and splutters, swinging his pale tusks uselessly, as if he might be able to tear himself free of his thick chains, but his efforts prove futile. One of Frank Sinclair's party strides across and snatches a black baton from the grasses at Pig's feet. The end of the baton flickers with electricity, and the man presses it against Pig's exposed flesh.

There is a prolonged squeal as Pig convulses, distorted through the hidden speaker, and when the violent convulsions subside his head drops again, limp against his chest.

Adam can feel his fists trembling. When he strikes the airlock there is a loud enough bang that Frank Sinclair and the rest of his party stumble backwards. Yet the glass holds. Blood rolls down Adam's knuckles, but he has caused not so much as a dent. The surprise in Frank Sinclair's face fades, and he begins to laugh. The laugh is a wretched, barking noise, and as it takes hold of him it rocks his soft frame, making his wrinkled flesh quiver. Adam strikes the airlock again, and again, ruining his fists with each useless strike, and he draws one of his pistols and shoots at it, making a black stain across it, but the glass holds; and the more he tries, raging against it, the harder Frank Sinclair laughs.

They all laugh together, all those naked people safe in their vault, and behind them Pig bleeds, with the pink petals of Eden's cherry tree gently settling upon his bruised shoulders.

* * *

Adam remembers wandering among the evergreens of Eden, until he came to a grassy clearing where there was a creature that he had not seen before. The creature had hooves, and coarse black hair, and curved white tusks, and rooted at the earth with its long snout, all the while grumbling and snuffling. Adam remembers that he went down on his knees and mimicked the creature until it noticed him, and that they then faced each other.

246

He recalls that the creature's tusks gleamed, pale and deadly, and that it trembled before it charged. Adam caught it by its tusks, then, and they both fell to the soft earth, a mess of limbs and hands and hooves, struggling and wrestling, until they were both exhausted and lay back in the grasses, breathing heavily. The creature made soft grumbling noises, and snuffled at Adam's hand when he offered it.

"My name is Adam," he told it, and he remembers running his fingers through its coarse hair until it stilled. "And your name is Pig."

The problem with the memory is that Adam remembers naming Pig in English, and try as he might, he is unable to shrug off the corruption. He has no recollection at all of Pig's name in Edenic, or any of the words he used to name everything in paradise.

*   *   *

There is too much stuff in Sinclair House. The walls are covered in damp and ruined paintings, and white marble statues loom from alcoves, stained with black mould, and there are bookcases and shelves in almost every room, cladding the walls like thick and musty insulation. The books are a perfect example, Adam thinks, of reading to confirm one's own beliefs: they are all theological in nature, and of a very particular slant. They speak to the superiority of man, and his God-given right to possess and exploit the world for his betterment. They give the reader permission to plunder all that is not man, interpreting ancient words for profit. Adam pulls books from shelves, spilling sheaves of notes, flicking through them and discarding them into the waters. Let the floods wash away those words, he thinks. Let those books become pulp. Let them remember that they were once trees, alive and thriving and heavy with leaves.

Nowhere can he find anything that resembles the code to the airlock.

In the game room, where the walls are hung with the heads of dead animals, Adam leans up against the snooker table and tries to order his thoughts. Glass eyes stare at him accusingly, each severed head so heavy with moisture that it droops low in the gloom. There are cabinets filled with antique rifles along the walls, and Adam considers them, but brute force has so far done nothing to damage the greenhouse. Adam's knuckles are a bloody ruin.

On the far wall there is a dartboard, which has had a hunting knife driven through it, pinning a piece of cardboard in place. Adam wanders across and pulls the knife from the wooden panelling, to free the postcard it has severed almost in two. On the front of the card is a picture of a pair of glassy-eyed elephants huddled at the back of a plastic enclosure too small for them, beneath the words BEIJING ZOO; and on the back, in Magpie's florid handwriting, is the message: "Dear Frank – Having a wonderful time at the zoo! Yours, Magnus." Adam frowns at the card, turning it over in his hands as if there might be some secret third side of it, but it remains cryptic. It's a taunt, he supposes. Pressing it back against the dartboard, Adam drives the hunting knife through it with enough force to split the wooden wall behind it.

Adam notices the sound of a helicopter approaching.

There is a thin staircase at the back of the main hall, and he uses it to make his way to the roof. There are chimneys up here among the ancient slates, and the storm seems to have tumbled a few, making a mess across the tiles. Adam disturbs the birds roosting in the gaps, and they flap away, leaving a clear space large enough for a helicopter to touch down comfortably at the centre. The helicopter in question is a sleek black affair, remaining dark even as it ceases to be a silhouette. Keeping his hands on his pistols, Adam watches it from behind an intact chimney stack. It's not much in the way of cover, but it might be good to block a couple of shots, he thinks.

More tiles slip from the edges of the roof as the helicopter descends. The door rolls back and three figures hop down, ducking, their clothes flapping wildly around them beneath the whirling blades. Adam emerges from behind his chimney stack as the helicopter departs, its pilot wisely deciding not to remain parked on loose tiles. "You made it," says Adam.

Crow straightens her clothes, her navy-blue coat and practical jeans, and smiles thinly, peering out over the ruined roof at the flooded estate. Butterfly seems more like herself again, dressed in bright reds and yellows and blues, with her rainbow hair plaited across her shoulder, and she passes Adam by, staring in wonder at the greenhouse rising like a lump of brilliant crystal at the rear of the house. Dressed darkly, Rook seems somehow taller than them both. He straightens his tie, which is today the colours of a peacock's tail, and strides up to Adam, gripping his briefcase so tightly that his knuckles are bloodless. "Where's Pig?" he asks.

"They've got him in the greenhouse."

"I see." Rook peers beyond Butterfly, at the enormous shatter-shard structure. "I've seen the blueprints. I trust you've had no luck getting inside?"

"Crab's looking around."

"Fine." Rook removes his little round spectacles and cleans them with a dark square of cloth. "Take me to the airlock, Adam. It's time this charade reached its conclusion."

The corridor leading to the airlock feels darker than before. The ceiling sags overhead, dripping with moisture. Ahead, waiting beyond the glass, are Frank Sinclair and the rest of his party. They stand, naked and brazen, chewing on bits of fruit and gathered nuts, their idle laughter crackling through the hidden speakers. They share little jokes, and Frank Sinclair bares his dog-teeth at Adam, casting his bloodshot eyes over Crow and Butterfly hungrily before settling upon Rook.

It is strange, Adam thinks, how much presence Rook has. He is small in stature, and he stands before the airlock in his sharp, well-tailored suit alone, holding his briefcase in both hands, yet whoever he turns his eyes upon shies away from him, as if they have been suddenly embarrassed by their nakedness.

Rook takes his time, inspecting the vault's contents as its occupants hurl ineffective insults his way. His gaze lingers upon the cherry tree and the figure chained to it. "Adam," he says, eventually. "A word, please." Adam wanders across and leans down, so that Rook can whisper confidentially into his ear. "Some of the trees. Some of the flowers. Perhaps some of the grass," he says, softly. "Am I mistaken, or are they very familiar?"

"They're from Eden," confirms Adam.

"I see." Rook frowns. "Once this situation has been resolved, I feel as if you and I need to have a longer conversation about the circumstances surrounding this place."

"I tried, for years and years, to paint it," says Butterfly, "but I always got it wrong. Eden, I mean." She stands before the airlock with a frown. "The main problem was the colours. I could never get the right pigments. The pigments I could get were made of common flower petals and beetle shells, and if I wanted to capture the real splendour of paradise, I needed pigments made of Eden's petals and Eden's beetle shells. I think my paintings were as much copies of Eden's flowers as Earthly flowers are, if you know what I mean. But this…" Her eyes slowly travel across the greenhouse. "This is it. It's crude, and flawed, and drawn by an inarticulate hand, but it's paradise. The colours are there. In the petals. In the grasses. In Pig's blood." At last, she faces the cherry tree, and her frown deepens. "It's beautiful, and it's vicious. You need to help him."

"Of course." Rook blinks, and clears his throat. Then he approaches the airlock. The jibes from the other side reach a crescendo, but all quieten as Rook flicks the switch on the intercom and speaks into it. "This has gone on for long enough," he says. "Allow me to introduce myself. You probably know me as Rook, which is my very real name. Today, however, I am here in my capacity as Roger Corvid, who is a senior partner in the Corvid & Corvid legal firm. As such, you may address me as 'Mister Corvid', should you so wish." Rook turns to Crow, and gestures at a nearby plinth, upon which stands an enormous antique vase. "If you would be so kind," he says.

Crow pushes the vase from the plinth, and it shatters across the carpet. Then she drags the wooden stand over to Rook. Returning to her place beside Adam, she makes certain to crunch across the shards of the broken vase.

Placing his briefcase upon the stand, Rook unlocks it and withdraws several pieces of paper. He takes his time, flicking through them. "Some of you were at the attack on my sister's funeral," he says. "You were sloppy. Scotland Yard identified the majority of you, and those who they did not identify I have identified myself through the use of private investigators. As such, you are all known to me. Further, your assets are known to me. I have spent the better part of the past few weeks cataloguing your estates. Some of you have protected your properties better than others, but rest assured that I have uncovered everything you have tried to conceal."

There is no more mirth in the faces beyond the airlock. All eyes follow the pieces of paper in Rook's hands. "You will be glad to know that I have come to an arrangement with Scotland Yard," he continues. "They have generously agreed to allow me authority over your assets, in return for the extensive evidence I have collected against you."

Rook straightens his papers. "To be clear," he says, "I have your money. Your bank accounts, local and abroad, have either been frozen or seized. I have your physical assets. Your houses, and cars, and tracts of land all belong to me. The horses, and dogs, and guns you used to attack my sister's funeral are now mine, and will be handed over as evidence. This house," he says, gesturing at the sodden walls, "is mine. The ground you stand on is mine. The fruit you are eating is mine. The jewellery you are wearing is mine. The very air you breathe is mine."

There is absolute silence from beyond the airlock.

"I will not return your assets to you," Rook continues. "You will never know the wealth and luxury you have enjoyed again. You have forfeited your rights to comfortable lives. However, I am well aware that most of you have offspring. You have children enrolled in various expensive institutes, and invested in various business ventures, who rely on you for your money. Your children, so far as I can see, have done nothing to deserve punishment for the crimes of their parents. As such, should you surrender immediately, I am inclined to allow them to inherit. Modestly." Rook lays the papers back in his briefcase, and seals it shut. "To be absolutely clear: you are to open this airlock, release your captive, and submit to arrest. Doing so will allow your offspring to inherit some of the money I have taken from you. I am certain that some of you will have questions, but I strongly suggest waiting until you have secured legal counsel for yourselves." Rook flicks the switch on the intercom, and steps back.

There is a long quiet in the greenhouse. Then all inside start talking at once.

Some yell at Rook, and others shout at each other. Arguments quickly become heated, and everyone suddenly seems very aware of their nakedness; they hide behind each other, wrinkled expanses of flesh reddening with embarrassment. Those with rifles wave them, or drop them. Some stare at their hands, or through the glass at Rook. Fights break out; fists are thrown, bruising bones. Blood is drawn, spattering the grasses. Then, all at once, there is a scrum for the airlock controls. A crowd gathers around it, punching in useless numbers to try and release the doors.

"I changed it!" cries a voice, louder than the rest. All eyes turn to see Frank Sinclair, stood at the rear of the crowd. He is holding a plastic and metal pistol-shaped object, and his eyes are wide and wild. "I knew you were all weak, so I changed the code. None of you are getting out without my permission." Some raise their rifles at him, and then lower them. The voices quieten again. "I have no children," growls Frank Sinclair. The crowd parts to let him through. "You can apply no leverage to me, fowl. Adam saw to that when he murdered my wife." When he is up against the glass, Frank Sinclair turns his plastic gun over in his hands, thoughtfully.

Adam advances on the door, so that he stands face-to-face with Frank Sinclair. He presses the intercom and speaks into it. "Open the door," he says. This close, he realises that the gun is a bolt gun. A pneumatic thing, used to slaughter cattle.

Frank Sinclair frowns. "When I was a boy," he says, "my father took me to Vatican City. We walked the streets, and there saw God's glory in the rich churches. It was in the statues of the saints, and the brilliant murals devoted to Christ's life, and the tall stained-glass windows. It was in the very architecture of the place – every stone of every arch devoted to God. At the end of the trip, my father brought me to see the Sistine Chapel, and there it was, Michelangelo's most precious offering to God, resplendent. I knew, then – I knew with absolute certainty – that

Michelangelo had been accepted into heaven. But do you know what else I thought, when I saw Michelangelo's finest work?" Frank Sinclair meets Adam's eye. "I thought: I can do better."

"Open the door," repeats Adam.

"You're not listening to me, Adam. I'm telling you that this place – this greenhouse – is a cathedral. I'm telling you that its every shard is devoted to the glory of God. I'm telling you that I am its architect, and its artist, and I have filled its walls with devotion greater than any mere mural or statue. I have rebuilt paradise. Do you understand me? I have rebuilt Eden, in God's honour."

When Adam thinks about God, he imagines it's a lot like thinking about an absent parent. There is the faintest idea at the back of his mind that there was a presence, once, which taught him things like how to walk and how to speak, but following that presence is a long and uninterrupted absence. Adam imagines that there might have been a time when he missed God, but that time has passed. "Open the door."

"You still don't understand. This is my cathedral, and I have built its walls strong. My congregation and I are safe in here, and God is with us. You will never be allowed inside. You forsook your chance when you killed my wife. You are too far fallen, Adam." Frank Sinclair turns to glare at Rook. "As for you, and all the rest of your kind – I am not merciless. I know how much you must long to return to your lost paradise. It wasn't your fault you were cast out. As such, I am willing to let you in, but only on my terms. On God's terms. As you were made." Hauling the lever back on the pneumatic gun, he arms it. Shouldering through his stunned party of friends, he strides through the grasses and up the hill. "Return to your true forms, and submit to my God-given dominion over you, and I will let you return home!" he shouts. He stamps the grasses down beneath his indelicate feet, leaving a trail in his wake, and the bolt gun swings precariously in his grip, his hair wisping around him wildly. All at the airlock watch, paralysed by indecision as Frank Sinclair approaches the cherry tree. Only then do a few break away, realising what it is that he intends; rushing after him too late. "This swine still refuses to submit. Look at it – still pretending to be a person!"

Pig's head is low, against his chest.

Frank Sinclair presses the bolt gun against Pig's temple, and his expression is disgust. "Watch now, first man, as I exercise my dominion."

The bolt gun bucks, and there is a soft thump.

XIII

Adam's first children were beautiful; helpless creatures emerging mewling into the light of the garden. When they learned how to crawl, they crawled among the reeds, and watched the fishes swim, and mimicked the billowing of their gills, mimicked the flicking of their tails. When they learned to stand, they ran beneath the trees and followed the birds, flapping their arms as if they might find a gust of air and fly. With patience, and time, they began to understand their own domain, the space between earth and sky, where they could stand and squirm their feet in the rich soil as if they might be trees burying their roots, growing tall by the sustenance of the earth. And grow like trees they did, taller and taller, and stronger, arms like branches, faces held up to the sun as if they might soak up all that light.

When his children began to wither, it took Adam by surprise. This weakness running through them, making them hunched and small and wrinkled, was new. Adam had never known weakness, and he did not know the cause of it in his children. Their flesh began to bunch up over their bones, and their eyelids drooped low over their eyes, and their knees buckled beneath them, and then the first of his children collapsed and did not rise. They tried everything they could, he and Eve: they fed the broken child water, and pieces of fruit, and they put it in the full face of the sun as if it was a wilted flower that might only rise with enough light. But then the flesh began to fall from its softened limbs, and the animals of the garden pecked and gnawed at it as if its skin was berries, and soon it resembled no child but a rotting heap of pulp and bones.

They had no name for what had happened to their child, so they called it death.

* * *

As days pass in the flooded mansion, it begins to feel like a tomb.

Butterfly spends her time wandering from room to room and drawing the curtains. The sky is dull, and what little sunlight leaks in through the gaps sparkles in the droplets of water that drip from the mansion's tall ceilings. She herself is a ghost, having exchanged her colours for drab, dark clothes scavenged from Ada Sinclair's wardrobes: great black shrouds that drag behind her and snag on the sodden floorboards until they are ragged. Sometimes Adam tries to follow her, to find her and ease her shivering silent sobs, but he always loses her in the gloom of the mansion's corridors. As days become nights become days, darkness grips the drowned corridors ever tighter, and rain patters intermittently against the windows, maintaining the waters engulfing the house.

Crow has taken to exploring the house's many bookshelves in search of sheet music. There is a grand piano in the partially submerged ballroom, standing with its feet in the water, and by the light reflected through the tall broken windows she plays the songs she finds. No matter where Adam is in the house, the music is always distant. Notes echo eerily from the waters, as if the piano is itself submerged. Sometimes, when Crow runs out of sheet music, she plays songs from memory instead. Adam recognises tunes from different times – long-forgotten songs by dead composers – and he is not sure which he prefers: the piano's mournful dirge, or the mansion's dripping silence.

Rook has housed himself in Frank Sinclair's study, where he has spread the papers contained in his suitcase as if he is building a nest out of them. The documents are in a muddle across the grand oak desk, and scattered over the thick, damp carpets, and pinned to the walls, and Rook has been working tirelessly at the words typed across them, searching desperately for the mistake that is not there. Fingertips stained with ink, he makes endless notes and revisions. One day, Adam sees him stood at the epicentre of the room, holding his rounded spectacles and peering at them as if they are a puzzle he is unable to solve. The frames have been crushed, and the lenses are cracked, and Rook's hands are speckled with splinters of glass.

From time to time Adam comes across a window yet to be curtained, and from there he can see Crab. Crab has exchanged his yellow coat for an old blue boiler suit and thick gardening gloves, and he works at the shining glass of the shatter-shard greenhouse resolutely. Sometimes Adam sees him emerge from the waters, dragging pieces of machinery and heavy tools, and the mansion's quiet is interrupted for a time by the electric whine and rhythmic thump of industry. At the end of the day, Adam sees Crab sitting atop one of the hills that rise from the floods on a scavenged deckchair, squinting thoughtfully at the greenhouse and chewing at an unlit pipe until the light fades from the sky.

Adam is having a lot of trouble dealing with Pig's death. To him, it is a new thorn of grief. The problem is that he feels the thorn so viscerally that he often becomes convinced that it must exist physically, embedded somewhere in his skin. Yet, try as he might, he is unable to find it and pluck it out. He spends his days standing before stained and rusted mirrors, turning and searching his skin for the prickling thorn he knows must be somewhere about him, and whenever he finds a trickle of water dripping from the ceiling, he stands beneath it and lets it wash over him as if it might somehow soothe the sharp needling. The mansion's wine cellar is filled with murky water, and Adam wades down there, letting the cold waters consume him completely in an effort to find some relief. There is no diminishing the thorn's sharpness, though. It continues to scratch at him constantly.

One day Adam sits in the ballroom upon a sodden bench and tries, by the eerie light leaking in through the gaps in the curtained windows, to read a novel he found in the mansion's ruined library. He is having a lot of trouble reading it because he is unable to draw the sentences together. Each sentence is an island, separated by a sea of meaninglessness. Meanwhile, beneath the ballroom's glinting chandelier, Crow attempts to remember a song she once knew, playing the first few notes over and over again in an effort to find the rest of it. Eventually, Adam chucks the useless novel into the waters, where it bobs for a while before it sinks, and Crow gives up on trying to remember the song, and they sit together in silence, listening to the muffled quiet of the house as it slowly falls in on itself.

There is a rhythmic splashing as someone approaches.

From the gloom of the corridor, Crab emerges. His gloves are blackened with oil, and his boiler suit is faded and threadbare around his joints, and there is something triumphant in his expression. He comes to a halt in the arched doorway and removes his gloves, rubbing his coarse hands together and clearing his throat. "All right," he says, and his voice sounds strange in the tomb-like quiet. These are the first words to have been spoken in the house in days. "I reckon I've got a way in."

* * *

Emerging from the house, Crow has the expression of a girl who has awoken from one dream only to find herself in another. Thick, whirling clouds snuff out the light of the sun, and up on the hilltops the trees are hunched silhouettes, as if they are cowering at the sight of that oppressive sky. There is no wind to tremble their dripping branches, and the waters of the floods at their feet are a glassy black that reflects nothing. The house has subsided, Adam notices; the wing they have emerged from is slowly sinking, as if it is dissolving in the waters. The silence outside is so absolute that Crow speaks in a whisper, as if she is afraid of breaking it. "That's a bad sky," she says. "You don't fly in a sky like that. You find somewhere safe to roost."

"You can stay here," Adam tells her.

"I'll go up one of the turrets," she says, "watch from there."

The house's turrets seem too close to the sky, Adam thinks – as if she might accidentally fall upwards into the clouds. "Be careful," he tells her.

"What are you going to do if you get inside?" she asks.

Crab is hunched over the engine of his little boat and hauling at the cord to get it started. Each time he does, the engine rumbles, and to Adam it sounds like distant thunder. Opening his satchel of pistols, he examines them; the silver of them gleams in the gloom. "I haven't decided yet," he says. Shouldering the satchel, he unties the boat, clambers inside and pushes it away from the shore. Crow remains in the arched doorway of the house, her pale face ghostly in what little light leaks down between the clouds, and as the boat drifts across the black waters she vanishes.

There is a snarl from the boat's engine.

The greenhouse is resplendent in the dark. Its every facet looks like a mirror reflecting an impossible summer. The bright light it casts makes the waters glitter in oily swirls, emphasising the gritty soil and metallic elements risen to the surface. Beyond the greenhouse glass lays a simulacrum of paradise so dazzling that Adam does not let his gaze linger long upon it. To be absorbed by the sight of it would be to invite corrupted memories he knows would overwhelm him. Leaning over the side of the boat, he sees himself reflected in the waters instead: a void of deeper darkness in the inky blackness.

The folds of Crab's face shadow his eyes completely, even as he steers the boat closer to the light of the greenhouse. He navigates around the crystalline construction's edge until he comes to a long section that looks like any other, and there he cuts the engine. Leaning over, he runs his coarse fingers down a length of the metal frame until they come to a cross-section between four panes, which rests just beneath the surface. "Right there," he says. "I wouldn't have noticed it if it weren't for the floods. You can see it better from the inside."

Leaning out, Adam tries to see the metal cross-section through the thick panes of the glass. The grass beyond the shatter-shard windows is a rich, healthy green, and blades brush up against the edge, almost hiding the outer shell completely; but there, between them, Adam sees the metal cross-section and the water dripping through it. The hole must be the size of a pinprick, he thinks – the result of a shoddy weld, revealed by the waters. It's not much of a weakness.

"What do you reckon?" rumbles Crab.

Beyond the glass, some of the garden's occupants are gathering. They stand upon the grassy hillside rise, some now wearing pieces of clothing, and others bearing rifles. For the first time since meeting them, Adam takes the time to really see them. He notices their withered flesh, their manicured hands and their fake tans, and he notices their expensive jewellery, and shining fake teeth, and plucked brows, and he notices how clean they are, as if they have scrubbed the outer world from themselves. There is no sign of Frank Sinclair.

"Think you can get through?" Adam asks.

Unzipping his boiler suit, Crab shrugs it from his shoulders. His skin really does look like a map of a mountain range, Adam thinks, and when Crab slips into the waters, which rise up his chest, he becomes an island. Exploring the greenhouse frame with his fingers, Crab hums to himself: a low rumble that sounds like the movements of the inner Earth. Then the skin of his arms begins to shift. It splits tectonically into hard plates, cracking into continents as he applies pressure against the frame. The metal groans, and the glass panes around it shudder, but it remains strong, resisting him. His palms divide, cracking as he forces the strength of a mountain against the weakness in the vault, becoming jagged as his hands crush into claws. The hum in his throat deepens into an earth-shake rumble as his features shift, hardening and splitting, rocky mandibles emerging. His dark eyes gleam in the fissures of his face, and the black waters splash over him, and the greenhouse frame moans, bubbles rising as it slowly twists inwards.

There is panic among the garden's occupants. They raise their rifles.

The waters around Crab churn as he tears into the greenhouse.

A gap emerges large enough for the floods to start rushing through, and they splash, oily and tainted across the pristine grasses. The tip of one of Crab's claws scrapes inside and the first shots from the garden's occupants ring out, ricocheting from the reinforced glass.

Adam finds himself moving automatically; opening his satchel and hauling his gun belts over his shoulders as Crab forces both of his claws into the gap, the metal screeching as he applies colossal pressure into widening it. The waters swirl around him now, flecked white as they pour into the greenhouse.

More bullets smack into the gap, but those that meet Crab's

claws only serve to crack his stony flesh. The greenhouse frame shakes, screeching as Crab shreds it, and then the plates of glass to either side of him finally twist away. The floods gush around him as he grinds himself inside.

Claws raised to his face, Crab shields himself from the gunfire aimed at him.

The waters must be freezing cold, Adam knows, but he does not feel it. The gap torn in the greenhouse wall is barely large enough for him to squeeze through, but he forces himself inside.

Then he is wading through the sodden grasses, and the greenery almost overwhelms him. There are the trees, and the flowers, and all the brilliant colours he remembers of paradise, inviting him to remember them, inviting him to forget about everything else – all those dark years spent beyond the garden. There are waters lapping at his legs, and bright mirrored sunshine being reflected upon him, and bees and wasps buzz as they flicker past. Except those aren't bees and wasps at all. They are bullets, and Adam is being shot at.

Rising from the waters, Adam tends to the garden.

The pistols feel so familiar in his hands that he barely needs to concentrate on taking shots. First, he fires upon those bearing rifles. Adam does not miss because he does not know how to miss; each shot is a mechanical process that his hands know better than he does.

Skulls shatter, spraying blood and bone across the rich grasses.

There is yelling, and screaming, and the stink of gunpowder, and bodies tumble.

When all eight pistols are spent, Adam recharges them automatically: powder, ball, ramrod. Reloaded, he cuts down those foolish enough to have not run from him.

Advancing to the apex of the hill, Adam expends the last of his pistols once more and waits a while, searching the greenhouse for movement. There is some in the distance, but everybody around him is dead. This time, when Adam reloads, there is no urgency.

Mounting the hill alongside him, Crab looks human again. There are welts across his skin where bullets struck him, but none have drawn blood. "You get that bastard Sinclair?" he asks.

"Not yet." Adam can see the cherry tree in the distance.

"You go on, lad," rumbles Crab. "I'll be right behind you." Rolling a body over with the tip of one of his boots, he takes a bloodied rifle and begins to wipe it clean.

Walking through the greenhouse is disorientating. The shape of some of the hills is all too reminiscent of paradise, enhanced by the trees that stand upon them. The sight is just as corrupted as Adam's grief-warped memories, though. For every piece of Eden here, there are so many other worldly plants at various stages of their limited lifespans. The recreation of paradise is only partial, and the recognition it evokes in Adam is flawed. He feels unsteady, as if the ground keeps shifting beneath his feet. Nevertheless, he advances, and when he reaches the foot of the hill bearing the cherry tree he draws two of his pistols, expecting at any moment to be fired upon.

There are no more shots. Nobody raises a rifle at him.

At the top of the hill a handful of the garden's occupants are gathered around a pink mound. They are unarmed men and women, and they cower at the sight of Adam, shrinking back from the muddled heap at their feet. Adam holsters his guns and examines their work. They have removed Pig's body from the cherry tree and covered in with twigs, and leaves, and a layer of bright pink petals. The burial is crude, and as Adam crouches beside it he can feel the new thorn of grief in him, piercing him sharply.

He glances around at the gathered people, whose expressions are twisted into masks of sorrow and regret, some possibly genuine. "Where's Sinclair?" he asks, and they raise their hands in unison. They are pointing at the airlock. The doors have been opened, a dark portal leading into the house. Adam rises to his feet.

"Adam," says a woman, her voice breaking. "We're sorry. We're all so sorry."

For a moment, Adam considers leaving them here at the foot of the cherry tree, where Pig's body lies cold. There should be mourners surrounding him, Adam thinks. Their tears should soak the soil, and the noise of their weeping should fill the air. They should dig him a proper grave, burying him deep in the earth among the roots of Eden's cherry tree, and each of them should lament for days and weeks and years over his loss. They should be allowed to grow old and die here, their every remaining moment tormented with regret and sorrow.

The moment is brief, and when it has passed Adam kills them all.

* * *

By moonlight, Adam considers his pistols. Blood glints like black pearls where it is spattered across the metalwork. The stink of powder is overwhelming, and each gun's handle is gritty and slippery.

Were he to kill Frank Sinclair with these, it would be a quick death.

Moonlight leaks in through a gap in the tall curtains of the house's grand entrance hall, and while it renders every white marble statue a pale figure in its allotted alcove, it does not reflect in the dark waters that engulf the ground floor. Adam stands on the balcony above that black pool and drops his pistols into it one by one, sending white ripples across the glassy surface.

Frank Sinclair deserves so much worse.

The walls groan, and the halls sigh, and the rafters creak, and moonlight illuminates the worst of the desolation: the sagging ceiling and peeling wallpaper. Where the wood panelling has come apart, it reveals the uneven brickwork hidden behind it. Once-proud faces stare down at Adam from the portraits, hollow eyes within tarnished frames, and a great many of them resemble Frank Sinclair, he thinks.

Rook is waiting before a thin staircase, ghostly in the gloom. Without his glasses, the deep shadows across his face make his features especially bird-like. "Are they all dead?" he asks.

"Almost all of them."

"Good." Rook nods at the stairs. "Frank is hiding in the attic."

The staircase is slender enough that Adam has to shuffle up it sideways.

"Adam?"

He pauses at the wooden hatch. "What is it?"

"You have no guns."

When Adam throws the hatch back, its rusted hinges moan. "They're not cruel enough," he says.

There are gaps in the roof where tiles have fallen. Beyond them is the looming sky, filled with whirling black clouds which have parted to reveal the full moon in all its glory. The moon glares like a great white eye, and Adam glares back, studying the wisps of clouds that swirl slowly across it. When he turns to the darker recesses of the attic, an after-image remains in his vision.

The attic is enormous. It seems to encompass the entire length of the house, and is filled with all manner of chests and furniture. The floorboards are dry, and they creak precariously as Adam slowly advances. He watches for movement in the deepest shadows.

All the remnants of the lives once lived in the house reside up here, and Adam reads them as he would a book. There are multiple television sets, and radios, and a handful of record players and gramophones. Pieces of damaged art badly in need of restoration are piled up together, and there are cots and toys and even a doll's house packed away in one corner. A shaft of bright moonlight illuminates a heap of birdcages, and hamster cages, and an elaborate rabbit's hutch, and there are multiple lengths of chicken wire still stained with guano. In some places the floor has fallen through, leaving great black gaps that Adam navigates around. The floorboards complain constantly as he makes his way through piles of ancient rugs, and chests brimming with clothes, and glass-fronted cupboards filled with old books and board games.

The blackened metal husk of a fireplace and its accompanying ornaments lie up against a chimney stack, and there among them is a garish sword rack holding a pair of crossed cutlasses. Heaving at the rack until it comes free, Adam bashes at the cutlasses to free them from their housing. They have been fused together with rust, so Adam snaps one in two and pulls the pieces of it apart from the other. The remaining cutlass was never meant to be used as a weapon: its blade is dull, and it is unbalanced and unwieldy, and its tip is a rough globule of rust. It is ideal, Adam thinks, for the agonies he plans to visit upon Frank Sinclair.

The further Adam makes his way through the attic, the less steady the floor is beneath him. The wooden boards give way to bare rafters with nothing but insulation between them, so that Adam has to tread carefully to make sure he doesn't put his foot through the floor. Those rafters are brittle with age, and the wood warps with each step he takes. There is still no sign of Frank Sinclair, only vague shapes in the dark that might be a man lying in wait, but Adam is meticulous. He moves from shadow to shadow, drawing aside old curtains and tapestries with the tip of his rusted cutlass, and crudely spearing the dark between splintered bits of furniture.

A clear space opens up beneath a particularly wide gap in the roof, and Adam pauses, turning about and studying the darkness of the attic. Nothing moves in the shadows, but the rafters beneath him sigh and shudder, struggling with his weight.

The slightest movement catches his eye, but it comes from outside.

Something flits at the edge of his vision, and he turns to be confronted by the enormous moon, revealed fully beyond the fallen tiles. A shape flutters across it; a shape with pale wings and slender antennae. It looks like a moth, Adam thinks. Except, it isn't a moth at all. It is a butterfly, made monochrome by the moon.

With a tortured moan, the floor gives way.

The darkness of the house opens beneath Adam as he falls.

With his free hand, he catches himself on one of the jutting rafters. Debris tumbles away on every side of him, smashing onto ballroom tiles far below. One of the huge hall's great chandeliers glints in the moonlight. He still has hold of his cutlass, but he's not sure how long the rafter will keep his weight. It shifts perilously beneath his grip as he hangs, suspended from the attic.

Before Adam is able to haul himself back up, a shape emerges from the shadows above. It is the end of a large-calibre rifle – the elephant gun – aimed at Adam's head, and from its barrel hangs Fox's brilliant brush.

With one wild eye to the sights of his oversized rifle, Frank Sinclair grimaces. He is dressed in antique clothes like one of the men from the many portraits hanging in the house, and his pale scalp is pitted like the moon that illuminates him. "You beast," he hisses. "I get it. I get it, now."

It would be easier to fall, Adam thinks. A few broken bones would be better than being shot in the head. Yet, as he considers his options, he notices a new darkness shrouding the moon. It is not a cloud, nor is it the silhouette of a butterfly. No, this shape is something else. It is a bird, Adam thinks – a bird approaching fast and silent with its claws outstretched.

"I thought it was the first true act of free will," continues Frank Sinclair, "but I was wrong. Now, I understand. You only took a bite because you were stupid and you were hungry."

As the silhouette grows larger, it unfurls its magnificent wings.

Frank Sinclair tightens his grip. "I would have made a better you than you!"

There is a chaotic burst of noise as the elephant gun fires, the roof implodes, and Owl screeches all at once. Splinters of wood and feathers rain down around Adam, and he feels the hot rip across his skull where the gun's shot skims him. Owl's enormous claws are embedded so deep in the floor that Adam can see them protruding through the ballroom's ceiling, dripping with an inky liquid that must be blood. The mighty creature, somewhere between man and bird, has eyes that are mostly pupil – two black expanses that glare at the screaming figure pinned beneath him. Owl screeches again, flicking his wings to remain balanced, before striking with his beak.

Throwing his cutlass across the rafters, Adam hauls himself up.

Frank Sinclair has been torn nearly in two. One of his legs is snapped beneath him, and his guts protrude glistening and black from his ripped belly. His eyes, wide and white, roll unseeing as he screams, wet hands fumbling uselessly at Owl's claws. Owl strips bits of flesh from him, ripping through his ruined clothes and swallowing glinting morsels.

Fetching his cutlass, Adam watches for a while as Frank Sinclair is devoured, considering how best to increase the small man's suffering. He is barely lucid, and his blood pours from him. It won't take long for him to die.

There is a cupboard full of clothes nearby, and Adam sifts through them until he finds some old belts and strips of cloth. Casting his cutlass aside, he carefully makes his way across. At first, Owl flicks his wings in warning, but he quickly settles again, returning to the feast at his feet.

Tearing away Frank Sinclair's clothes, Adam begins to tie tourniquets around the ruined man's bleeding limbs and sliced torso. When enough of the bleeding has stopped, he slaps the dying man's cheeks until he rises momentarily from his delirium. "What…" Frank Sinclair's voice gurgles in his throat. "What are you doing?"

"You're right," says Adam.

"What?"

"You're right. I was stupid, and I was hungry."

Owl strikes again with his beak, tearing out a chunk of Frank Sinclair's chest. The dying man wails, and gurgles, and tries to grip hold of Adam's coat, but his hands are too slippery and they fall away. Owl strikes again, and again, and Adam wanders back over to the wardrobe, leaning up against it to watch as Frank Sinclair is slowly devoured. From time to time he returns, binds the worst of Frank Sinclair's wounds, and finds creative ways to make sure the dying man remains aware of what is happening to him, but after what must be an hour or so it seems pointless. There simply isn't enough of him left. And with a final well-placed peck, Owl punctures Frank Sinclair's heart.

With the clothes of the dead man's ancestors, Adam wipes the blood from his hands. The elephant gun is nearby, and he delicately removes Fox's brush from the barrel. In the light of the moon, the tail gleams wetly, blood beaded across it.

The last time Adam saw Fox, he was living up in the Hida Highlands. There was a famine at the time, and though the crops down in the valleys were failing, and though many thousands were starving, Adam's plum trees still grew tall, and bloomed bountifully, and, as the year progressed, bore heavy dark fruits. Adam shared his crop of fruit with anybody who made the journey up the high hills to his small farm, and after each feast he buried the stones in his fields, so that more plum trees would sprout next spring. One misty morning he woke to distant shouting, and went out to his trees to find a group of skeletal men tearing them from the earth. They were raking at the roots, binding lengths of rope around the trunks, and hauling them onto crude carts. It did not take long for Adam to stop them: they were all starved, and weak, and bore blunt tools. Afterwards, he sat among the wreckage and looked out over the valleys – at the way the mists pooled in the valleys around the green hills – and it was from those mists that she emerged: Fox, her fur agleam with the same dew that glinted on the grasses. She yipped, he remembers – a solemn greeting that broke the silence that had settled over everything like the mists. Then she sat with him a while, and licked the blood and plum juice from his fingers.

XIV

On the day that Eden's twin trees burned, there was a storm.

There had never been a storm in paradise before. The winds and rains had always been gentle, and Adam had enjoyed the feel of them across his skin, and the way they played through the trees, rustling their leaves. Adam knew Eden's weather as well as he knew the songs of all the birds, and the calls of all the creatures that called the forests and plains of paradise their home. Now, the winds and the rains made an unfamiliar music. The trees groaned, their branches heaving and whipping, and the rains were sharp and stung at Adam's skin, pattering noisily against the sodden ground. The clouds were thick and dark in a way he had never seen before, and he had no name for it all, so he called it a storm. Eden's creatures hid in the gaps between roots, and the knots of trees, and cried plaintively to Adam, asking him in their various voices for relief.

As night fell, the storm gathered its strength.

Light fell from the sky, and the clouds bellowed, and Adam cowered from them both. The bright strikes that left streaks across his vision he called lightning, and the great crashing boom that echoed across Eden's valleys he called thunder, and from his crude shelter between an oak and a sycamore he could see the lightning, raking the hill at the very centre of Eden again and again with its terrifying magnificence. Soon, a new light billowed out over paradise, which looked, to Adam, like the sudden unfurling of a flower made of colours that he did not recognise. The strange new colours illuminated all of Eden with their eerie, shifting magnificence, and Adam felt himself drawn towards them. With the storm buffeting him, and with all of Eden's creatures following in his wake, Adam made his way there, to where the twin trees stood, wisdom and life, at Eden's heart.

Both trees were on fire. The light from them was brilliant and hypnotic, constantly shifting between all the colours that Adam had named in paradise, and revealing yet more, ever stranger colours, as they were consumed. The heat from them was fierce, and the rains hissed as they struck the blackened branches. The fruits of the trees warped and darkened as they caught fire, burning up in weird twists of coloured light, and crackling branches fell, still smouldering and crumbling into ashes among the trees' tangled roots. Before long, even those very roots burned, until both trees were conflagrations, searing streaked after-images into Adam's vision that would never really leave him. Adam turned from the dazzling vision to see that most of Eden's occupants had come to witness the burning trees. He could see the fires reflected in all their eyes, even in the darkness of the forests that lined the base of the hill.

Eve arrived, then, and took his hand, and together they watched the trees burn.

After a while, she left him, and began to advance up the

hill. Adam could see the way that the terrible heat affected her: heavy droplets of sweat rolled down her skin, each refracting the endless shifting colours of the fire, so that Eve gleamed with their burning. Still she ascended, each step drawing her closer to the place between the trees – that nest of tangled roots where she and Adam had slept so often, tangled up in each other. Adam wanted to go after her, wanted to run up the hill and join her there, perhaps burn with her, but something kept him at the base of the hill: the weight of his responsibility for all those that watched and waited with him, the animals of Eden, whose lives were each so beloved to him. Eve drew close enough to the trees that the flames licked at her skin, and with each gush of wind it seemed as if the guttering fires should consume her, but they did not. At the hill's summit she stooped, and there she grabbed the untouched end of a burning branch, turning and raising it over her head.

When Eve descended the hill, the eyes of all of Eden's creatures followed her. At the base of the hill, she took Adam's hand and smiled up at him, a smile that assured him that whatever happened she would always be there, and they would face it together. Eden's creatures gathered before them, and so too did their children, and by the light of the burning trees, and the burning branch in Eve's hand, they weathered the long night and the storm. By morning, the trees were ashes.

* * *

Adam buries Pig. It is a bright day, and a cold winter sun pierces the panes of the grand greenhouse, warming nothing. He digs a deep ditch at the foot of the cherry tree, so close to its base that he has to spend a while gently untangling its roots from the earth. When Pig lies among those roots, Adam makes certain that he is settled into a comfortable position before covering him. That night, Adam slumbers atop the grave with his back against the tree, and in the morning he wakes to find that someone has placed a patchwork blanket over his shoulders.

It takes weeks for the floods to subside. Frost grips the ground instead, freezing what remains of the waters. Adam often wanders through the ruins of the valley during the day, crunching through the wreckage of the estate. He sits on rocky outcroppings between the frozen bodies of dead sheep, watching the soft glow of the clouds. Sometimes, he sifts through the rotting fruit fallen from the trees of the ruined orchards in search of viable seeds, and when he finds them he digs holes in the hard earth and plants them. Most won't take, he knows, but there is a chance that a few will.

Butterfly is the first to take residence in the greenhouse. Adam watches her for hours – the way she flutters among Eden's flowers. Sometimes he kneels down beside the artificial stream, cupping his hands and offering her a still surface to drink from. Her tongue is long, and scarlet, and her feet tickle his scarred skin, and when she is satisfied she stays a while, gently opening and closing her brilliant wings before flitting away.

Crow, too, begins to roost in the greenhouse. Adam hears her long before he sees her, her voice echoing over the rolling hills. One day he notices her circling high above, close enough to the panes of the ceiling that the tips of her wings brush against the glass, and he follows her back to her nest – a half-finished thatch-work high among the branches of Eden's silver birch. From then on, whenever he notices a fallen twig he takes it to her, leaving it like an offering at the base of her birch. From time to time she peers out over the edge of her nest and croaks at him, beady black eye agleam.

Owl takes up residence near the doorways between the inside and the outside. Adam spies him preening himself among the branches of the cherry tree, overlooking the airlock that leads into the house. There aren't many good perches beside the torn section of metal frame, so he soars around it, wings shimmering copper and brass as he patrols. Mostly, however, Adam notices him standing sentinel beside the greenhouse's loading doors – an enormous, glass-panelled airlock hidden at the very rear of the vault, large enough that trees might be hauled through them. Those doors have been broken open from the inside, and cold winter winds gust through them, so that Owl puffs up his chest as he perches over them. His wide eyes spy every twitch of movement – every errant leaf that dares to cross the boundary from outside.

Crab, meanwhile, remains in the house. Having cleared the greenhouse of corpses, he seems to be demolishing all that remains of the estate. There is a clattering and hammering, and the splintering sound of sawing, and the whine of machine drilling at all hours, accompanied by noisy whistling and singing. The house shudders, and rocks, and seems to get smaller every day. Sometimes there is a crash, and an entire wing collapses, revealing ever-greater expanses of sky.

Rook remains in the shape of a man, and Adam often notices him rambling the high hills that surround the estate. Wrapped up in a long black coat, and with his hair swept back across his head, he seems to have regained some of his stature. He is wearing a new pair of spectacles – spares recovered from his briefcase, perhaps. One day, when the overcast clouds are so thin that they make for a remarkable display, Adam joins Rook on one of his walks, ascending the steepest of hills as if they might somehow draw closer to that dramatic sky.

"How's business?" Adam asks.

"Oh, I'm taking a small break," he says. "Corvid & Corvid basically runs itself these days, anyway. All I do is put out fires."

Adam glances back at the greenhouse, resplendent at the heart of the valley. "Do you think you'll join them?"

Rook's smile is gentle. "It's tempting, isn't it?"

"I thought it could be a kind of safe place."

"A sanctuary. Yes. I had the same thought."

At the top of the hill they stop and rest a while. Soon, the distant rumbling of engines becomes apparent, followed not long after by the sight of white trucks on the road that leads up the house. An entire convoy.

"What do you think this is?" asks Rook, hands buried deep in the pockets of his coat.

"More trouble, maybe."

"Perhaps." Rook frowns. "I'm not sure what it could be, though. All of Frank Sinclair's friends are dead, and I have Scotland Yard chasing their ghosts across the world. Nobody's paying attention to this place except us."

As they descend, Adam expects to hear the clamouring of gunfire. It seems inevitable at this point. Yet, as they reach the base of the hill, there is nothing but the yelled exchanges of drivers trying to coordinate their parking, and the slow quietening of engines as they are switched off. Doors are rolled back and thrown wide, to reveal the greenery contained in every truck. There are trees tied up on flat-beds, and flowers carefully wrapped up in individual pots, and whole expanses of wild grasses cut up into careful squares. The men and women of the convoy are wearing thick gloves, and some of them carry shovels and trowels and heavier pieces of gardening equipment.

"Are you Mister Corvid?" A woman with a clipboard approaches.

"Pardon?" Rook frowns. Then, "Oh, yes. Of course."

"You need to sign here." She offers the clipboard.

Rook scrawls his signature reflexively. "What is all this?"

"You weren't told?"

"The phone lines have been down."

"Delivery," says the woman, "From…" She checks. "… another Mister Corvid."

"Mister Corvid?"

"Magpie," says Adam.

The army of gardeners unloading plants from the convoy are handling pieces of Eden. Hundreds of them. Thousands of them. So many that Adam feels dizzy, overwhelmed by the sheer magnitude of it all. He had thought that the stadium garden was the extent of Magpie's collection – that all in his possession now stood in the greenhouse vault. But there is so much more here.

Enough pieces of paradise to fill several stadiums – enough to fill the greenhouse from pane to distant pane.

"These are…" says Rook, as realisation reaches him at last.

"Yes," says Adam.

"All of it?"

"All of it." Adam remembers the hidden greenhouse in the basement of Owl's house, and wonders how many more secret greenhouses Magpie must have, hidden everywhere. The sheer scale of the operation is dazzling.

"This is what my brother has been doing all this time?"

"He only showed me the stuff in the vault. But yes, I think so. Collecting it all together."

Rook runs his hand through a patch of grass, feeling the blades. "It's… magnificent." Then, frowning, he withdraws his hand. "He has a lot to answer for."

It would be easy to grab a trowel, Adam knows; to haul trees and flowers and all of Eden's greenery into the vault. There is nothing Adam wants more, in fact, than to lose himself in the reconstruction of the garden. But there is something he knows he must do first. Rook is right: Magpie has a lot to answer for. Pulling his torn and stained coat around him, Adam takes one last look at the convoy. It *is* a magnificent sight, he thinks: all those pieces of Eden, reunited again. Then he turns and starts to make his way up the track, crunching through frozen puddles. It's time to find Magpie.

* * *

Adam stops at a garden centre.

The car park is so full that the queue of cars vying for space is preventing anyone from leaving. Vehicles are laden with so much wood that it sticks out of their windows, and doors idle at awkward angles, drivers gesturing uselessly at the unmoving traffic. Adam manoeuvres around it all, shuffling past overburdened trolleys. He saw the garden centre from the side of the motorway and felt drawn to it, distracted from his initial destination. It would be worth picking up some new tools, he thinks, for when he returns to the greenhouse.

The garden centre is cavernous, and echoes with the voices and footfalls of its busy occupants. They haul planks of timber, and trellises, and enormous bags of nails onto trolleys. The aisles devoted to wood seem to be mostly depleted of stock, so a few enterprising folk are purchasing entire sheds and carrying them in small teams. With all this wood, Adam imagines they will try and repair the damage done by the flood.

As he skirts the queues at the tills, Adam considers the forest of trees that died for all this wood. He wonders how long ago those trees were felled; how long ago they sprouted from acorns and seeds; how long ago the trees that dropped those acorns and seeds took root themselves. He considers the forest back through the generations, all the way back to those first trees, the progenitors that dropped the acorns that would grow through centuries and centuries to become these planks and sheds, converted from a living forest into unliving human structures.

There are no hammers, but there are plenty of shovels. There is quite the selection, in fact, and while each shovel has a metal blade, the hafts vary from plastic to wood to metal. There are long shovels, and short shovels, and spare parts – blades and handles and sharpening kits. Adam decides to avoid plastic because it warps too easily, which leaves him with a choice between metal and wood. Taking a metal shovel in one hand, and a wooden shovel in the other, he weighs them. Metal bends, he thinks, and wood splinters.

As he considers the shovels, Adam realises that for the first time in a long time he feels happy. No, not happy – content. The kind of contentment that comes with being completely absorbed in a pleasant activity. He remains standing there for a while longer, a shovel in each hand, letting the noise of the garden centre rush around him. He can still feel the wreath of grief gripping his thoughts, but today it feels like the sun is shining down upon the rich green leaves of the thorny tangle.

"If you ask me, you should just buy both." Magpie is stood at the end of the aisle, hands buried deep in the pockets of his enormous brown shearling jacket, with a grin that makes him look as if he has a mouth full of pearls. Gone is his deadly silver smile; the crowns he wears are the same white as the rest of his teeth, making him seem symmetrical. "Hello, Adam," he says.

"What are you doing here?"

"I figured you'd try and find me, so I thought I'd save you the trouble." He rolls his sleeve back and checks his watch. "I'm on a tight schedule, I'm afraid, but I have time for a quick chat. There's a conservatory café attached to this place that does some splendid scones. The scones themselves are a little dry and floury, and the butter comes in those dreadful pre-packed oblongs, but the jam is excellent and they are quite generous with it."

Adam replaces his shovels. "You make it sound like you've tried every café in Scotland."

"Most of them," he concedes.

The conservatory is warm and bustling with calmer shoppers. It is pleasant to walk among the out-of-season plants, Adam thinks, no matter how strange it is to have flowers blooming so late in the year. The vivid colours of them are soothing. The café is positioned between trellises covered in varieties of ivy so thick that they almost completely engulf the glass walls, and the tables are of an awkward white metal designed for outdoor use, impractical for balancing cups and saucers upon. Adam's chair is uncomfortable, no matter which position he takes on it.

Magpie returns from the counter with a tray of tea and a stack of scones. "The jam is homemade, apparently, but the lady behind the counter won't tell me her recipe. Credit to her, I suppose. It keeps me coming back." He cracks open a scone, smears it with a thin layer of butter, and pours jam onto it straight from the jar. When he bites into it, jam oozes from the corner of his mouth and drips onto his plate, and when he grins there are tiny red seeds clinging to his pearly teeth. "Marvellous," he says. "Simply marvellous."

Adam tries a scone. The jam is good, he thinks. "I buried Pig beneath the cherry tree," he says.

Magpie's smile softens. The cheerful noise filling the conservatory seems to lull, fading with his smile, until Adam can hear the gentle clinking of the wind-chimes for sale outside.

When all trace of his teeth has gone, and his expression has settled into something sombre, the network of scars across Magpie's face became so much more apparent. They are the silver of spider silk, Adam thinks.

"Do you remember," says Magpie, gently, and his eyes follow the stir of his spoon as it swirls his tea, "the time we went to the Alps together?"

Adam thinks he remembers the sky – an unbroken white the same colour as the snow. "We went in winter."

"That's right. You read about skiing in an almanac and wanted to give it a go, but you were no good at it. We spent a good few months up there in a cabin. Every day you'd go out and sink into the snow, and every night you'd go into the forest and find dead boughs to cut down so we had something for the fire. Do you remember the day I brought peaches back from the village?"

"Peaches?"

"Yes. I was traipsing around the market, miserable as anything, filling a pack with all kinds of salted meats and scraggly dried vegetables, when I came across a stall selling peaches. They were completely out of place. The colour, the freshness, the size of them. It was the middle of winter, and there were peaches. Of course I bought them all, and dragged them back up the mountain, and puzzled over them for days, poring over them while you were out struggling with your skis. The thing about them, beside the fact that they were completely out of season, was that the taste of them was so damn familiar, but I couldn't for the life of me work out why.

"Then, one clear day, I went out and stretched my wings for a while, circling the big white frozen sky until the tips of my wings went numb. When I came back, starving hungry, I decided to peck at a peach. And that's when it came back to me. That's when I realised that I had tasted these peaches before, all the way back in the garden. It was a revelation, of course. The existence of the peaches meant that the peach tree had survived, just like we had. And if the peach tree had survived, well… what else might have? How much of Eden was still out there?

"The next day I went back down to the village and found the stall that had sold me the peaches. It was run by this fair young man by the name of Matteo, and I flattered him into showing me his farm. We traipsed all the miles down to it together, and he introduced me to his father and his mother, who were both pleased to show me their humble orchards in return for a generous purse. Those orchards were half buried in snow, each tree leafless and hibernating through the winter. Except, of course, for a single peach tree, settled on a low rise, still clothed in green, with pink and orange peaches dangling engorged from its branches. It was wonderful to behold."

"Did you steal it?"

Magpie sips at his tea. "No," he says, and his smile slowly returns. "I married Matteo."

"I don't remember that."

"By the time of the wedding, you were long gone. Through to Constantinople, I think. But yes: I married Matteo in a tiny little private ceremony. Just the two of us, and the promises between us. And I lived on his farm with him until he died. We were together for the better half of a century before I inherited the farm from him, peach tree and all." Magpie's eyes are agleam with his recollection. "It never mattered to him that I was a bird. He loved to watch me fly. I mourned for him a long time after he was gone. I still mourn for him today. A few months after he passed, I decided to see just how many pieces of Eden were still out there."

"A lot."

"More than I had imagined." Magpie checks his watch again. "Anyway. I can't stay. I need to catch a train down to London, so I can take the Eurostar through to Belgium. There are rumours that a convent of nuns outside Antwerp have in their possession an undying gorse bush." He wipes the crumbs from his face with a napkin. "Before I go, though, I have a gift for you." He slips an envelope onto the table. "A souvenir," he says, with a wink.

The envelope is small, but heavy. Adam tears it open and pours the contents out. Silver crowns tumble onto his palm: molars and incisors, and even a couple of canines. Half a mouthful of teeth. He sifts through them with his thumb as he might seeds – as if trees might grow from them. Maybe he can plant them in the greenhouse vault, he thinks, before realising that he still has questions he was meaning to ask. But when he looks up, Magpie is gone.

Adam remains in the café while his tea cools and the butter turns greasy in the warmth. He waits for his thoughts to still before pocketing the crowns, and then begins to consider the shovels again. The metal shovel was a decent weight, he thinks, but the wooden shovel was covered in a good quality varnish that would prevent it from splintering for a few seasons. Before he takes his leave, Adam goes to the counter and buys a few jars of jam: strawberry, and raspberry, and blackcurrant. Crow will appreciate them, he thinks. She likes sweet things just as much as her brother does.

* * *

Adam tends to the garden.

Days and weeks pass, and from time to time Rook arrives with someone new. The first is Kingfisher, whose whirring colours serve only to accentuate the sumptuous brightness of the garden. Then there is Lynx, who emerges from Eden's reconstructed forests every night and slumbers curled up beside Adam, rumbling his ribs with her purr. When Crane arrives, she casts her broad shadow long over the garden. So, too, come so many others, until the vault is noisy with their calls. Yet each time Rook returns with someone new, Adam finds that he is disappointed. And as weeks turn into months, he begins to examine his disappointment. The problem is that he keeps expecting Eve to arrive, he thinks. And yet… somewhere deep inside him, he knows that she never will.

One day, after a lot of thought, he emerges from the greenhouse.

The valley outside has been transformed by spring. All the seeds Adam planted over winter have started to sprout, filling the basin from edge to edge with green. Tall grasses have consumed the worst of the shattered greenhouses of the farm, and Adam wades through them towards the upturned shape of the yacht. The ruined craft has been transformed, as well: it now resembles a kind of shack, covered in a layer of moss, with grasses sticking from the cracks in its hull. Lying outside it on a deckchair is Crab, soaking up the sunshine as bees buzz around him.

"You're living out here?" asks Adam.

"Aye, lad. I'll be around a small while longer, I reckon, then I'll be gone."

"You're not staying?"

"You ain't got nothing but a pond in there, lad. What's a pond compared to the open sea?"

"Fair enough." Adam has brought a box with him, and inside it is the rose planted in a small amount of soil, its petals pale and resplendent in the sunlight.

"What's that for?" asks Crab.

Adam considers his answer. "Do you still have your boat?" he asks.

"Aye, lad. There's a river across the way."

"Can you take me up north? To Eve?"

Crab's stormy brows rise. "I can," he says. "If that's what you want."

It's hot enough that Crab wears only a pair of beaten jeans along with some sandals, and in the bright sunlight his coarse skin is slowly reddening. He steers his little tub of a boat gently along, north and upriver through Scotland, towards the glens at the country's heart. Spring is everywhere, and Adam watches it pass by – the fresh leaves unfurling on the branches of all the trees.

"You remembered, then?" rumbles Crab, eventually.

"I think I always knew," says Adam. "Something Rook said just threw me off for a while."

"Aye," says Crab. "He reckons it's kinder on you to let you forget."

For the past few weeks, Adam has been gently probing the cause of his broken memories. And what he found there surprised him. It was a rose – Eden's own white rose. All his thorns of grief belonged to an enormous, overgrown rosebush. "I don't remember the details," he says, "but I know where she is. How long ago did it happen?"

"Oh," Crab frowns, thoughtfully. "Centuries ago, now."

"How did it happen?"

"You sure you want to know?"

The rose is so light, in its box. Adam turns it around, filling his mind with the wonderful shape of it. He knows all too well the power of ignorance, but it's time, he thinks, that he confronted the rosebush binding his memories. "Tell me," he says.

"It was you, lad. You did it."

"I killed her?"

"She asked you to."

Adam remembers, then, the weight of the knife; the strength it took to push it between her ribs and into the heart caged within them. He remembers her breath against his neck as it stilled, the wetness of her blood across his knees, and the way her hands slowly lost their grip on his as she died. "I killed her," he says. There were bees, because he had been keeping bees at the time – his skin too tough for their stingers – and they filled the air with their humming. There were dandelion seeds, as well, drifting with the breeze. Yet, for all the bees and seeds and winds, there was such a stillness.

"I won't be gone," she had told him. "My heart will still beat in your chest."

Except, she was gone.

It had taken her centuries to weather down the granite of his resolve with her gentle determination. They had come to Fife, so she could work at the new university at St Andrews, and it proved just as disappointing as all the others. For the longest time, Eve had been struggling with the world. She had grown more and more convinced that she had learned all she could learn from it, and that there was only one mystery left to solve: the mystery of death. She had failed to find a cure for it, or a satisfactory answer for it, and it was something that every living thing not made in Eden experienced. An experience she wanted for herself. At first, it had been an idle suggestion – she wondered what it might be like to die. Then, as the years turned into decades turned into centuries, she became determined to find out.

It had to be Adam who did it. Nobody else would have been strong enough. But it had broken him, muddling his mind with so much grief that it had become a knot of thorns. Without Eve, what joy was there in the world? Without her there to remind him how to love them and forgive them their countless everyday cruelties, why should Adam care for his descendants? Why shouldn't he just join her in death?

Crab hums gently to himself as he steers, and as Adam listens to the song, he knows why he's still alive. He's alive for Crab, and for Crow, and Rook and Butterfly, Owl and Magpie. He's alive for Kingfisher, and Lynx, and Crane, and all the others who still survive of Eden. It is his honour to know them, and love them, and care for them still, even after all this time. Even without Eve to help him.

Eventually, Crab navigates to the edge of a stream and pulls his little boat up the embankment. "She's just up there," he says. "Over the ridge. You buried her here. There was a church, but I don't reckon there's a congregation any more. You want company?"

"I should do this alone."

"Of course, lad." Crab settles down on the bank, and removes his sandals, paddling in the stream. Then, he begins to hum a low song. As Adam climbs the steep embankment, he realises that he recognises the tune. It's another old shanty, he knows, but this one is for lost friends. It's a funeral song, but not an unhappy one: a song to celebrate a long life well lived.

At the top of the ridge, Adam sees the ruins of the church.

It was a modest building, built mostly out of stone, and appears to have tumbled into itself a long time ago. Spring has been kind to it, filling the small field with daisies and dandelions. A fitting place, Adam thinks as he makes his way through the grasses. It takes him a while, pausing at every sunken gravestone, until he finds the one he's looking for.

Time has worn away every word once etched into it, but that doesn't matter. Adam knows that it's Eve's grave. For a while, he sits up against it and talks to her. He tells her about Magpie, and about the Sinclairs, and about Pig, and he tells her about the

293

restoration of the garden. He tells her about the lives he has been living, and he tells her about all the lives he's taken. Then, when he's told her as much as he is able, he crouches over her grave and plants the rose above it.

Eden's rose, to mark Eve's final resting place. And with its planting, he feels the thorns binding his memories slip away. At least for the moment.

The grasses and flowers here will rise and die, rise and die. The church and all the gravestones will be worn away. The valley itself will subside, shaped by the river that runs through it. The mountains in the distance will be ground low by time. And the rose will survive it all. It will be here when all of Adam's descendants are dead, and the land is occupied by whatever comes after. It will be here until the end of time, every bit as perfect as the day it was made.

On his way back to Crab, Adam realises that he's not going to stay in the reconstructed garden either. He'll stay long enough to finish his work on it, but there are still too many lives he would like to live out in the world that his children have made. He will visit, he knows, but there's still too much on Earth that he wants to see.

It's just like the time he left Eden, he thinks:

What's a pond compared to the open sea?

ACKNOWLEDGEMENTS

Some books take months to write, and some take years. *Birds of Paradise* took just over a decade to write, and I have so much gratitude for all those who helped me along the way.

To everyone at Titan: thank you. I am eternally grateful for George Sandison's vision and passion for the book, and without Davi Lancett there would be no Fox. The book is beautiful inside and out because of Julia Lloyd, and the brilliant interior illustration is the work of Darren Kerrigan. Dan Coxon and Andy Hawes made certain that everything was where it should be.

To all my readers: thank you. Robert Dinsdale's endless kindness and advice was invaluable as I worked through various drafts, and Tam Moules' wise and patient council was instrumental as I worked on this final version. Aliya Whiteley was kind enough to help me to untangle some of the earlier chapters, and Zoe Strachan gave me some much-needed encouragement at a critical moment. I hope you'll be able to see some of Cynthia Rogerson's enthusiasm in these pages, along with Michel Faber's critical eye. Kirsty Gunn, Jim Stewart and Eddie Small had so much influence on this book, as did Rob Maslen and all the Fantasy Phoenixes. Paul Davies, James White and Ross Weryk were all kind enough to give me feedback on very early drafts, and I am grateful to everyone who gave me encouragement during the days when I was calling it *Eden Rose*.

Sometimes, it takes a long time for a piece of creative work to come together. *Birds of Paradise* took long enough that some of those who were instrumental in its making did not live to see its completion. This book is in honour of them.

Oliver K. Langmead lives and writes in Glasgow. His long-form poem, *Dark Star*, featured in the Guardian's Best Books of 2015. Oliver is currently a doctoral candidate at the University of Glasgow, where he is researching terraforming and ecological philosophy, and in late 2018 he was the writer in residence at the European Space Agency's Astronaut Centre in Cologne.

For more fantastic fiction, author events,
exclusive excerpts, competitions, limited editions and more

VISIT OUR WEBSITE
titanbooks.com

LIKE US ON FACEBOOK
facebook.com/titanbooks

FOLLOW US ON TWITTER AND INSTAGRAM
@TitanBooks

EMAIL US
readerfeedback@titanemail.com